P9-EDN-160

A JOURNEY TO SAHALIN

A JOURNEY
TO SAHALIN

by James McConkey

COWARD, McCANN & GEOGHEGAN, INC.

NEW YORK

Dedications such as "For God, Man and Yale" seem archaic to us, I suppose, because we've become uncertain about all three of the elements involved. But I think that a Brangwen, my fictional university, can still serve as a valid element in a dedication if we as a people can maintain both a search for a transcendent order we obscurely intuit within ourselves, and a feeling of compassion for our fellows. It is in this sense that I dedicate this novel

FOR COLERIDGE, CHEKHOV, AND BRANGWEN.

If such a phrase seems presumptuous, I can say in my defense that I thought of it while writing the book in a villa just outside Florence, my own most glorious Sahalin (no prison camp there: from my desk I looked out at a nearby slope of olive trees and grapevines and, in the distance, the blue mountains of Tuscany topped for many months of the year with snow), and believed from my retreat that anything was possible. I am grateful to the John Simon Guggenheim Foundation for providing the wherewithal necessary for such physical and spiritual perspectives.

This is a novel about the interrelationship of public and

. . . BOMB CURB WASTES AMERICAN LIVES: LE

private matters. My involvement in the disturbing events at Cornell University in 1968–69 gave me some insight into the way public events affect our personal lives and the way our personal lives in turn affect what we do or say in public. But this novel, as an imaginative rendering of experience, constructs its own history, its own people, and its own institutions. Brangwen University and the residents of Philippa, New York, are constructions of a mind that felt the need to prove to itself that individuals (whatever the evidence to the contrary) remain responsible for their personal destinies and are involved in the destiny of their nation.

JAMES MC CONKEY

Trumansburg, New York
New Year's Day, 1971

PART I

What he was dreaming was this: his house was on fire and his daughter Mary burning; his house was on fire in some other wing (in his dreams the old house was always larger than it really was, something he even vaguely knew while dreaming), and Mary, her hair burning, her flimsy nightgown ablaze, came screaming through the halls and into his room—the room where he lay with Stella—and fell between them. He put out the fire with his pillow and blanket and kissed her seared eyelids while she sobbed. He was cross with Stella for not being concerned enough to wake up.

Toward morning he had another dream—a vision of God— which made him later remember the first dream as only some sort of nagging anxiety about Mary, who was off in Massachusetts, in college, apparently still too caught up in private problems to study. In this second dream, God had just created the world and peopled it, but he, George Chambers, angered by God's complacency, said, "Tell me, God, what's your justification for yourself?" And God said, "You are, my son." He said, "Come off it, God, and level with me. What's your *real* justification?" And God, who was simply a radiant face, turned that face to look at another radiant face behind him, saying, "He is;" and that second face turned to a third, saying, "He is;" and so it went, throughout infinity. The last voice he heard came from very far off.

Not knowing whether he was pleased or near despair, but deciding on the former, Chambers awoke to God—the morning sun—in his eyes. It was still early, but Stella was gone from the bed. After he dressed, he went downstairs into the kitchen, smelling burned coffee (last night's coffee had been put on the stove to heat, but had boiled away); without giving it much thought he prepared a fresh pot and while it began to perk he wandered out through the woodshed (replacing, as he went, the garbage can lid: "It's not that I'm neat," he said aloud to himself, for he really wasn't; it was just that with the town dump half a mile away one had to do whatever one could to keep the rats there) and into the backyard. Once an open field, it seemed almost one again, for the weeds grew high in the uncut grass; Stella sat on her stool in the middle of it, surrounded by blue blooms on the tall stalks of chicory. A cat dozed in her lap, two more near her feet. She was wearing her dressing robe over her nightgown, and was too intent with her watercolors to notice him. In the distance, on the Wilcox farm, cows were bellowing: Hayden was late with his milking, as usual. George came up behind his wife. "Hello, Stella," he said, giving her a kiss on her sun-warmed cheek.

She jumped. "Oh, my Lord," she said, for she had dropped a puddle of brown in a corner of the paper. "Good morning," she said, and looked ruefully at her painting, an abstraction mainly in greenish-brown and yellow. "Maybe it's better with it," she said of the dark brown, and rapidly and haphazardly increased the smear with her brush. "An ugly mess of brown shows I know the rest is all sentimentality. I can't quite get what I'm after. When I first saw the sky, there was this greenish streamer of a cloud and this—this indescribable haze as the sun came up."

"Smog from the dump."

"Call it what you like—it was remarkable." Stella sighed, crumpling her watercolor and tossing it to the ground. "Hand me another sheet—there, in that book by my left foot—would you, George? I don't want to disturb Miranda."

"Maybe you ought to paint your dreams," Chambers said. He gave her the sheet, scratching the cat's ears as he did so.

"When I'm nervous," Stella said thoughtfully, "I sometimes see the strangest patterns; but always a moment before I fall asleep, too late to do anything about it . . . I see colors in my sleep, nothing terrifying or clever about them like your dreams, George—just beautiful colors, but they don't exist, at least not on this earth."

"I had a dream this morning," he said cheerfully. "One face after another."

"You simply can't do the human form anymore. Neither in entirety nor in part."

"I don't see why not. When you come down to it, it's still attractive enough, and I really don't see what else we've got to take much pride in."

She grimaced. "But it's already been done, as an ideal I mean. The Greeks and Michelangelo—all that." She waved vaguely at the past, pained to have to attack a cliché with an argument that was in itself another. "Epochs of generous breasts and handsome buttocks and noble brows and cute little penises."

"Is that last an ideal?"

"No luck for you, old boy." Stella gave him a wicked smile. "It was the way the sculptor had to assert his own sexuality before those domineering bronze and marble thighs. *He* wasn't going to be squelched by the size of his creations. If you want to find the secret behind the golden age of sculpture, look to the penis."

"Oh, come now, Stella," he protested. "That's pretty silly, you know." But he laughed, liking his wife. What he liked at this moment was, in a way, a pose—her ironic, artistic self. She was almost his age, mother of a girl in college and a son in his last year of high school; she was beginning to get stout, her hair was starting to gray; but here she could be sitting outdoors in her nightgown and robe at eight in the morning, solemnly making

BLACKS MOVE OUT OF FORMER RIOT AREA IN

outrageous theories about art. "If what you say is true," he said, willing to go along with it in spite of all, "then what you as a modern with your can't-draw-people complex—what you need is only some secret of your own to set you up. Didn't Maynard"— Maynard was a local artist on the art faculty of the university —"have some luck with human figures for a time? He was fond of pinheads. Doesn't he think of himself as an intellectual?"

"That ass!" Stella hissed in indignation, half rising from her stool; the cat jumped down and stalked away. "He drew one self-portrait after another without knowing it. Didn't I beat him out at the May show with my sepias? Oh, George, you can't do anything with a brush, some paints, and a sneer."

"*You're* sneering."

"I'm not painting." She sat back and crossed her arms.

"I know when it's time to go." He started to leave, looking back to the house, and saw the trail he'd made in the dew. "My shoes are soaked," he said. "Why is it that Mark hasn't cut the grass? All he has to do is sit in the seat and *drive*."

"Maybe he likes the chicory blossoms," Stella said. "So do I." She reached down to pick a stalk at random, and looked at the blossom. "They've got such an intense, idiotic color. Stare at one and—I don't know—it becomes the universe—blue and beautiful and—and pitiless." Her eyes were wet. "For God's sake I'm getting paranoid," and she tossed the flower away.

He felt both tender and uneasy; but when he spoke, he was unexpectedly speaking of his daughter. "I wish Mary would write," he said.

"So do I." Stella was wiping her eyes.

"But she won't."

"I expect not."

"She really didn't have to leave home so early. In July, I mean."

"She had her heart set on that summer camp near her school."

"Do you really believe that?" Chambers asked.

"No."

"Well," he said, dawdling, unwilling to leave, "if the grass isn't cut before the first snow, it will all mat down; and what will we have for a lawn next year?"

Stella brightened. "A whole field of chicory, perhaps?" She feigned absolute joy at the prospect.

He sighed. "At least the roots are said to be good in coffee."

"I left some coffee for you, warming on the stove."

"I know; I'll get it." He jogged off to the house, having never told her about his dream, but her chicory blossoms were not, after all, much different from his God faces. He dreamed and Stella saw; his nights often were a bother, and her days. He had the better of it there.

Mark sat at the kitchen table, eating cornflakes and staring at at the box. Chambers poured a cup of coffee and sat opposite his son. "Good morning," he said.

Mark pushed his hair away from his eyes but said nothing. Chambers drank his coffee, watching Mark. His son was a thin boy, rather small for his age. He had large eyes and a large and sensitive mouth. Fine blond strands curled from his upper lip and cheeks; they gave him the look of having just poked his face through a cobweb. His brown hair fell down all around his head; the tips of his ears were pink rocks in a murky flood. Why was it, Chambers asked himself, that such a face would be impossible to paint anymore? Would it be sentimental? One could give emphasis to the raw blotch on the chin: Mark had stood before the bathroom mirror, forgetting to comb his hair in his ceaseless war against pimples. Was it that his son was simply like all adolescent sons, a type, and types have been done to death, reduced to the cliché? He was touched, the father was— by what? Not by the cliché, but by what was hidden from him —by all that was disguised, all the worries and dreams that an adolescent keeps to himself; touched perhaps by his own memory of himself at that age. But what he was remembering, drinking his coffee, was himself at an earlier age, the time he had been running up the school stairs in the seventh grade, going back to the art room to pick up the Brontosaurus he had carved

WOMEN, PSYCHOLOGISTS REPORT . . . AIR

from Ivory soap, and had felt himself having an erection, the first one he'd ever been conscious of, just as two teachers were passing . . . Mark looked up once, to see if his father was watching him; finding out that he was, he turned quickly back to the cereal box.

Chambers said at last, "Do you want to come home on the bus or wait for me?"

"Wait for you in front of Sears. Six o'clock."

"I can't promise to be there on the dot. Woudn't it be better if you came on the bus? You'd have time to mow the grass."

Mark took a spoonful of cereal. "Can't mow the grass."

"Why not?"

"We're going to see about Phil."

"Who's Phil?"

"Guy I know. In my class."

"Professor Durant's son?"

"Yeah."

"Where's Phil?"

"In jail."

"In *jail?*" A dialogue with his son, Chambers thought, was stichomythia; he felt himself a character in an unfolding myth he'd never heard of before.

"That's what I said."

"What's he doing there?"

Mark gave him a look of irritation. "What do you do in jail? *Wait*, I guess. Phil is *waiting* in jail, that's what he's doing."

"I mean, for God's sake, what did he do to get *put* in jail? You must know what I meant—"

"Well, you don't need to get so mad."

"I'm not mad," Chambers said. "I'm just interested in why a friend of yours would be in jail."

"You don't need to be so intense about it."

"And you needn't be so defensive."

"Why should *I* be defensive?"

"I don't know why."

POLLUTION DOWN 25% IN NEW YORK CITY,

"Well, I'm not defensive," Mark said. "I didn't do anything. If you thought I did anything—"

"It was the furthest thought from my mind."

"You were just sitting there, *staring* at me."

"When I came in?"

"Yes."

Chambers laughed.

"What are you laughing at?" Mark asked.

"I guess I'm embarrassed. Do you really want to know what I was thinking?"

"What?"

"I was remembering my first erection."

"No kidding!" Mark looked at him with interest. "That's a funny thing to be remembering. How old were you?"

"Twelve or so. I was going after a soap sculpture I had made, a dinosaur—"

"Kids used to get quite aroused over things like dinosaurs in your day, I guess."

"Oh, cut it out, Mark. I was just wondering if you were worried about some sexual problem—"

Mark smiled indulgently, pushing his hair back. "No; it was just this terribly stupid thing that Phil did . . . He painted a peace symbol on the courthouse wall."

"There might be stupider things to paint."

"Well, he also wrote, in big block letters, 'Alleluia, I'm a bum.' "

"What made him write that?"

"I said it was *stupid*, didn't I? It's all very complicated. The sheriff called the principal who knew it had to be one of us—one of the guys interested in music as well as politics—because of the way he spelled 'alleluia.' Phil confessed, though of course he didn't have to, so they put him in a cell with a junkie and a pervert."

"They did *what?*" Chambers rose from his chair, astonished by the violence in himself.

"I said—"

MAYOR CLAIMS . . . SCUBA ARCHAEOLOGISTS

"How do you know that's what they are?"

"You *look*. It's written all over them. Just call them old creeps if it makes you feel better."

"You went to the jail?"

"Yesterday, with Mr. Ferguson."

"Your principal?"

"The same."

"For God's sake, you might have told me."

"Don't get mad, huh?" Mark pushed his hair back.

"I'm not angry at *you*." Chambers paced the room. "Listen, does your friend have a lawyer? I'll call Bolgano. He'd be perfect in a case like this; he does most of the work for the Civil Liberties Union—"

Mark got up and rinsed his cereal bowl in the sink. "All that happened is that Phil did this silly thing, and they did this silly thing back. Either they took him at his word—I mean, that he was a bum—or they didn't want him to be one and so locked him up for a week with a couple who were. Either way, isn't that how the system works? It isn't your responsibility; we're taking care of it." He looked out the window. "Oh, Lord I'm late again," he said cheerfully, glad to avoid further questioning, and grabbing some texts and tattered papers from the hall table, ran out the door to the waiting school bus.

Chambers watched the bus lumber down the country lane. It mollified him somewhat. *He* liked school buses, which were part of the system; he liked the way they drove down remote roads as well as highways, picking up the little kids who—different from boys Mark's age—were always waiting expectantly by the mailboxes, holding school books in both hands, their mothers usually by their side; yes, he liked yellow school buses, which were phenomenally punctual considering the weather, the way trains used to be; and he liked the yellow snowplows as well, the plows which, on silent winter nights, came thundering past, slicing through the drifts before his country house, red lights pulsing like hearts on the high roofs of the cabs. He was, he supposed, enough of an administrator to appreciate such rolling

FIND SHIP SUNK IN TIME OF ALEXANDER THE

stock of the local polity; at any rate, buses and plows made one think, in their passing, that all was well. On his grave he would like to see a stone with these words:

Here lies
GEORGE CHAMBERS, minor administrator,
who, whatever his faults,
loved his wife Stella
and
his children Mary and Mark;
and whose
affection for school buses and snowplows
remained ever steadfast

Possibly Stella could do a drawing of it, to hang above his desk, to keep him from forgetting.

Chambers laughed.

Yet a moment ago, hearing about a jailed high school student, his heart had been beating as if he were face to face, in that homely and familiar farmhouse kitchen, with an opponent—sheriff or judge or school principal—whom he might strangle. Why should *he*, in a sense a public official himself, turn suddenly in such outright hostility upon those who represented the public order? Ten or even five years ago his response to some similar news would have been one of incredulity. Throughout his adult life, Chambers had been freer of rage and hostility than most people, without ever taking pride in the fact; perhaps he had simply been able to control them better, recognizing them as emotions which normally lowered his self-esteem. It surprised him, the degree to which he could almost revel in hostility, when his sense of social injustice gave him permission. A person's own desire for generosity of soul, for fairness in human relationships, could become, in uncertain times, the key which liberated the beast from its cage.

He wandered upstairs, bothered by such thoughts; he was vaguely in pursuit of a clean handkerchief and the change and fountain pen on his dresser top. A sheet of paper skittered across

GREAT . . . LINDSAY DECRIES RACIAL AND

the hallway floor in the morning wind. Mark's window was open; it had come from his desk, for other papers were fluttering on its littered surface. He picked up the sheet, holding it as he went to shut the window; and he saw that it was an unfinished letter in Mark's handwriting, and that it was to Mary. "I shouldn't," Chambers said; but he was a father like any other father, and so he did, reading rapidly and with guilt:

In my room, 7 A.M.

DEAR MARY,

I woke up early as you can see. Bad night.

If what you said yesterday on the phone is true, I think you ought to come home. You aren't a boy and wouldn't be drafted for saying the hell with it, and if you can't study or even go to classes you wouldn't be missing much. As for the peanut butter crackers, you can eat them here all day as well as you can in your dumb room there.

I know we all miss you here, Mom in her own way as much as Dad and I ("me" sounds better) and you could certainly help with the housework. As you know Dad doesn't believe in servants any more than you or I do, but if anybody needs help it is our mother who is outside *right now* in her p.j.'s painting away. By the way I heard some awful coughing the other night after I had gone to bed and looked through that hot air grating, the one you told me you used to use to spy on the dining room when you were a kid. Can you believe they—*our* parents!—were passing a joint back and forth, holding their noses so they could get the smoke down and making awful faces and coughing and giggling? I know the smell from after school. There's a new little jar marked "Exotic Spices" on the shelf and it has dried leaves in it. I think Mom must have planted some somewhere. Isn't that like her though? You need to come home and take hold.

But what I really want to talk about is something else. You know that Information Please club you formed as a pressure group to make the school give us something more than the old garbage like the *Reader's Digest?* You thought it had folded before the term was up. Well school's hardly begun but IP's going strong after a summer's sleep, Phoenix reborn and all that. We have no officers

RELIGIOUS TENSION AS TEACHERS' STRIKE

(participatory democracy), but if anybody is responsible it is your brother. Thinking of what happened to you in Washington (I know you don't want to remember it, but you've got to, Mary, if you ever want to get back your old zip) I had to do something *political*. I just had to, Mary. We started it with that group in music class (a select few because you've got to be nuts to take a twelfth-grade music elective) and Mrs. Peard who's the new music teacher turned out to be very sympatico (sp?). But we have to go underground without an adviser now because Ferguson is scared as you can imagine on account of a stupid and wholly unauthorized (by the IP) thing that Phil Durant did. (He's the son of Prof. Durant in philosophy at the U.) Phil's in jail for defacing the courthouse. The judge said it would cost ten thousand dollars to sandblast the words off the bricks, but after school today the IP group is going to try paint remover and Spic and Span and water.

We're going to need all the help we can get this year with IP, and since you started it in the first place you can come home and give us the benefit of your experience. That would be good for you and good for us, so why not?

When you call me at the Rooster Thursday, you'll have this letter and can let me know how you feel about it. I'll finish this tonight and let you know if we got rid of the words and have sprung Phil.

Chambers put the letter on Mark's desk, under a disassembled transistor radio, shouted good-bye out the window to Stella, and started off to work in the VW, having first had to wipe off the moisture the morning mist had left on the distributor points. He didn't mind such activity; it gave him the sense of mastery over a complex piece of equipment whenever he could make it operate with a few massages of a dry rag. The distributor cap snapped off and snapped back on in a satisfactory way. On particularly cold winter mornings, he snapped off the air cleaner, which had a similar spring catch, pushed the spray button of a pressurized can a couple of times, squirting ether into the carburetor to make the reluctant engine start. It set him up much the way that massaging the points did. One morning the previous winter, even the ether hadn't worked; he had some sort of crucial meeting with the president and the assembled vice-presidents, but no way to get to it (the engine of Stella's Dodge wouldn't turn over even once—just an idiotic cluck when he turned the key), so he had simply aimed the spray toward his nose, squirted once, and had felt quite fine. There was something to be said about modern technological advances; but Chambers decided, as his car bounced past the dump entrance, that maybe they weren't worth the litter. Transparent plastic bags were impaled on the hedges and white pines; plastic Clorox bottles and aluminum beer cans filled the ditch; a yellow plastic bag of the fifty-gallon variety lay in the middle of the road, run over already, the grapefruit rinds and a viscous fluid spilling from its mouth like the sour contents of some animal's mangled guts.

People were pretty goddamned messy; he was upset by Mark's letter no doubt, but still he had never dribbled his garbage down the road. His house was the closest one to the dump, so he had more reason for care; nevertheless, one could tell something about the nature of mankind from the manner in which people tended to their refuse. Cats covered their feces; men flushed them down toilets, but if they were out in the woods . . . He remembered suddenly and with distaste a soiled newspaper he'd come across as a child in a park somewhere.

"Oh, for Christ's sake, Chambers," he said; feces were a distressing image so early in the day. Upset because of Mary, his thoughts had been veering away from her, but now he preferred the worries she brought. What was the terrible thing that had happened to Mary in Washington? He had driven her and some college students to the Washington March in the Dodge that year, and she had stayed on to visit her cousin who studied foreign relations at the International University. Had something happened that day to account for her sullen withdrawal, her loss not only of appetite but of any kind of apparent joy, her poor showing at college? But he dismissed the questions almost as soon as they came, for they were too painful, and anyway the

ONASSIS AFTER CEREMONY ON GREEK ISLE . . .

answers were temporarily withheld from him. He beguiled himself by seeing Mary at twelve or thirteen, smiling as she ran toward him through a field of oats, her blond hair almost the color of the ripe grain, her eyes bright with some kind of prospective mischief—for Chambers, who disliked cameras, was his own Polaroid, knowing the precise instant at which his mind would catch for a lifetime flowing hair and an expression of the eyes. Out of fear of sentimentality or triteness, one might not wish to paint or even photograph such a moment; but the mind frames it with all experience, and there it exists, God knows, with a burning boy in the newspaper and a soldier shot through the belly who in his unclear agony prays to Jesus for a bowel movement. Chambers shook away these images to see Mary as a three-year-old, being pushed off the porch on her tricycle by that six-year-old who used to bully all the smaller children in the Floral Street neighborhood. How he had wanted—still wanted—to shake that sly little bastard with his obsequious smiles for all adults! His heart began to beat as it had earlier in the kitchen.

Floral Street had been Chambers' experiment in living with the poor, but he had moved to the country—a fact which he readily admitted to anybody—as soon as his salary had permitted him a gracious old farmhouse for his family. Floral Street and his social conscience had something to do with his ambivalent feelings toward the town dump. He had known it to be there when he bought the house (though then it had been small enough to be hidden from the road) and in fact had welcomed its presence. Somebody, probably a poet, had said that a study ought to have a window facing a garden and another window facing a dump. Democracy, whatever else it might be, was more a town dump than a formal garden.

Chambers had turned from his little county road onto the state highway and drove with the sun splashing gold against the dust of his windshield, thinking of the folly of non-returnable containers. Dumps were filling up all over America because of (1) the increasing population and (2) the increasing use of non-returnable plastic and aluminum containers. Capitalism, being a fairly mindless affair, turned out aluminum Budweiser cans (who cares that the supplies of bauxite are dwindling?) and plastic Coca-Cola bottles because consumers like Chambers himself were increasing in numbers and prosperity (a growing population makes for a growing economy) and would rather toss away a container than collect a penny or two for returning a glass bottle. What a piece of human stupidity that was! He ought to stop drinking beer unless he had the option of returning the bottle or can, or perhaps he ought rather to begin a campaign.

As he envisioned his campaign, all Americans would be asked to stock their non-returnable containers in their basements and garages. On Non-Returnable Container Day—NRCD—they would drive to their neighborhood supermarkets and fill every aisle with them; non-returnables would rise up in waves, cascading over the Tide and Joy and Gleem, rising over the pyramids of Skippy Peanut Butter, sliding down in glittering and tinkling avalanches over the cash registers themselves. If the bottles and cans overflowed the stores, then into the parking lots with them, into the streets, into the courthouses, into the jails, into the homes of the manufacturers of Budweiser and Coca-Cola and Schlitz, into the homes of the importers of Schweppes' Tonic, into the White House and the halls of Congress.

Chambers, engrossed as he was and blinded by the sun, went over the rise without seeing the school bus; his VW barged into the massive bumper, its little hood capsizing in the car's effort to slide beneath; Chambers, caught in the wreckage, lost consciousness, thinking, "Thank God, I didn't hit one of them."

ADVANCE AGAINST BIAFRAN CAPITAL . . .

2

George Chambers did not die, though he was close enough to death for a day or so to know what it was all about, which was nothing. He lay without pain, without sensation of any kind except for the awareness of a cave or a well at the end or bottom of which there was a flickering—some aurora borealis of the nerve tips—and the buzzing of a chain saw or a Volkswagen engine. He had angered something that was separate from his mind, something that dwelt in the cave. "I'm sorry," his mind finally told whatever it was that was so distraught; the buzzing lessened and he slowly began to mend. A splintered rib had almost pierced his heart; he had a neat little incision on his chest—a fragment of bone had been removed—which, while the bandage was being changed, looked as if it could be zipped open some day for an examination of the workings and a possible replacement of defective parts. He had also broken his leg.

His first visitors were Stella and Mark. They came into his room with that guise of cheerfulness which hides dismay at the sight of glucose bottles and swollen faces. Stella brought him a bouquet of chicory blossoms. "Oh, George, they're already withering," she said, bending down to give him a kiss. "Chicory's best in the grass."

O'BOYLE SUPPORTS CHURCH STAND ON BIRTH

"I mowed the yard," Mark said. He stood uncomfortably, hands in the back pockets of his jeans.

"What else have you been doing?" Chambers said. They couldn't hear him; his voice was a whisper. He motioned for Mark to come closer. "Were you able to wash off the words?" he asked.

Mark said, "You read my letter."

"I've paid for my sins."

"We got it off all right," Mark said. "Sandblasting for ten thousand dollars! We hardly needed the paint remover. We had to stall around until the photographer came." He took a *Philippa Daily Express* clipping out of his wallet and gave it to Chambers. There was a picture of seven or eight high school students, the boys all with hair as long as Mark's, the girls as well as the boys dressed in jeans and T-shirts. It was a posed shot of them standing in a row and scrubbing away at a clean wall. Chambers read the news account:

> Students of a high school leftist organization, "Information Please," yesterday afternoon washed off a sign painted on the north wall of the courthouse by one of their members, Philip Durant, Jr., 18, son of Dr. and Mrs. Philip Durant, 115 Craft Lane, Lakeview Heights.
>
> The Durant youth had been jailed for defacing the public building, but was released into the custody of his parents after Sheriff Oscar Delaney told Judge Horace Casey that friends of the boy had managed to remove the paint.
>
> Judge Casey, in commending the "Information Please" group for its action on behalf of one of its members, asked if the group felt an equal responsibility toward the city and the country as well.
>
> "If young people like these banded together in support of decency and public order," he said, "the problems of America would be solved."
>
> A leader of the student group, Mark Chambers, 17, accused the sheriff of jailing the Durant youth in a cell with a man held on a sexual offense and another who is being bound over to the Grand Jury on charges of trafficking in narcotics.

CONTROL METHODS . . . SPOCK SAYS NIXON

"Is this the way Judge Casey thinks the city is going to turn its youth into responsible adults?" he asked. He is the son of Mr. and Mrs. George Chambers, R.D. 1.

The courthouse sign was composed of a peace symbol and the words, "Hallelujah, I'm a bum." According to High School Principal Thomas Ferguson, the sign "was of no apparent significance." He termed "Information Please" an organization of "bright students, mainly children of Brangwen University personnel" whose "energies have been diverted, rightly or wrongly, into protest, and who need adult guidance."

Chambers handed back the clipping. "I see you're a leftist," he said.

"Newspapers! Do you see they said Phil was eighteen? That's to protect the sheriff. Phil's my age. You're supposed to be eighteen to be put in jail. They didn't even get 'alleluia' right, and I spelled it for them."

"You wanted the publicity?"

Mark shrugged. "Why not?"

"It appeals to the prejudices of everybody in town who thinks the university makes nothing but trouble."

"It tells off the judge, doesn't it? Shouldn't I have said that?"

Chambers began a topic of greater concern to him. "You seemed to want Mary home very much," he said.

"In my letter? I never mailed it."

"I thought that maybe—maybe she would come when she heard I was in the hospital." He found it even more difficult to say the sentence than the soreness of his chest justified.

"We phoned her," Stella said. "She wanted us to let her know right away if you took a condition—how do those awful phrases go?—'if you took a condition for the worse.' "

" 'Take a condition' sounds like a willful choice, like 'taking a wife,' " Chambers said. "I take a condition, if it's up to me, to get the hell out of here."

"If there *happened* to be an emergency, Mary would be on the next plane out of Boston," Stella said. "You can count on that. Or 'you can rest assured.' Oh, George, when I'm upset all

WILL   WIN   BUT   IT   DOESN'T   MATTER   .   .   .

I can *do* is talk in clichés. That's what everybody does, visiting in the hospital."

"Mary's staying near a telephone, as a matter of fact," Mark said. "We're going to call her as soon as we get home."

"Of course I was never in any real danger," Chambers said; he felt his eyes filling with tears. "I would have thought though—"

"Oh, cut it out, Dad," Mark said, hitting his fist against his other hand. He stared at the ceiling.

"I was only about to make a joke," Chambers said. "I was about to say that I thought Mary might want to come home to bury the Volkswagen; she used to love it so. I taught her to drive in it—"

"She never said a word about the car," Mark said miserably. "It was *you* she— Oh, never mind."

"I want you both to know I'm here out of my stupidity," Chambers said. "I was dreaming of a campaign to return non-returnable cans and bottles. I had them filling the White House and Congress—"

"And up the stairs of the Pentagon?" Mark laughed, and then caught himself.

"What happened to Mary in Washington, Mark?"

"I promised not to tell."

"But I'm her *father*, for Christ's sake."

"And I'm her brother. It was something told in full confidence. You wouldn't want me to break a vow, would you?"

"Let's none of us use such abominable phrases," Stella said brightly. "Let us vow, never again. Let me tell George who called—"

"Listen, Mark," Chambers said. "It's quite possible that I hit that school bus because I *wanted* to get hurt, you know? To bring Mary back. I read your letter and was upset—"

"You're trying to take advantage of your accident to make me break a confidence."

"I still want to know."

"When she wants to tell you, she'll tell you, I guess. You

HUMPHREY GAINS, LATEST POLL SHOWS . . .

always said we should keep confidences and be honest. That was one of *your* virtues, I thought."

Chambers smiled at his son's earnestness. "All right, I don't want you to tell me." He reached for Mark's hand. "Whatever your leftist tendencies, you're a good son."

"For Christ's sake," said Mark, blushing, and pulled his hand away.

"The president called," Stella said. "He says he needs your help and why did you do this thing to him. He says there are problems coming up with the militant blacks and the radical whites."

"That sounds like the president," Chambers said. "He reads the newspapers too much, looking for his latest speech. What's a 'militant'? What's a 'radical'? Can you show me one? Do you remember that party at Bolgano's—"

"*He* called too. Jimmy called."

"—when I had only one drink, but got this revelation: There is no such thing as a radical anymore. There may be kooks, nuts, self-serving idiots, adolescent Maoists, young Christs looking everywhere for their crosses, I don't know; but there aren't any radicals. Do you know why?"

"You shouldn't excite yourself, George." Stella bent down over him, frowning and feeling his forehead as if he were a delirious child. "And Phyllis called."

"Because it takes a sane world for there to be radicals. It takes good earth. Radical comes from 'root.' A radical gets down to the essence, but there has to be an essence to be got . . . Does Phyllis miss me?"

"You know she does. You know how she dislikes taking orders from that young crew-cut fellow who wants to marry her. I think Phyllis is in *love* with you, George."

"Of course she is. Who else called?" He was shamelessly enjoying this list of worrying people.

Stella hesitated. "Well, Cecil Maynard asked about you."

"That's surprising."

NO RESPONSE FROM HANOI ON NEW PEACE

"Actually, he called to see if I'd have lunch with him to-morrow."

"I thought you hated Maynard. One of the last things you said to me was that he was a pinhead."

"He's cynical—but after all, why shouldn't he be? His wife left him for that manager of the supermarket who was being transferred. I haven't done anything like that but you're full of cynicism anyway—"

"I am not." He would have been outraged, had his chest not hurt; as it was, he simply gave her an appealing look.

"All about that lack of good earth. But no, you're too senti-mental to be a cynic." She patted his hand. "You insist that people be better than they are. It would be better for you if you had a little cynicism."

"So now you prefer Maynard to me because he sneers better?"

"I didn't say that, George. Don't be a baby. I thought that Maynard disliked my work, but apparently he doesn't. He said I deserved to win in the May show. He invited me to lunch to talk about business."

"What do artists have to do with business?"

"Have you read about the way doctors all over the country are banding together, incorporating themselves? Why, they're doing it right here in town. I bet you don't even know who operated on you; it depends on the day. Somebody else will take out the stitches, whoever is responsible for stitches on the day they have you written down for that. *If* they remembered to write you down. If not, you'll have to ask. It has something to do with taxes. They can retire at a hundred thousand a year instead of twenty—"

"Artists like you and Maynard don't make five hundred a year." He felt that he was really becoming feverish; Stella was babbling on about somebody she knew who was a prostitute, no, who was not, who was a good artist, one whose work had sud-denly become famous because of the governor of New York or Jackie Kennedy Onassis or maybe it had been the Shah of Iran;

PROPOSAL . . . EXPERTS PREDICT RACIAL STRIFE

as she talked her head seemed to grow and shrink, to waver as if it were under water.

"Stella," he said, "I think you're drowning."

"What?" But she went on, excited by some idea Maynard had given her. Art had become an investment, a means of profit like oil wells, and why had artists always sold their best work, the labor of a lifetime, for a glass of wine? Artists should look after their own interests, incorporate themselves—

"Mark," Chambers said, dazed, "is your mother making sense?"

"It sounds like a business cooperative," Mark said. "If somebody hits the jackpot, they all get a share and cheat the government in the process. If that leads to socialism, it's probably a good idea."

"I know what's not a good idea," Chambers said. "Progressive hospitals, full of incorporated doctors, where they let visitors in at any hour to chatter on as long as they like. I love you both, but if I don't go to sleep, I'm going to throw up."

They left, and instantly he was in a long and peaceful slumber.

He spent ten days in the hospital. The routine of hospital life, which at first had seemed to him, in his drugged and early convalescent state, strange and remarkable and aimed solely at his personal recovery, came to seem commonplace. Like all other institutions, the hospital had a reality and conventions of its own. Truth here was cleanliness and efficiency; the starched uniforms of the nurses crackled early in the morning like static electricity or dried locust shells remembered from his childhood. There was the customary hierarchy of any institution: here the unseen hospital management and board of trustees responsible to the county taxpayers, then the various ranks of the seen, the doctors, interns, nurses, nurse's aides, orderlies, and custodians, a busy and disciplined army around whose activities the volunteer ladies of the hospital guild skirted with a certain

EXCEEDING SUMMER GHETTO VIOLENCE . . .

sweet but bewildered obsequiousness, pushing little carts loaded with candy and cigarettes and reading material.

Trundling himself down the corridor toward the potted ferns of the sunroom in a wheelchair, his cast (to which Stella had imparted an only partly abstract female form in wild colors) stuck out before him like the decorated prow of a nineteenth-century whaling ship, he passed the geriatrics ward where the patients, their cheeks sunken, mumbled to themselves, drooling, their arms and legs and heads sometimes violently shaking as if the film—for they were but images and reflections of lost identities—had slipped on its sprocket, their eyes half-blinded with cataracts or just age; all of them mercifully oblivious not only to the prow of his Pequod but to the sheeted corpse being wheeled from their midst by a radiantly blond-haired athlete to where? To a frozen locker? To wherever they took the dead who had lived too long. And when, back in his room, he listened despite himself to the incessant bickering of the roommate brought in to occupy the empty bed—a middle-aged storekeeper suffering from emphysema—and that roommate's wife, a series of bitter incriminations, masked by the proper hospital smiles, covering such topics as expenses, clothing needs, long-distance telephone calls, undelivered promises and the relegation of responsibility for ungrateful and bratty offspring, he knew that any point there might be in life could not survive such dreary enmity.

And yet what bothered him most was how, after he listened to such poison from puckered lips, it began to make no further impression upon him. He could accept it, just as he accepted the hospital routine, the silly (from his point of view) awakening at dawn of a corridor of patients better off asleep to get their respective faces washed, their respective temperatures taken. He ate, dutifully, his breakfast, though he never had more than coffee at home; he waited for his morning backrub and the eleven o'clock visit from his doctor. And so his day went. What had been strange had become familiar, he had adjusted to it even as he had adjusted to a stiffness in his chest and a leg encased in plaster, and no doubt he would feel deprived of something—pills? cold toast? the buzzer behind his bed?—when he went home. A baby born in the maternity ward could be transferred to pediatrics and, at the proper age (if the child was the proper sex and certain alterations in hospital procedures were first made), be transferred back to maternity to deliver an infant of her own; thence onward through gynecology and minor and major surgery to the ultimate goal of geriatrics. The little notice in the hospital newspaper acknowledging with regret the end could refer to the equanimity of the deceased, her eternal trust in the administration and staff, and her cheerful adherence to the code of cleanliness and efficiency—as attested to by the fact that she had always awakened with a smile to the approach of washcloth and thermometer. In short, her life would have had societal meaning.

This kind of adjustment to, or simple acceptance of, environmental or cultural or social reality no matter what, which once had seemed to Chambers of inestimable value, accounting for men's stubborn perseverance and endurance despite all hardship and pain (he remembered, for example, having been touched by the suffering eyes in a newspaper photograph of a Blue Star mother who would "go on" adding to her huge ball of tinfoil for the war effort, although her only child had been killed on Omaha Beach) now suddenly appeared as something quite the reverse, as the most impressive argument possible for human pointlessness. One could see the human race mindlessly adapting to an Earth whose land masses were continuous New Yorks or Tokyos, whose atmosphere was forever gray with soot and whose waters—viscid with green slime—contained only slender metallic fish equipped with deadly explosive darts. The unchanging good that we dimly perceive now and again, the ultimate order, the universal laws, were humanistic illusions to mock us and make us strangers to ourselves; meanings, values, were to be found not in what all people shared, but rather in what separated them: the particular environments (however ugly, however changing) and traditions they had inherited or slipped into, the skins they had been born with.

Sitting in his wheelchair in a corner of the sunroom, Chambers looked from the homely toes at the end of his cast to the dusty fern at his elbow and thought that a letter to his Senator —for an idea that might aid in the integration of working-class neighborhoods had occurred to him some weeks before—might be a release for him, and so he began to write with haste:

DEAR SENATOR JAVITS:

I limit myself in this letter to some considerations of property. The Catholic Church, as you must know, once thought of property as an extension of personality; if such a view can be considered a reasonable one, the Church itself (judging from its insatiable need for ever larger holdings in the medieval period and later) must have been undergoing a severe identity crisis. Nevertheless we should begin to understand—

No, no, that would never do. What could possess him to begin a letter about racial integration to a liberal Jew with an attack on the Catholic Church? He deliberated whether or not he should tear up the sheet and swallow all the pieces, but ended up making of it too tight a wad for a prying custodian to want to untangle and buried it deep in the dirt of the fern.

It was a passing thing, this empty despair. He'd had moments like this in the past and had managed to vanquish them. *They* were something he shared with mankind.

On his next to the last day as a hospital patient, he had an unexpected visitor, Fred Henry, a black student at Brangwen. Chambers was alone in the room, reading; he hadn't known he had a visitor in the chair until Henry mildly said, as if he were continuing a discussion from that morning and not the previous year, "Mr. Chambers, I figured out an answer to that problem."

He looked up, startled and then gratified. "Oh, hello, Fred," he said, dropping his book and propping himself up against the pillow. "Which problem?" He smiled. "I remember a lot of them."

"Not *those* problems—later than that." Henry did not return

ENEMY SAILORS AS GOODWILL GESTURE . . .

the smile; he would not even play at their former relationship. In his underclass years, at the time the university began its efforts to enroll students from the ghettos, he had held a working scholarship, serving as a student aid in Chambers' office. Toward the end of his sophomore year, he had quit the job—out of hopelessness with it perhaps, but doubtless more out of a sense of misplaced allegiance; he had been working to organize the black students and had become, even before he renounced the job, the first president of the League of Black Students. "That literary problem," he said. "We were having coffee at the Union last spring, and you were looking through my short story text; we got into an argument over Pynchon and Joyce."

"What was my position? I remember, it was over 'Araby,'" Chambers said. "That swoon at the end. All of those little religious details. And the train ride and the dead-end street and the bicycle pump and *The Memoirs of Vidocq*. I said it was melodramatic but more than that, it was hopelessly contrived. And you argued that Pynchon's story, which I was defending, was even more contrived—"

"Well, isn't it? There's all this action going on in two places, this cat with the lease-breaking party on one floor and this other cat on the floor above him trying to nurse a bird back to health. The party sort of peters out and so does the bird. The whole thing—all the talk, all the petering out, you know?—the whole thing turns on this idea of entropy. You admitted it was more contrived than 'Araby' but said the contrivance didn't matter. Why would that be? Why would you argue against contrivance in one story and say it didn't matter in another?"

"That's the way I argue, I guess," Chambers said cheerfully.

"Well, what you said irritated me because it was so illogical and still seemed true . . . I've been thinking about it. Contrivances don't matter when people don't matter. That kid in Joyce's story is so adolescent you might want to forget the whole thing; but you can't, you still got to consider his feelings—"

"His loneliness?"

"He's got these dreams—all right, these idealistic illusions, the hang-up of Christianity in Ireland—which he thinks ought to come true out there in the world, but they can't, which of course is why he's lonely. I mean, if a boy seems *real*, you don't want this sense of a writer carefully laying everything up in symbols."

"But in the other story the people are *intended* to be types, examples of an idea about civilization or society—"

"Exactly, that's what I'm saying." Henry stared at him, softly drawling his words as he did whenever he was impatient. "You contrive your people, you can contrive anything else you want and nobody cares. You could say that Joyce wanted the boy to be a type too—a type to represent paralysis instead of entropy; but if he had been only that, why, then the melodrama and the arty symbolic shit wouldn't have mattered. You wouldn't have had a thing to complain about."

"Then the fact that I object to the contrivance—"

"Means that you care about the kid more than you do about the lease-breaker or the bird-nurser. Now you dig."

Chambers smiled. "You certainly reversed my argument. Only—"

"Only what?"

"What if the idea about entropy is true?"

"You mean, suppose that civilization has just about had it?" Henry sucked in his cheeks. "Black people know that whites feel that down in their guts. Oh, shit, man. Can't we forget the politics and keep this conversation on a high literary plane?" He half-rose from the chair. "If not, I got to go."

"How about an artistic plane?" Chambers asked. He tapped his cast. "What do you think of my painting?"

"Did your wife do that?"

"I didn't know you knew she painted."

"I saw her show at the museum."

Chambers was pleased. "Not many students went. Did you like it?"

"Not especially. This is better."

"It's the first human figure she's done in ages."

Henry sat back, lacing his fingers behind his head. "President

Johnny Doran would never let Mabel do a female figure on his cast. He might get himself a decal of the university seal, though."

Chambers sighed. "Good-bye to the literary and artistic planes."

"They invited all of us disadvantaged types to a party at their house in my freshman year. It was to get the new program off to an auspicious start, remember? Fifteen blacks from Harlem and the South and one lost little Puerto Rican who thought Sam Duncan was going to slip a knife into his liver."

"Did Sam bring along a knife?"

"His switchblade fell on the floor when he was looking for his cigarettes, he was so nervous. Old Johnny must have seen it. But he stood under his chandelier, being the hearty liberal president of a liberal university—"

"Oh, for Christ's sake, Fred. Nobody can win when you think like that."

"I wanted him to be himself, not the hearty president of a prestigious eastern school."

"I don't know. I think I'd have a pretty hard time being myself if I gave a party and my guests brought switchblades."

"Only Sam." Henry started tapping his feet on the floor. "That kind of exaggeration can lead to real trouble."

"You're touchy. I thought you and I were beyond that." Chambers felt—or imagined he felt—a sudden hostility radiating from Fred. "You were attacking the president for not being himself. How about you? Were you being yourself?"

"How could I be, holding a teacup in my hand? It rattled— da-da-da-da—every time I put it in the saucer. The whole thing was comical . . . Let's forget it."

"I ask, because sometimes it's difficult to behave according to what you think you are. Right now, how should I behave? There's some sort of tension between us—"

"You don't like me calling him 'Johnny,' do you?"

"Maybe that's what's making me uneasy."

SPLASHDOWN COMPLETES "PERFECT MISSION";

"Why? Because he's the president of the university and you're his dean of students?"

"I don't think so." Chambers considered the question as best he could; his attention was on Henry's nervous tapping. "Are you trying to make me part of the Establishment? I guess when you say 'Johnny,' I get uneasy because I don't want to acquiesce —you know, in silence—to anybody else's opinion."

"You mean, you don't want to take the view of the black student body?"

"I simply mean that *I* don't have any animosity toward him."

"The young instructors—and of course I mean white, what else is there?—the young white instructors in the Arts College don't mind hearing me say 'Johnny'; they got better names of their own for him. For that matter, some of the older professors, like Durant in philosophy, make public condemnations of him, don't they?"

"He's attacked on both the left and the right, which shows, I suppose, that he's neither—"

"You don't have any criticisms of him?"

"If I did, would it be right of me to cry on your shoulder about them?"

"Why not? It just might be you're not so free as you think you are."

"It's a personal choice on my part to say No, I won't attack the president in front of you or anybody else at this moment in my life. Why should I? I've always liked you, Fred, but what I won't do is this: I won't criticize *him* simply to win *your* esteem." He felt angry. "What are you getting at, anyway?"

"Nothing really. Nothing about Doran, at any rate." Henry looked depressed; he had stopped his tapping. "But you know people are at least partly what they think they're supposed to be. Even you—being dean of students and all—I'm just wondering how much a part of you that is."

"You worry about yourself, I'll worry about me."

"Don't bite me, man: one of us may be rabid." But Henry smiled at last. "That's what I'm doing, really. I'm thinking of the League and I'm thinking of me." He rose quickly. "Well good-bye, I've got business."

The brief but engaging smile, reminding Chambers as it did that Henry had once been more open and lighthearted, made him think now that Henry might not be well; standing by the bed, he looked thinner than Chambers had first noticed. "Are you in trouble, Fred?" he asked.

"There's something going on at this moment—"

"What?"

Henry started to say something; he took a breath instead, and a look of irony came to his eyes. When he did speak, he drawled his words in a bitter and self-mocking way. "Didn't you know, Mr. Chambers, that trouble's what us folks is born to?"

In the morning Stella came for Chambers, signing him out of the hospital and helping him—he was awkward—into the back seat of the station wagon. Before she started the engine, she gave him a letter from Mary.

3

Sitting sideways in the rear seat, his cast on the cushion and his back pressed against the opposite corner, Chambers held the envelope, still sealed, in his hand, trying to see if he could read the words through the paper. Stella, concentrating on her driving, looked briefly at him through the rear-view mirror. "Why don't you open it," she said.

"Why did she address it just to me?" Chambers asked. "That isn't like her."

"You were the one in the hospital."

"Maybe it's just a bulky get-well card."

"Do they have humorous verses for fathers who bang into school buses?" She shifted into second gear to pass a slow-moving truck on an upgrade.

> "Oh my Dad I feel so sad
> You hit the bus;
> Will the cop now jail my Pop?
> Oh cuss, cuss, cuss."

"That's not very good, you know," Chambers said. He felt defensive.

"But it's apt," Stella said. "You did get a summons."

He was silent, thinking of the bother of it: a leg in a cast for a month or so, a court summons (would he lose his license?), and the fact that whether he lost his license or not he would need somebody to drive him to work and home every day for a while.

"We have to get another car," Stella said.

"Not if I lose my license."

"Oh, you won't, George." Stella smiled at him in the mirror. "There never was a 'school bus station ahead' sign before that hill, it was a disgrace the county neglected it for so long, but there's a sign there now, and you ought to get a medal for injuring yourself to save the lives of future children. What if it had been a Greyhound instead of a VW? Look at it that way. And anyway, you're the dean of students at Brangwen. The paper never even carried a story—"

"To protect me? That means they thought it a disgrace, doesn't it? They shouldn't give me special treatment."

He could tell, just looking at Stella's neck, that she was annoyed.

"What are you going to do?" she asked. "*Demand* that the judge take away your license? That would make things hard for me and Phyllis."

"Why for you and Phyllis?" Phyllis Christy was his secretary.

"It means that I would forever be driving you to work and Phyllis would be forever driving you back. But how would even that work, when Phyllis doesn't even own a car? I can't drive you home most days. We have to get a car, so Phyllis can drive you home until you can drive again yourself. I've ordered it already, we pay only fifty dollars above the dealer's cost. Wasn't that clever of me? Why don't you read your letter?"

But he wasn't ready to. The feel of the letter in his hand made his heart jump, but he wasn't going to look at it until some other things were resolved. He couldn't bear to look at it—was he just putting it off? bad news?—until he understood where he was. It was as if things had gotten away from him, maybe long before he had entered the hospital, and that perhaps the fault lay in him. He meant to be on top of his problems. He felt stubborn and perverse, demanding to know about cars and being driven by Stella and Phyllis while the letter remained unopened in his hand; and Stella, who didn't like to bother over details, was upset by his insistence.

He asked, "Phyllis will take the new car home with her?"

"Don't be *petulant*, George. I thought you would be pleased. It will be a help for her and a help for us."

"What kind of car?"

"That new orangy color."

"I mean, the *make*."

"A Ford or Chevrolet or something like that . . . Something that doesn't have much shiny stuff in front or taillights that look like arrows pointing to Johnny's All-Night Dining Car. Phyllis and I are going to Syracuse tomorrow night to pick it up. Of course we don't *have* to do it. I told the man I'd have to ask you—"

"Why aren't we buying one here in town?"

"You get them cheaper if you buy away. Cecil Maynard told me. You call a dealer in Syracuse or someplace, say you don't live there and normally would be buying at home, but if he's willing to give a good price—"

"I'd rather do business here in town."

"I told Cecil you'd say it was a shoddy trick, but he said to tell you the people in Syracuse get the same deal by coming here, to Philippa, which is a smaller town, so the local dealers have the best of it by far . . . Do you mind?"

"If you ask me, you and Maynard are getting awfully chummy in your joint mercenary concerns."

"That incorporation business? You thought that was silly, but listen, George, Cecil has an architect friend who has the contract for remodeling a half dozen or so tuberculosis sanitoriums or sanitoria or whatever they are, in some Midwestern state, turning them over into mental hospitals and rehabilitation centers for juveniles—"

"Do you see that hay wagon?"

"Of course." She swerved around it, swinging the wheel as if she were skipper of an ocean liner, still talking. "The idea is to

WRONG . . . CUSHING SAYS JACKIE'S WEDDING

make them as cheerful and attractive as possible, murals and sculpture and all that, and Maynard may get the subcontract for all the art work; he's thinking of a team of local artists—"

"So you'd go off to Nebraska or some place with Maynard, if you had the chance?"

"It's only a possibility, George. And with Marjory Feidelman and Doris Banks—"

"Old Pinhead and his incorporated harem."

Stella laughed. "Oh, George, you're losing your hospital spiritual pallor at last. I thought you might be turning into some kind of grouchy old invalid bear. What does Mary say?"

"I'm up to date on *you*. What about Mark?"

"All right . . ." Stella sounded depressed. She brushed some strands of hair from her eyes. "Mr. Ferguson insists that Information Please doesn't exist; he's like the State Department on Red China. They invited a South African boy, that white student at Brangwen who wants to claim asylum somewhere and is about to have a breakdown because he can't think of a place in the world he wants to claim it—"

"It's a metaphysical problem."

"Mark says he's full of guilt, because he thinks he ought to go back to South Africa and fight against apartheid, but he knows he'd simply be thrown into jail. Well, Information Please invited him to give a talk on apartheid, but there wasn't a room scheduled for the talk because Information Please doesn't officially exist and so they met on the lawn in front of school and attracted more people that way then they ever would have inside, teachers and the football team on the way to practice and all that, including the principal, and Mark asked him—the South African—what he thought of what some bank president said, that if American business withdrew all its investments from South Africa it would hurt the blacks more than it would help. The South African responded with all the obscenities a stay in a modern American university could provide him with. He was cursing Mark, you see, thinking that *he* agreed with the bank

NO GROUND FOR EXCOMMUNICATION . . .

president. Things do get confused these days. Poor Mark, I heard this from Margene, not Mark—"

"Margene?"

"Margene Court, Maryjane's mother. Maryjane's in Information Please, as is that Durant boy, and *his* father is furious, by the way, both at you and Mark—"

"What did Margene tell you?"

"That Mark responded with his own supply of obscenity—"

"He doesn't *have* any, for God's sake."

"In an emergency he must be able to dig up an appropriate word or two. He was trying, Maryjane told Margene, to prove he wasn't on the bank president's side but the South African's; and because he said whatever he said the principal was shocked into a recognition that a subversive organization, by golly, *did* exist and he confiscated some news clippings that Mark had put on the social studies bulletin board and some members of the football team knocked Mark against a locker after gym."

"Oh, shit," said Chambers.

"There you go, identifying yourself with the younger generation again."

"Don't be facetious, for God's sake, Stella." He crumpled the letter in his hand without thinking of what he was doing, and then, looking down at the envelope, carefully rubbed at the wrinkles. "It's just the hypocrisy . . . Can anyone tell me with a straight face that the football coach or the members of the football team—what do they call them? jocks?—say 'Gee whiz' when they lose a game?" In his mind he was seeing his son surrounded by all those helmets and padded shoulders; his anger was making him dizzy.

"Maybe it was his hair they were objecting to," Stella said. "Or maybe they don't direct *their* obscenities toward the president of the Chase Manhattan Bank or whoever it was."

"What do *you* think of Mark's political activities?"

Stella gave him a look in the mirror that was both inquisitive and worried. "I don't want him to get hurt, do you? That's as far as I think about it . . ."

DELAY DECISION ON ENGLISH CHANNEL TUNNEL

"Do you think I've encouraged him too much? My God, I'm
no subversive and neither is he. I just know things can't go on
as they have in the past. You can't be in a university these
days—"

"It was Mary before Mark—"

"And I drove her to Washington. But what kind of hypocrite
would I have been if I'd refused? I approved of the March, you
know that—"

"I'm not accusing you of anything."

"At least I did take a political stand."

"Listen, George, I may not be so consciously political as you
think I ought to be—"

"I'm not accusing you of anything either."

"Artists—and that's what in happy moments I think I am, an
artist—"

"Of course you are. Have I ever denied it?"

"—ought to stay clear of politics in their lives as well as their
work. At least that's what I say of middle-aged female artists
of a suggestive disposition. I suppose we could make signs and
even carry them; but that sort of thing would creep into our
paintings—"

"What's wrong with that?" He was irritated.

"It just seems to me that in an age like ours the politics, even
the politics of dissent, aren't true enough for art. If you wanted
to work with political ideas, you would either have to be wholly
negative, which is not art as I know it, or sentimental. I've got
to explore my own vision, private and limited as it might seem
to you. Would you rather have me do the Socialist Realist
thing? A giant poster of Lenin or Nixon or Mao? Of a farmer
in Lower Siberia or one perhaps of our very own and very
absentminded Hayden Wilcox, who forgets to latch the gate
against his cows?"

"Don't poke fun at Hayden."

"I'm not. I'm just asking you to see him as a heroic social or
political figure."

"I'm not saying you ought to do a big canvas or sculpture of

. . . CUBANS HELD IN BOMBINGS . . . GRANDSON

Hayden. How did we get on him? I don't see why, though, you couldn't do something more with *people*. You managed something or other, a girl, on my cast—"

"The excitement of a new medium."

"I can see, for example, a perfectly fine statue of Martin Luther King."

"Disowned by his fellow blacks up to the moment of his assassination for preaching the white man's Jesus."

"By *some* of them."

She looked at him peevishly; she didn't like to be forced into negation, which all discussions of art and politics eventually brought her to. "Can any reasonable man believe in the white man's Jesus? Do you?"

"I believe in love not hate."

"You say that in a spiteful way."

"Oh, come now, Stella." And yet he had made them both defensive. What it was of course was that he felt he never should have driven Mary and the two college students to Washington, that he felt responsible for encouraging both Mary and Mark in their political activities; but why should he make Stella defensive for being apolitical, for being subjective and individual and abstract in her paintings?

"Stella—"

"What?" She jumped in alarm at the urgency in his voice.

"Oh, nothing." But what he had suddenly in mind—had he the will to say it—was that if she wanted to have an affair with old Pinhead, for God's sake she should go ahead and not feel guilty about it: she didn't need to foist his secretary on *him* to justify her adventures. No, that was an improper thought, unworthy of either of them; and because it shamed him he said nothing to her about it.

He headed off on a wild new tack. "I was talking with a black student the other day, a boy who has turned much more antagonistic than Fred Henry."

"Who's Fred Henry?"

He saw, in the mirror, how upset Stella had become. But she

was concentrating both on her driving and what he was saying, though Fred Henry couldn't possibly have any importance for her at the moment. He felt unreal (as he deserved to feel, for having had pernicious thoughts). He said, "Fred Henry came to see me in the hospital yesterday. He was out for dinner once last year."

"That thin-boned boy? With the lovely eyes?" She rubbed at her own.

He cleared his throat, looking again at the back of her neck. It was as if they were talking on the telephone. "But I'm not talking about *him*. I'm talking about Joe Collier who, as a matter of fact, replaced Fred as president of the League. Joe Collier asked me what I thought of guns. Just like that. I told him I'd killed a German boy the only time I'd fired one in combat. I told him I hated guns, that I didn't own one, that I never would, that I never went hunting with anything but field glasses and the Peterson *Guide*, that I had never allowed Mark to have even a toy pistol; and he said, 'That's a typical white middle-class hang-up of people your age.' "

"I dislike expressions like 'typical white middle-class hang-up,' though isn't it odd that a black boy would say it in reference to your not liking guns and killing. At one time it might have referred to a brutal white preference for mass lynchings, Negroes on a line like laundry. Excuse me if I seem to be playing with words, but I think I'm serious." Her voice quavered. "I don't know where you're taking this conversation, really—"

"I suppose he was attacking a liberalism that stops short of violence when it encounters injustice."

"Liberalism that espouses violence isn't liberalism, is it, George?"

"It gets complicated. If by condemning violence I allow other violence to continue—I mean in Vietnam or against the blacks— what am I doing but patting myself on the back for being a good man who does nothing?"

"That strikes me as a specious argument. Why would you attack your own ideas like that?"

HIJACKING OF PLANE . . . BERKELEY STUDENTS

"I was just trying to paraphrase what Joe Collier probably meant; I wasn't agreeing with him. At least—" But his was a hopeless confusion of motives; it was what one got for not being absolutely honest from the start. He really didn't like Joe Collier and he detested violence, his life should have been devoted to fending it off, to the saving of his children and all children from it; and yet here he had been attacking his own emotional convictions through a half-assed advocacy of what Collier had probably meant by a hang-up on guns. What was really bothering him was his concealed jealousy and the way his defensiveness had driven him to attack Stella's art. He had enough generational hang-ups without adding guns to their number (he thought it a flaw in himself that he used credit cards, had an inadequate savings account, and that he had such a grim passion to be so loyal in marriage: why shouldn't Stella have a fling? Why not? If it helped her sense of herself as an artist— that precarious identity for this aging housewife that he loved, this mother of two, who wanted so much to be carefree, to be gay, and to do the masterpiece that lay beyond her ability and her time). These thoughts tumbled about in his mind in no particular order; how could he possibly tell Stella all that?

"All I can say, Stella," he said, almost bitterly, opening his eyes, "is that I love you."

"What?" Stella said. "What?" She was trying to wipe her eyes with what she had found in her purse, a mislaid parking ticket from whose corner a caught hairpin dangled.

"I was jealous, for God's sake," Chambers said. "That's all."

"Jealous?"

"About why you and Maynard were in such a hurry to get me a new car, and why you had arranged to have Phyllis drive me home."

"George." Stella cried and giggled and was near hysteria.

"Oh, God," Chambers said; his own eyes had become wet. "I thought maybe you and Maynard were trying to find me a substitute."

"Oh, George," Stella said. "The president called yesterday in a panic: I was trying to keep it from you until at least you'd read the letter, I thought enough was enough. He wanted to know when you'd be back. There was a demonstration yesterday, something that promises to be mean—"

"Was it the League?"

"I think so; it was too late for last night's paper, you can probably read about it tonight. But I thought we'd have to make arrangements right away; that's why I called Phyllis, that's why I called Cecil Maynard. He bought a car last month and I didn't know a thing about cars or where to buy them."

"And you did all that for me."

"That's what I *thought*. I didn't think you'd want the bother yourself . . . Oh, George," she said, looking at him in the mirror, her eyes brimming, "did I really—did I *really*—make you jealous? I never thought I could manage that."

"Was it a controlled demonstration or was it a riot, Stella?" He smiled at her in the mirror.

"I don't know; I really don't know." She began to laugh, and so did he; he had never thought he would laugh at the thought of a demonstration or a riot, that he would actually be pleased for the moment; that there ever could be such an insane relationship between public events and private feelings.

As they turned into the driveway, he still had Mary's letter to read.

4

DEAR GEORGE,

You don't know how long it has taken me just to make sure it was "George" I was writing to. I started I don't know how many letters, beginning some of them "Dear Father," but *those* all got stilted, I don't know why, as if I were addressing somebody with an old-fashioned mustache who was very proper and to whom I would have to be extremely careful about what I would say; I tried "Dear Dad," but that sounded flip which I am not; I even began one "Dear Dean Chambers," thinking that I might be able to write truthfully if I thought of you, my father, as a stranger. When I was very little, I called you "George," do you remember? because that was what Mother (and she has always been "Mother," I've never had any trouble with that) called you, and so did all your adult friends. When I got to junior high —or maybe it was while I was still in the sixth grade at Floral Elementary—my friends laughed at me for calling my father by his first name, and I got self-conscious about it. It used to bother me not to know what to call you; I used to say just "Hello." Did you know you were "Hello" to me for years, that when I said "Hello" I was really calling you by a secret name? Young girls who feel particularly close to their fathers always have trouble knowing what to call them. I know I was jealous of Mark, who could say "Daddy" almost from the start: I wanted to be able to make that kind of claim on you, but I also wanted you to respect me as you would an adult. Anyway, now that I've grown up I can call you "George" again, this time as a daughter old enough to know her own illusions and to know as well that her future simply has to be decided by her own mind.

Now I'm writing simply what comes into my head, hoping to be honest with you that way and not get myself all involved in false ideals (rationalizations) and self-deception. It's known as automatic writing, or *almost* automatic. Almost as soon as school started, my roommate Sylvia Bannister got so blocked she couldn't do her essay writing for freshman English, so we sat at opposite sides of the same desk and practiced automatic writing. I threw away what I wrote, but she turned in hers to her creative writing teacher who was so horrified by her sado-masochism and her death wishes that he gave her an "A." Sylvia's problem is that her parents hate each other too much to give each other the release of a divorce. Sylvia thinks she's ugly (she's really very pretty, or could be) and that everybody finds her hateful, because her parents resent her as proof they once were intimate. Sylvia I guess has been my only friend, but a few weeks ago she left the dorm in violation of the regulations and rented an apartment in town to be by herself. Which is one reason I've been calling up Mark at the Rooster and listening to his problems and telling him mine. But my problems are mainly over with, as you will later see. *Don't worry about me.* I wouldn't want you, with your broken leg and operation and all, to have any more anxieties. I feel guilty enough for not coming to see you in the hospital.

It would have killed me too if you had died in the hospital, Daddy (oops, look what I slipped into) and me not there. I'm not trying to say it would have been all right for you to die *had* I been there. (Oh my ego makes me so mad at myself.) But I couldn't come, I looked so awful. I know this sounds terribly vain, but I couldn't stand to have you and Mother and Mark—

but especially you, all hurt the way you were—see me so pasty and fat and stupid. For that matter I was already putting on weight at home this past summer which was one reason I left in July to go to that dumb camp in Vermont I pretended so much I wanted to go to, and then on to that week of college orientation learning songs to be sung at football games, etc. After school started, I went to classes for a time but they were large lectures and— Oh, I don't know: I started lying around in my room, doing nothing but talking to Sylvia and sleeping and drinking Cokes from the machine and eating Skippy peanut butter and Ritz crackers. Well, I must admit your accident really shook me up. I'm not coming home, not for a good long time, but not just because of the way I look. I'm not coming home until I can prove to myself I'm worth something. It's got to be through my own ACTIONS and not your love and understanding and so you can see my not coming home really doesn't have anything—at least from this moment on—to do with my being fat which is anyway just a symptom of being sorry for myself. With your permission I'm going to Europe with Sylvia. I thank God I don't have parents like Sylvia's, but at least her father sees this Europe trip as her salvation—he's going to write you about it—and I see it as mine.

The day you were hurt I was all in a turmoil about staying in my room, I was worried about my awful self-centeredness, and so I looked up Sylvia even though she had rejected me to hurt herself (I think) and found her barricaded in a corner of her apartment. I mean, she had taken all her furniture—her mattress, her bedsprings, the sofa, the rolled-up rug, the mirror off the wall, the broken chair, even the little fridge—and made a kind of zoo or cave out of it all; and there she was hiding, back behind it all. She had been letting some fraternity boys—there's more evil in people when they're in a group (fraternity, sorority, Mafia, national political parties, nations) than *you* ever let me know, George—letting these creeps make love to her because she wanted to debase herself, and afterward she had been on drugs she'd gotten from them, LSD or something, and no food.

If I'm all fat, she's nothing but bone. What a pair we'll make in Europe! More on this later.

Remember Trip, our little dog on Floral St. who got run over and how I found his body in the gutter with the eyes all bulged out from the pressure and how I couldn't sleep for weeks? What made me get so hysterical the way I did wasn't Trip—though I loved him—but *Death*. My own death. I was self-centered even then. You knew what scared me. You said that children and young people (I've heard you say it since too, but always remember back to that moment when I was ten or maybe eleven and you talked to me for the first time as if I were old enough to understand what you yourself believed) worry more about their Death than older people do, and I wondered why that would be so, older people being so much nearer to it, and you said (was this a year or so later?) that when a person got older what bothered him about Death was not that he personally would die but that those he loved would. You said in Death's favor that if life were eternal—if relationships were forever—there couldn't be any love, so that the whole thing about Death was a standoff and you guessed (being able to joke about it) that we had to live with it as long as we could.

I remember, on Floral St., how you used to shout at the drivers who went too fast and how once you shouted what must have been an insult at a gravel truck and the man, a Negro (we'd say a black now) who lived in the next block, stopped his truck and got into an argument with you about safe driving in a neighborhood full of children (he had four or five of his own), and whether or not the truck could have stopped in time if a kid had darted out between the parked cars, and how he insisted on driving around the block again at the same speed while you hid behind a car in some unexpected spot, sending Mark's old tricycle—the one that used to be mine—out at him, to see if he could stop in time; and how you pushed it out so hard you hurt your shoulder and the gravel flew up and down on the truck cab like hail he slammed on the brakes so hard, but the tricycle got caught under his bumper just the same. He said you cheated and you said you had *not* and Mark began to cry about his tricycle and Mother came out of the house pleased to see that for once you were acting like a child and a whole mob from the neighborhood came and then the police who tried to find the body and there was nearly a riot when the police tried to haul off the Negro for having bald tires even though they could find no corpse and you had to admit you had pushed the tricycle into the street and the police thought you were another nut from the college on the hill and went home; and you and the truck driver sat on our porch steps drinking beer and talking about bomb shelters and you said that no matter what Kennedy or his advisers said you were not going to build your family one, you had to draw the line somewhere and that was it.

Because that was the time that Kennedy, whatever his fine inauguration with Robert Frost there, had been trying to get Americans to build bomb shelters which was why I guess you were out in the street all the time shouting at speeding drivers; and you said later to Mother (I was listening in the next room for you had started to cry, which you do I think more than most men, which I think is fine and OK because you and Mother are happy enough in marriage so that you aren't afraid of losing, the way some men are, your precious masculinity), you said to Mother that the President's encouragement of bomb shelter building was all gamesmanship, a way of getting around the nuclear deadlock, for if Americans had bomb shelters the Russians could see that some of us could survive a nuclear attack by them which meant that our own nuclear weapons weren't paralyzed after all and so they'd better be careful about West Berlin and places like that. And you said to Mother that *anybody* who tried to take devious advantage of *your* love, whether he was a President or a funeral parlor director, had your contempt, and that you'd rather have us—your family—dead than to have us moles who had helped bring about a nuclear war with our blind digging.

That was a crucial moment in my life, George, for though the shelter boom fizzled and there have been many things much

THOUSANDS CHEER WALLACE IN GARDEN RALLY

more terrible since, it was the day that I first thought of politics as unreal and insane and a threat to personal values. Why was it that man could once find meaning in wars and violence, could pride himself on his strategies and deceptions, and could somehow justify or at least ignore all the cruelty and brutishness about him? And yet this thing that's called alienation—this knowledge that what *I* am is not to be found *out there*—has been developing for a long time, hasn't it? Maybe ever since the Renaissance? (This last question comes out of my so-called college education, I guess.)

But to change the subject. Mark wanted me to come home to work with him on Information Please as sort of a graduate adviser or something, and though I still believe that what is called idealism is the only practical course we have (for we must get beyond greed and personal interest simply to go on existing for a few decades), I just can't get excited anymore about getting information to high school kids on the Causes of the Vietnam War or on the Industrial-Military Complex and How it Affects Foreign Policy or Cuba Under Castro or Alternatives to Capitalism or Discriminatory Practices in Upstate New York Communities or any of the other suggestions for courses or at least lectures I horrified Mr. Ferguson with when I started Information Please in my senior year. It's not only that something like IP can't do anything but arouse the fury of the Taxpayers' League and end up causing people like Ferguson to behave more like reactionaries than they want to (he's not a bad guy, after all) but that I *just can't get excited*. It's something that's been happening to me slowly like I guess when you're freezing to death but don't really feel the numbness spreading. (I know about it now, so don't worry.)

Maybe you remember how last year I went up to some of the Brangwen SDS meetings to get ideas for Information Please. They were trying to get the university to do something about housing for the poor (because the very fact that the university is in town, with all those kids able to pay high rent, three or four of them in a ratty apartment at $60 a head, means the poor

. . . HEART PATIENT DIES AFTER TRANSPLANT

are squeezed more and more), but when the university agreed
to give land and to help the poor get mortgages to build houses
SDS as an organization felt betrayed (they wanted a confrontation to expose the evils of Capitalism and what did all this agita-
tion for housing lead to but a strengthening of Capitalism and to
a desire for property by the poor) and stopped pressuring Brangwen to see it through which meant the university could take its
sweet time and now the poor who had their hopes raised for
their families are still waiting. I know the university has financial problems and there are new problems (with the blacks)
and all sorts of trouble with the city bureaucrats: I'm not blam-
ing Brangwen. My point is simply that it was as wrong for the
SDS to take advantage of the hopes of the poor families in
Philippa as it was for Kennedy to propose bomb shelters, and
anyway even if we managed to make the U. S. a Socialist state
and to build houses like crazy it wouldn't finally help because as
anybody knows who wants to think about it (most people don't)
babies are being born too fast. There are already about as many
of us in the world (except maybe for Australia and places like
that) as we can take even if there was a reasonable political
structure encompassing the whole world; and the more we do
to make conditions better the more of us there will be and anybody who doesn't see the connection between population increase and problems like pollution and the inability of any of
us to feel our own importance and the horrible life in the slums
must have holes in the head. But when I stood up in an SDS
meeting and proposed to them that maybe they ought to be
working for birth control (which I thought transcended politics) I was told I was a racist high school kid and any such talk
would alienate the blacks from the movement because in fifty
years or so the blacks won't be a minority anymore. Of course
that isn't true, all of us middle-class whites have too much of a
headstart.

I am perfectly aware that no doubt I have been using apocalyptic visions as a means of justifying my own selfish inability
to get excited by *anything*, for the way I got discouraged with

Information Please and was morose last summer and for not going to classes now that I'm fortunate enough to be in college and for not writing letters (though *this* one ought to make up some for that, it's 3 A.M. and cold and so quiet in my room my pen makes a loud swishing noise) and for refusing dates and for thinking I'll never get married and bless you and Mother with grandchildren, and even for getting fat and ugly; I know it's wrong the way I look for signs of doom and remember things I read years ago in Huxley about population growth or that terrible apocalyptic ending in *Confessions of Zeno* (published in the 1920's I think) I read in high school, or the way (when I went regularly to the clinic because of some recurring pains in my stomach that I never told you about and were never really there) I always looked for the same tattered copy of the magazine that had an article by Fred Hoyle saying that though man had discovered nuclear energy just in time to learn how to use it after oil and coal were gone he apparently had no way of controlling his breeding and hence had lost control of his destiny and was apparently doomed to cycles of breeding and cataclysm until some day in the distant future the survivors would be wise enough at last to know what to do. I suppose astronomers can afford to take a longer view of things than I can. I know it's wrong of me, I know it's wrong to go about feeling nothing but what that character in "Gooseberries" feels, that he wants to go knocking furiously with a hammer on everybody's door who feels happy, thinking they have no *right* to be happy; but you do have to admit at least that the problems are real ones so that *you* as a father don't have anything to do with what goes on in my stupid and confused head.

I want you to know that because, Daddy, Mark told me on the phone when he wanted me to come home because you were hurt that he thought that you thought you somehow felt guilty for whatever it was that was bothering *me*, that you thought you had protected me from ugliness and being hurt too much and encouraged me in my quote idealism unquote too much and maybe even had loved me too much: which of course is about

HUMPHREY DECLARES NIXON "IRRESPONSIBLE"

as stupid and confused a way of thinking as my own, if you'll
excuse me. It should make *you* feel better to know that it was
your accident (and my realization of how much I *do* love you,
in spite of what I said about not feeling anything: I hope you
can tell in this letter the difference between what I *have been*
and what I *am* as I write) that made me see my own selfishness,
that got me if not home (oh damn those Ritz crackers) at least
out of my room and over to Sylvia's apartment, so that I was
able to help her (she's sleeping like a baby in my bed right now,
the housemother brought me up a mattress because the people
at the clinic told her to, they think I'm helping to bring Sylvia
around). She's looking forward to going to Europe with me and
even has been reconciled with her father who of course came
right away when I phoned him and who is a rich N.Y. psychiatrist who approves of our plan if we promise to stop over at
some Swiss clinic run by a friend of his and he—Sylvia's father—
is paying all our expenses and will buy us a little sports car; we
won't leave of course until Sylvia is able to. I've already applied
for a leave of absence, which is better than staying here (I'd
flunk the term) and will stay in N.Y. at her father's apt. (her
mother's not living there) with Sylvia until we leave. What I'm
trying to say is that in helping Sylvia I'm helping myself which
proves you've always been right about human relationships and
the importance of love. That maybe I'm not so selfish as I've
thought is a help to me. I know that when I first heard of your
accident and thought maybe you might die, I wished it was *me*
and remembered too what you said about the way older people
feel about Death; which shows, if there's any doubt, that I'm
getting to be an Older Person.

As for what happened in Washington, which Mark says you
are positively neurotic about (probably because I didn't want
you to know and so your imagination no doubt makes too much
of it), I want you to know that the evening we drove down, you
and me and those two college girls, was probably the happiest
time in my life, I'll always remember it. I mean, how we sang
songs and listened to the radio and watched the stars and

IN ARMS STAND . . . 32 DIE IN NEW HAMPSHIRE

stopped for hamburgers and how that one girl Frances was so proud that her rich but liberal relatives near Baltimore approved of what we were doing and were planning to put us up for the night and give us breakfast, and how we got lost and found the house way out in the fox-hunting district about two in the morning but the house was dark and Frances got the idea that maybe they wanted us in the guest cottage, the door being wide open, and how we found those two mattresses side by side on the floor and Frances (who must not have been so sure after all about her rich liberal relatives) got all enthused about how they must have planned that for us, and wasn't it thoughtful, and how they must have intended the Oriental rug, which was rolled up at the foot of the mattresses, for a covering; and how, because the rest of us were not only sorry for Frances but all giddy from driving and happy—oh I don't know—not only said but *thought* it was the finest bed imaginable and crawled on the mattresses wrapped up in our coats and pulled the rug over us; and how the girls teased you, saying what would the president say if he knew his dean was in bed with his girl students; and I couldn't sleep, I was so happy (and cold!). In the morning, of course, we found that the boys in the family had been doing gymnastics in the cottage and that Frances' relatives had beds for us in the house but that the maid had turned off the light at 1:30 A.M.; still, it was better the way it turned out. It's almost as good writing all this down to make you remember it as it actually *was* for me that night.

What happened the next day was *all my fault* and happened only because I *deliberately disobeyed* you. You remember that after we crossed the bridge you took us out of the March, saying this was as far as we ought to go; you had heard there might be trouble in front of the Pentagon. I could see that Frances and the other girl were disappointed, but after all you *were* responsible for all of us. Anyway, I walked back across the bridge with you and them and then said good-bye, because you said it was OK for me to meet Geraldine and stay with her and miss a couple of days of school to see Washington (which was all right, since all my high school grades had been A's). Anyway, to make a long story short (for this is going to be brief now, I promise) after I found Geraldine by the Lincoln Memorial as planned we decided to hang around a while and ended back in the March and finally found ourselves not only at the Pentagon but in the front row facing that line of soldiers. I suppose we wanted to be there, I won't deny that. They looked so young, just like us, and so miserable holding those heavy rifles and it seemed as if it would be so easy for them to just drop those guns and stop defending that awful building and join us, that maybe if we could get them to do that simple thing it really would be the start of a nationwide movement, soldiers and civilians alike, that would bring Johnson to his senses (for you can't make war without soldiers) and those soldiers *did* seem to be wavering and you could tell they were listening even if they tried to be impassive to the crowd telling them about the need to stop killing and how mankind had to love and there was this soldier just opposite me who had big awkward feet and there were tears in his eyes I was sure of that and I was thinking unless this whole thing is stopped now it will be my brother Mark who someday will have to be holding a gun and being that terribly miserable about it and I did, I honestly did, feel then this real rush of love for that soldier and I ran out of the line, carried away I guess by *everything*, and gave him a kiss on his cheek but I guess I was wrong about him or was a threat to his precious masculinity and honor as a soldier or something because he hit me as hard as he could in the stomach with the butt of his rifle and all I remember then is him standing there in the sun as impassive as ever and I was on the ground and I guess vomiting because Geraldine who got some boys to help me to her apartment had to send my sweater and pants to the cleaner's.

So now you know why I looked so odd when I finally got home and you can put much more importance on this than it has and if you insist on seeing this as explaining everything about my problems, including why I've been eating Skippy peanut butter (the crunchy kind) and Ritz crackers this year I

TURKEY . . . CLIFFORD SAYS U.S. TO KEEP

suppose it's your privilege but please remember the Washington March was in Oct. and that it was only *after* I got back that I began to get Mr. Ferguson hysterical with my Information Please plans and to go up to Brangwen to sit in on their SDS meetings and it wasn't until summer came and I was finished with high school that I began to get really depressed and even though being away at college hasn't been very great I'm still able to believe sufficiently in love (in the important large sense) and am after all saving myself because of it.

Here it is dawn and the heat's finally gurgling in the radiator and I'm ravenous and if this letter has been so long it was because truthfully I wanted you to know what happened at Washington and still didn't want you to know, but I'm glad you do and happy you're recovering so nicely (so I don't have to feel guilty for not coming home) and now I'm going out to the cafeteria and bring back a tray of food for Sylvia and myself. Tell Mark I wish him well in starting up Information Please again, but that I won't be joining him (since he only wanted me to for my sake, and I really don't need help), and tell yourself and Mother and Mark how much I love you all even though I'm not coming home now (please don't try to argue about *that*) and I promise to write from N.Y. and regularly from Europe.

Love,
MARY

5

One day in the fall of 1968—the day that Fred Henry had come to see George Chambers in the hospital—eighty black students of both sexes danced on the tables of the coffee shop in the basement of the Architecture School at Brangwen University to the beat of a large soup spoon applied to the bottom of an empty lard tin. Upon being applauded by the other students there (who, overcoming their initial bafflement and alarm at the intrusion, had left the tables for a corner of the room where they had followed the dance as if it were some entertainment at a night club), the black students, forming a snake line much as in a pep rally, left the coffee shop. Following their drummer and accompanied by an ever-increasing number of excited dogs, they crossed University Road several times, stopping traffic while they jogged in convoluted patterns around the cars; one nervous young member of the music department—John Ormsby, a violinist—who was showing his visiting grandmother the campus, thought a riot was in progress, and, making a violent U-turn in his new BMW, nearly ran down half a dozen students.

While the file circled the statue of Silas Brangwen, two of the blacks shinnied up his bronze Victorian coat to fasten a sign around his neck. BLACK STUDIES NOW, it read. Then the students divided into three groups. Still led by the drummer, the largest

. . . U.S. AND BRITAIN ABSTAIN IN UNITED

group went to the door of the president's suite in the Administration Building, arriving just at tea time; refused admission by
the president because of their number, they were told that one
or two could see him. After an earnest consultation among their
leaders, they decided against such a move. Offered tea and
cookies in the anteroom by the President's secretary—if they
would wait for her to boil more water—they refused. Chanting
"Black Studies *now*," they left. The second group entered the
library, each student going to the stacks and taking an armful
of books; they dropped the books on the floor by the main desk
explaining to the clerk in charge that they were "not relevant."
Perhaps through some mistake in planning or at least in execution, the third group entered the Old Dental Building. Scheduled for demolition in the early 1970's, Old Dent was used
exclusively for offices of graduate assistants and instructors without tenure who taught sections of the Core Course in Humanities required of all students in Agriculture and Engineering.
The afternoon being Friday and the university reasonably convenient by a low-fare weekend Greyhound to New York City,
the building was nearly deserted. This group pounded on doors,
dribbled the debris from waste baskets (banana peels and the
like from lunches packed by the wives of the graduate assistants) down the steps, and, in the men's room, ripped a dispenser for Scott towels off the wall and tossed it through the
frosted glass of the window.

As fortune would have it, a member of the campus patrol was
using one of the stalls and was able to identify three of the
students. In his deposition, Officer Torgeson stated that it was
his belief that the group of approximately ten black students, at
least two of whom were women, had come into the men's room
by accident, thinking it an exit; alarmed at finding themselves
not only in a *cul de sac* but facing a more or less uniformed
policeman seated in one of the stalls (there were no doors to
the cubicles in the men's room of Old Dent) had broken the
window with the paper towel dispenser as an act of bravado and
then fled.

NATIONS VOTE ON RHODESIA . . . CURFEW

Later President Doran said that the academic year would have been altogether different had not a patrolman been using the men's room; or, in any event, if George Chambers had not broken his leg. It was true enough that if Chambers had been on duty, Officer Torgeson's deposition would not have been fed into the judicial machinery of the university; it was Chambers' young assistant, Terence O'Brien, whose duties normally consisted of serving as a liaison between the administration and the fraternities and sororities (for they attempted to govern themselves, imposing penalties through their Pan-Hellenic Board on errant units), who in Chambers' absence had made the decision to submit the deposition.

But to find in any particular episode the origin of the disasters at Brangwen was, as President Doran himself knew, to simplify a complex problem. All that could be said with precision was that at 4:35 P.M. on a Friday afternoon, Officer Torgeson reported to Proctor Warren who reported to Assistant Dean of Students O'Brien that at 3:55 P.M. of that same day ten black students had entered the men's room of Old Dent and that three of them —Henry Osgood, Thomas Potter, and Jack Johnson—had been identified in the act of breaking a window with a plastic Scott towel dispenser. At 5:15 P.M., Assistant Dean O'Brien turned over Officer Torgeson's deposition to the chairman of the Student Judicial Board, Stephen Harcourt, a senior majoring in sociology; on the following Monday the Board mailed to each of the three students a notice requesting them to attend a hearing on the alleged offenses. The three students failed to appear at the hearing, at which time, in accordance with Board practice, a second and final hearing was scheduled. A second notice was delivered by campus messenger to each of the students, giving the new date as the first Wednesday in December and declaring that failure to attend would result in automatic suspension from the university; the messenger reported that each of the students, upon receipt of the notice, responded with the same phrase, "We ain't going, man."

The reason for their refusal became clear in a letter which

FOLLOWS OUTBREAK OF VIOLENCE IN PEEKSKILL

appeared in the Brangwen *Daily Sentinel* two days before the second hearing:

DEAR EDITOR:

On Friday, Oct. 30, the Black Students League, concerned by the refusal of the administration to take meaningful action on a commitment to the Black students for a program of Black Studies at Brangwen University, engaged in a controlled nonviolent demonstration. As a consequence of their participation in that demonstration, three Black students out of the total of eighty involved have been singled out for punishment of their alleged offenses. Upon the advice of the membership of the Black Students League, the three students refuse to appear before the Judicial Board for the following reasons:

1. They were engaged in a political action of the League. Responsibility for that action lies not with them as individuals but with the League as an organization. It would be a mockery of justice to try these three students for their participation in a significant political action while continuing the traditional practice of disciplining fraternities and sororities—those notoriously discriminatory and racist social organizations—as *units* for the contemptible and decadent behavior of individual members during what is euphemistically termed on the official calendar a "week-end social function;" a discipline, furthermore, that is effected by these social organizations themselves and not by the Student Judicial Board.

2. As a totally White body in a predominantly White university, a university that, whatever its stated views on equality and justice, is part of the complex of institutions of a racist America, the Student Judicial Board is, in our view, illegitimate. In this respect we point to the fact that the present judicial system was planned and put into operation without the participation to our knowledge of a single member of a non-White race.

To us, the validity of both of these points is beyond argumentation. We call for the immediate withdrawal of charges against these students. Upon such a withdrawal, we shall willingly work with our White counterparts to achieve a system of justice equitable for White and Black alike.

. . . ISRAEL BOMBS EGYPTIAN REFINERIES . . .

The above statement has been approved without dissenting vote by

THE MEMBERSHIP OF THE BLACK STUDENTS LEAGUE

So the matter of a paper towel dispenser thrown through a window became the matter of the legitimacy of an institution's judicial system—and perhaps by extension, of the legitimacy of the entire judicial structure of the United States, which traditionally had favored the well-to-do above the poor, the white above the black.

Once charges had been filed, once the judicial machinery had begun to turn, the process was almost unstoppable. This was part of the purity and incorruptibility of the system which appealed to its supporters. By charter, the Board of Trustees had granted the president jurisdiction over matters of student conduct; but both by tradition and legislation that jurisdiction had been transferred to the faculty, and that body in turn had delegated its powers in this sphere to the Student Judicial Board. Such shifting of responsibility for their own conduct to the students had been part of an enlightened student code designed at least a decade previously by a group under the direction of Morris Freedman of the Law School. The Board had the power to pass judgments without interference, so long as they were made in strict conformity with the Code.

Theoretically, the president—having first telephoned the chairman of the Board of Trustees to explain his reasons—could have revoked the jurisdiction granted the faculty and by them to the Judicial Board, but had he done so he most certainly would have provoked the enmity of the majority of the faculty, who were not used to infringements upon their traditional rights. Indeed, it was the check upon his power that had prevented the president from making quicker decisions on the nature of the Black Studies program (the questions of course credit, qualifications of the black professors to be appointed, and—most difficult question of all—the degree of autonomy to be allowed the program, were currently being deliberated by a committee of the faculty) and had led to the demonstration.

In the understandable absence, then, of direct presidential action, the only group that might have managed to subvert the judicial proceedings was the Committee on Student Affairs, a policy-making group of faculty members, administrators, and students. The vice-president for student affairs, Martin Niemeyer, was on the committee, as was, by virtue of his office, George Chambers. The chairman was Philip Durant, whose son had been briefly jailed for scribbling on the courthouse wall. Another member was Morris Freedman, who, as chief architect of the Code, was the Committee's authority upon its rules and implications. The president had communicated to Vice-president Niemeyer his wish to find a quick means of forgetting the charges, a wish that Chambers was in agreement with; but the chairman was not about to be pushed into a major reversal of policy by pressure from the administration.

"Policy formulated to meet an emergency," Chairman Durant opened the meeting by saying, "is less policy than strategy, and a withdrawal of charges for some trumped-up reason—even if we could invent one—is simply a strategic withdrawal, which must be what the president has in mind. But the case is, after all, before the Board. If the charges aren't valid, their verdict will show it." To which Morris Freedman added his agreement, saying, "What we have to decide is simply whether—on the basis of an allegation of flaws in a judicial system—we declare the system no longer applicable in a certain case; or whether we stand firm in support of a continuing system of justice while showing our sincere willingness to work with anybody to correct whatever flaws it *conceivably* may contain."

The committee was divided. Durant, Freedman, and the other two faculty members—one a child psychologist, the other a historian—believed the integrity of the judicial system had to be protected whatever the cost. Chambers, Niemeyer, and the two students held that the particular problem was based on such a trivial offense that the case should be forgotten. The

230 NORTH VIETNAMESE SLAIN IN SURPRISE

very triviality of the offense, in the view of Morris Freedman, made the principles stand out more clearly; in the view of Chambers, inflexible principles always stood in the way of insight into complex human problems.

"Well, as it stands now," Freedman said, "it's *their* sense of principles against ours. Should we assume theirs has priority?"

Durant agreed. "To say what George says," he told the committee as if it were a class, "is to excuse all actions in the final analysis . . . To permit an act to go unchallenged because you see a psychological or social explanation for it is—is, why, it's *permissiveness*. You can see what that's already done in our society."

"I don't excuse all actions," Chambers said firmly. "I would never excuse somebody who engaged in an act that he knew would damage or destroy another person. Anything done out of simple selfishness or cruelty to another—no, no, I'd resist that as long as I could."

Durant smiled. "But damage to an institution you can take lightly?"

But Chambers did not see this particular case that way. He agreed that the Black Students League had been engaged in a political action directed at the university, but he felt that its purpose had not been basically destructive. To insist on punishing three students for breaking a window was, to his mind, to demean or to deny the larger act of which it was a part; the refusal of the three to appear was apparently part of a BSL decision to force the university to respond to the political motivation. Now, if one were to isolate the window damage from the rest of the day's protests (and despite the BSL he was as much in favor of doing that as was any supporter of the judicial procedures), one would see that an incredible row was being made over five dollars' worth of breakage. Didn't that suggest, whatever anybody said to the contrary, that the three blacks were really being held accountable for a perceived threat in the combined acts of eighty black students? Was it honest to deny a political act and still punish three people for it? He spoke with

ATTACK . . . BISHOP URGES U.S. AID TO BIAFRA

conviction, hoping through his effort to end a matter which had
become a tangle because of his absence from office at a crucial
moment. The committee as a whole regretted that the charges
had been made. But to Freedman and Durant, the kind of
reasoning Chambers was using had ceased to matter the moment
the judicial processes had been invoked. The line had been
drawn.

Since the committee could do nothing but argue, the secretary
—Phyllis Christy, normally Chambers' secretary—was asked not
to keep minutes. But the inability of the committee to come to
any agreement was a victory for the chairman and Morris
Freedman, since inconclusive debate meant no alteration in
policy.

At the hearing of the Student Judicial Board that Wednesday,
the three accused blacks did appear, but they were accompanied by the other seventy-seven members of the League who
had also participated in the demonstration. The president of the
League, Joe Collier, stood on a chair to read to the jurors the
letter that had appeared in the newspaper. That letter, he declared, constituted the defense of the three accused students;
they had therefore appeared before the court, as they had been
requested to do—a concession not found in the letter, but one
that suggested their concern for the welfare of the university—
and would now adjourn to the corridor with the other members
of the League to await the decision. Despite the urgent plea of
Chairman Harcourt of the Student Judicial Board that they disperse, since their presence gave at least an implication of a
threat to the proceedings, they refused to do so. "Why, we're as
peaceful as you can get," said Collier calmly. "We're just here
because we're interested in what's going to happen to our
brothers. It's a Christian way to act, man." His remark drew
laughter from those near him.

While the Board deliberated beyond locked doors its response
to the unprecedented state of affairs, the black students sat on
the floor and on the nearby steps; some of them read, some of
them played cards, and some of them talked in small groups.

. . . FEDERAL BEAUTY COUNCIL ASKS FOR

After three hours of debate, the jurors were unable to reach a decision. Harcourt told Collier and the three white journalists present (one from the student newspaper, one from the city newspaper, and the third from a weekly newsmagazine planning a feature on student unrest) that, because of the unusual nature of the case, the Board was turning it over to the Committee on Student Affairs. "Do you mean," asked the reporter for the magazine, "that you want *them* to make the decision for you?"

"On an issue of this sort," said Harcourt (his tie was loose and his hair rumpled), "one that has serious implications for the whole university . . ." His voice momentarily faded. "Hmmm, that's an interesting question . . . Oh God, what we need is some sort of guideline not found in the Code, a policy clarification. What's the position of the administration? What's the advice of the Student Affairs Committee? Nobody in this place seems to be giving *direction* anymore, they leave it all up to us . . . You might add," he said suddenly, "that I—yes, that I'm resigning at this moment from the Student Judicial Board to protest the lack of direction I find in this spineless university. I mean, what's a president for?" The black students who overheard him cheered and applauded and began to form a snake line in the corridor similar to the one of the day of their protest. "Goddamn it," cried Harcourt, incensed, "that's a *personal* decision, not a political one; it implies nothing about the merits of *your* case, I'm neither supporting it nor attacking it." He sighed; he was near tears. "Oh, fuck it all," he said.

Though racial tension had been apparent earlier, such were the beginnings of the active phase of the troubles at Brangwen University in the academic year 1968–69. George Chambers thought if this particular episode hadn't ignited some highly inflammable gases, another probably would have. He could understand how hostile the blacks could become to a president, a dean, a committee, a code, to any symbol of authority: for in his own mind was affixed the image of a soldier in the act of thrusting a gun butt into the stomach of his own daughter.

ACTION . . . EXPERT SAYS ATLANTIC OCEAN

6

"If I had the decision to do over again," said Terence O'Brien mournfully, putting his hands behind his head and staring out the window, "I can't say that I would have decided differently."

"I *told* you not to act so quickly, that George would be back in a few days," said Phyllis Christy.

"I would have phoned George at the hospital, but *you* said—"

"I know," said Phyllis, tapping her foot.

"It's not that I'm a racist, for God's sake," said Terry.

"Nobody's accusing you of that."

George Chambers sat behind his desk, his cast resting on a stained pine footstool brought from home (Mark had made it in junior high). He sipped at his coffee and listened to his assistant dean and his secretary bicker. They sat facing him on a new divan with chromium tubular arms and legs. On the low table before them was a copy of the Brangwen *Daily Sentinel*, showing a picture of Stephen Harcourt, his arm raised in anger or despair at some black students; above him the main headline read:

JUDICIAL BOARD POSTPONES ACTION;
CHAIRMAN RESIGNS, ACCUSES DORAN

They were having a staff conference—which meant that since a lull had come to the activities of the dean's office (as often

GOOD FOR WASTE DISPOSAL . . . "INSTANT"

happened immediately after any major event) they were chatting over coffee. Chambers was, of course, disquieted by what had taken place; but what chiefly bothered him was not a need to absolve himself from a sense of guilt, a process which Phyllis was making difficult for Terry, but something harder to define: a sense of dissatisfaction that was not yet despair though he felt it could yield to that, a wish on his part to return to some stage of innocence or at least of ignorance—to some period in his life not only before the demonstration, but before Mary had been struck in the stomach by the butt of a gun. Actually, to find something to hold on to, he had to go further back—to the times when his children had been much younger. He was thinking of a camping trip his family had made to the West—of driving a car late at night in a rainstorm. He remembered the glow of the dashboard dial, the sound of Mary's guitar, the rest of them laughing at some joke . . . What bothered him now, he thought, was his sense that everywhere events were taking precedence over people. He felt a personal threat in this, that whatever he was or might like to be was endangered. Were people as individuals unimportant, puppets caught up in some movement toward doom of which the present social unrest was but the preliminary tide? What he, or anybody, might say to friends or at a committee meeting had become almost an irrelevance. The truth of any matter was not what a person felt but the event itself. One discovered truth then by reading a newspaper.

Chambers welcomed this momentary chatter, this lull. He was glad to focus on Terry and Phyllis, individuals with idiosyncracies and characteristics which defined them as surely as he and Stella and Mark and Mary were defined. Terry, for example, wore a tweed jacket and an ascot. He looked to be the fraternity boy he once had been; and clearly nostalgia for his old campus and a way of life no longer to be found in it had sent him back to Brangwen after a period in a brokerage house. He lit a cigarette—as always it was of the English kind, Players —with a slim lighter and went on talking to Phyllis. Terry rented

a furnished room from an elderly woman, the widow of an ento-
mologist, in a Victorian house downtown; he spent some of his
spare hours weeding the flower beds for his landlady and occasionally taking her to the movies. A week or two before Chambers' accident he had told Chambers that he simply had to find
a new room, since his landlady, who insisted on giving him
breakfast, invariably cut into the rind whenever she prepared
his grapefruit. It comforted Chambers to think of Terry's attitude toward wedges of grapefruit that contained rind. If you
looked at Terry that way, you could tell, at least, that his decision to bring charges against the blacks was fully in character.

Terry suddenly addressed himself to Chambers. "What you
need to know, George, if I haven't already told you," he said,
"is that *before* I got the deposition, even before the demonstration was over, the damned phone calls started coming in. This
fellow that plays the violin—"

"Ormsby," Phyllis said.

"This fellow Ormsby called; he was *frantic*. 'For God's sake,
my grandmother has a heart condition and there's a riot going
on. What are you people *doing* about it?' he said; and then a
girl who was quite hysterical called from the coffee shop. And
somebody phoned to say the blacks were beating up another
black who had refused to join them. This person who called
said he thought it was Fred Henry being hit—"

"Fred was seeing me at the hospital then," Chambers said.

"It was all just a rumor," Phyllis said. "It turned out to be a
Pakistani graduate student in nutrition and nobody hit him at
all. He apparently shouted something at the demonstrators and
they just circled around him, shaking their fists; it was like a
dance, that's what Anne—you know, Marty Niemeyer's secretary—said; she followed them around, having a marvelous time."

"But Phyllis," Terry said, hurt, "I *did* get the call and you've
got to remember the tension we were feeling in the office. It's
easy enough to be offhand about it *now*."

Chambers smiled at them both. Phyllis too was in character:
she often rebuffed Terry like that. She was thirty—a few years

older than Terry—and she had a three-year-old daughter whom she called Spider. Spider was a fragile child with straight black hair. Talking about her child to Chambers or Terry, Phyllis behaved as if Spider were an interesting little human being that it had somehow fallen her lot to take care of and be amused by; but Phyllis gave all of her available time to Spider, bought her expensive toys, took Spider to the doctor at the first sign of a cold, and was thinking of starting her at the violin by the Suzuki method. Phyllis thought Spider had great artistic ability. Phyllis' husband had been in his first job after graduate school, an assistant professor in government. Apparently in the best of health, generally admired as a bright young man dedicated to reforms in the federal government, he might have managed something of real value either in politics or as a critic of the system, or so Phyllis believed; but he had complained one day of a severe headache and died the next of a cerebral hemorrhage.

Terry, of course, would have been so glad to marry Phyllis that he would have swept Spider as well as Phyllis into his arms. But she wouldn't have him, even though—at least in superficial matters—they were similar. Clothes, for example, were important to Phyllis too. Chambers, who normally had no idea of what people were wearing, always could look back upon any given day in his office and remember how Phyllis was dressed. Like Terry, she liked informal clothes; today she wore a short skirt and high plastic boots. Chambers thought that to both of them clothes probably were an assertion of a life they aspired to rather than had.

Terry was caught up in his continuing self-justification. "—and Warren had just brought in Torgeson's deposition when that Englishman Garmonsway—you know, the adviser for SDS, though why an English mathematician is the adviser of an American radical group is beyond me—when Garmonsway called in to say that he understood we were prosecuting the blacks and if that were the case it was a pretty s-h-i-t-t-y thing—"

LEAVE U.S., AGNEW SAYS . . . POLICE SLOWDOWN

"You needn't spell it out for my sake," Phyllis said, and then she gave all her brightness to Chambers. "Does he need to spell it out for yours, George?"

"No," Chambers said.

Terry flushed. "I—" he began. "Oh, hell," he said.

Chambers felt sorry for Terry; Phyllis was being inexcusably cruel to him today. It wasn't really the complexity of the racial problem that was bothering Phyllis. She knew that Chambers was disturbed, and so she became bitchy with Terry for having made things more difficult for Chambers. In a way, Chambers represented for her the dead husband, or at least the virtues of that husband transferred into some older man who was in the best of health and likely to survive (barring further accidents) as long as Bertrand Russell; he had known that from the beginning. He had given her a job when she needed one, even though at the start the letters she wrote from dictation had been as quaint and mysterious as the notes found in Chinese fortune cookies. She was loyal to him. He gave her a kind of security that Terry couldn't.

And so there they were: Terry, Phyllis, and he, the entire staff of the dean's office, a little world within a world. If forces, destiny or whatever you called it, tended to make individuals anonymous, to wipe out identity, still the people were *there* under the events and each was full of insecurity and he supposed loneliness and anguish. And it was no solace to know that. Life struck him suddenly as almost unbearable. What he *ought* perhaps to be saying to Phyllis was, "I think you two ought to marry," though of course it would be a meddlesome thing to say and she would consider it crass, a slap in the face. "I don't like the color of this room," he said, for at the moment it did appall him. He felt himself carried away in a wave of pettiness that on any other day would have been astonishing to him. "Why weren't we consulted? And I really don't care for chrome furniture or metal desks. What was wrong with what we had?"

It was such an irrelevant intrusion that Terry looked at him in alarm. Phyllis, though, giggled. "Listen," she said, "the decoration in the Ad building was all Marty Niemeyer's project. He's leaving, did you know that? You can put back things the way they were—"

"Who said he was leaving?" Chambers asked.

"Anne told me. He's got a job as president of a college in Wisconsin. President Doran doesn't want him to announce it now, it would sound as if there's dissension among the ranks of vice-presidents in a time of crisis. Who wants to be the new vice-president for Student Affairs?"

"Not I."

"You're the logical choice."

"A vice-president," said Chambers with a sigh, "is accountable to the president; he can't say anything in public that is contrary to presidential policy; and even if he does it in private, it's a betrayal of trust."

"A vice-president can redecorate the dean's office without asking the dean a thing."

"Let me tell you an anecdote, Phyllis," he said; for he felt lonely himself, whatever his sense of family, as lonely as he imagined Phyllis and Terry to be. He wished her to understand —she with all her ambitions for him—what he as an older man felt. "Last year a boy came to see me. He was a senior in the English honors program, which I understand is a rigorous pre-professional program. This boy was bright, he had for that matter the best record of anybody in the program; but he'd gotten into an argument with an instructor over a paper he'd done. Instead of the typical scholarly exercise he'd written something he felt was unusual and original; the instructor, whom he thought pedantic and I guess unimaginative, had told him, yes, it was so wildly original it was a farce." Chambers tapped aimlessly at his cast. "At any rate, the boy became so sour and depressed he did no further work in the class and was about to be flunked out of the program. I told him, of course, that it was stupid of him to let the remark of one person—particularly of a man he apparently didn't respect—ruin a prospective career. The boy gave me the most conspiratorial stare imaginable. 'You

INSTINCTIVE   AND   LEARNED,   BEHAVIORIST

are advising me, then, Dean Chambers,' he asked, 'to do well in
my classes so I can go to an Ivy graduate school and make a
fine record so that I can get a good job in a first-rate school like
this one?' He said it of course with full awareness of the irony.
He thought, you see, that was what my advice would be, what
a dean would be expected to say. But what was so terrible to
me was that he *wanted* me to say it, because he had already
made that kind of decision in his own head and wanted it
stamped with the official university seal. It was a revelation to
me, how depressed I became. 'No,' I said, 'no, not at all; I don't
recommend anything.' "

"Is that the end of the story?" Phyllis asked.

"Does it strike you as pointless?" Chambers sighed again.
"Here's another story, then. When I was a child I thought the
way all children did, how fine and remarkable it would be to
become, or even to meet, the President of the United States.
Even when I was in high school I had a dream in which President Roosevelt came to my town to pay a particular visit to *me*.
'I've always wanted to meet you,' he said. 'That letter you wrote
to Secretary Morgenthau came to my attention—' You see, Phyllis, Morgenthau was Secretary of the Treasury then—"

"Who's Secretary of the Treasury now?"

"I forget; but we knew the names of all the Cabinet members
then—Ickes and Hull and Wallace—names that mean nothing to
you . . . But I *had* actually written a letter to Secretary Morgenthau. It seemed to me terribly simple to bring real prosperity to
America, to do away utterly with poverty, just by freezing all
prices for eternity and then pumping a great deal of money into
the economy, and by having a tax to keep the rich from getting
too rich; and in my dream President Roosevelt said to me that
he had read my letter and had it under advisement. He stayed
for supper and shook hands with me and my mother and father
. . . And in my dream I was telling my civics teacher and the
principal that President Roosevelt had come to see me and had
stayed for supper, and I wanted to be as solemn as the fact demanded, but my face, despite myself, broke out into the proud-

est smile. Waking up, I was so happy I can hardly believe it." Remembering, as he talked, his happiness, Chambers had been reflecting the proud smile of his dream; and when he looked toward Phyllis and Terry, he saw that both of them were smiling with him.

Phyllis said, "I like the second story better."

"Do you find it as pointless as the first one?" asked Chambers. "The thing is that at some time, I don't know when—if you asked me now I suppose I would say when Truman ordered the bombs dropped on Japan, but I know that's not really so, I didn't begin to understand how I felt about that until much later—I began to lose not only respect for leaders as symbolic figures of authority but what sense of meaning you get through identification with any institution—with a business or even a nation or a university . . . I know I'm not describing anything unique, the only thing that separates me from the students who walk in this door—the ones, I mean, who are restless and dissatisfied but want to do more than inflate their own egos; the ones, I mean, that I like—is that they never had a President to respect, except maybe briefly Kennedy; and he—"

"Nobody can reform anything, can they? If they simply say that institutions compromise them," Phyllis said; her voice was suddenly sharp. "I don't think anybody ought to use institutions as an excuse or apology for himself." She rose from the divan, frowning. "You didn't like that one boy because you thought he'd made a compact with himself—'all right, if they won't buy my originality, I'll knuckle down like all the rest, I'll do what I'm told and go through the system for the sake of a soft job at a prestigious university.' So he deserved to get thrown out of the office on his ear; one doesn't *have* to sell out, after all."

Chambers leaned forward, putting both hands under his cast, shifting it; his back had commenced to ache. "It just seems to me that if I were to accept this theoretical post of vice-president you just offered me, I'd be selling out, too . . . I got my master's in sociology but backed out of that kind of career; I had instructors too of the kind that boy talked about, in fact they were all that way. Maybe I was envious, seeing that boy—he *was* clever, you know—going on and up, chairman of the department at Yale, head of a new college in California, something like that . . . But no, his life would be from my point of view without meaning. Ambitious, meaningless people are a threat to me, Phyllis," he said earnestly. "What I like about the dean's office here is that it's really in a kind of eddy; we're appointed by the administration—at least I was, two presidents back—but represent as best we can the interests and welfare of the students—"

"Brave Terry pulled us right out of the eddy," Phyllis said, looking at Terry at last more sympathetically than in reproof. "We're out in the middle of the stream—"

"Help, I'm drowning," said Terry in a faint voice. "Mother made me play the violin but never taught me how to swim—"

"But the point is," said Chambers, "that we have the freedom to say what we think; you can argue if you want to that we have that freedom because from an administrative or faculty point of view we really don't belong to either and aren't important enough to worry over anyway, but still I would say that because we're free to speak our own minds, because we work with human problems and not with institutional ones"—his voice began to rise—"we're happier and are of more value by far than we would be if all three of us were swooped up and put down in Niemeyer's office with a private phone line connecting us to the other vice-presidents and to the president's desk."

"All right," said Phyllis, "I withdraw my offer." She strode toward the anteroom, a secretary with business to do; at the door she stopped. "Terry can be vice-president," she said, and shut the door sharply.

Chambers was disturbed. "I'm too long-winded," he said to Terry. "We left you, didn't we, in the middle of an explanation—"

"Let's leave it there," Terry said, rising.

Chambers didn't want him to go. "It was some complaint Garmonsway made."

"He said it was a shitty thing we were prosecuting the blacks when we were doing nothing about some Aggies who had cut the hair of the only shaggy boy in the Ag School. I only brought it up because if it seemed inevitable to the adviser of SDS that we would be sending the case of the blacks to court, it seemed likely enough that I *should*." Terry looked at him unhappily. "I made a mistake; why should I try to say I didn't? I'm going to tell Phyllis." He followed her into the anteroom.

Chambers reached down for his crutch. He got himself upright with it and hobbled over to the window. The leaves had left the campus trees; he had a view not only down the hill to the city and the lake but to the factories on the hill to the left; and far off and straight ahead to the blue rise beyond which his own house lay. The view, which often had pleased him with a sense of openness, today seemed confining, even oppressive; was it because of the mists that lay upon the lake, the grayness of the sky encompassing everything he saw? A sordid town in a beastly climate, if one were objective about it. Soon it would be winter . . . Speaking to Phyllis, he had been surprised at how easily the anecdotes had come to his lips and had thought with pleasure that he was saying something simple and profound. He ought to have said nothing; or if he had to justify himself, to have said only that his view of life was based on human relationships. How fatuous and absurd he must have been!

A black limousine drew into the parking circle beneath his window. The chauffeur disappeared at a trot beneath him; he reappeared with a suitcase. President Doran, attaché case in hand, walked briskly behind him; he was off, no doubt, for a consultation or a speech in Washington or New York or Philadelphia. Just before he reached the car, a quartet of students came out of the bushes to his left. They raised their arms, clenching their fists in the manner some of the SDS members had recently found to their liking. Somebody lifted a sign: DORAN TRAVELS WHILE CAMPUS BURNS. Momentarily startled, the president looked at them. He saw the sign, took it as a joke, and laughed, waving to them like an experienced politician. The jeering and fist-shaking continued. He got in the car and was driven away. A gust of wind, bringing sleet mixed with rain, shook the window; the students vanished as if blown away.

The incident, trivial as it was, had set Chambers' heart beating hard. It seemed to him a stupid piece of harassment carrying what the town newspaper would call "a veiled threat": the kind of act which would make more difficult the task of resolving the issue of the three blacks. Stupidity and accident ruled; malice and bitterness echoed in the empty air. Resentment was the modern disease: it lay behind the shearing of an Aggie's hair, behind the clenching of fists and the jeers he had just witnessed; it lay deep in a man like Garmonsway, that highly paid refugee from upper-class England disturbed not only by the elegance of numbers but by his inability at forty to add anything to mathematical knowledge. He had felt the oppressive weight of resentment in the university atmosphere upon his return to work: bitter young instructors at lunch, attacking tenure policies or the extent to which federal funds granted for scientific research had made the university a tool of an evil foreign policy, humanists attacking in the student newspaper the hypocrisy of the president for paying lip service to their needs, an adolescent voice from the statue of Silas Brangwen shrieking out, "We need *more* Vietnams: the more we get, the sooner the Capitalistic monster will fall" (but what about the dying and the dead, what about those left to grieve, what about the hungry wandering aimlessly in a ravaged land?).

Resentment had taken a ludicrous moment in a men's room and made of it a bitter symbolic design—a proof, on one hand, of the intolerable racist nature of white America and the hypocrisy of its liberal institutions; and a test, on the other, of the integrity of a judicial system, of all that opposed chaos while permitting rational judgment and the operation of democracy itself.

Chambers wished he could resolve this particular dilemma. Responsibility for minor acts of vandalism at one time would have been within his small domain. But whatever he had said to Phyllis, whatever his approval of eddies, he knew that personal relationships alone did not suffice any longer. No, a person could not resolve an issue in any personal interview if the emotions were so far in excess of the act which had engendered them that to talk reasonably about the act to the contending parties was to appear unreasonable and politically naïve and possibly even gratuitous. Some central seed of belief had fled, vanished to the stars from which it had perhaps originally come; and what was left behind was simply an immense void within which the individual soul (including his own) was a red ember, smoldering with dissatisfaction at something so abstract as to seem inane: the human condition itself. Chambers, who was loyal to his wife and family; who disliked violence and the exploitation of man by man; who in the past had been an exemplary dean because he liked students and took pleasure in alleviating their problems, because his word was trusted, because he was opposed to injustice of a bureaucratic or any other kind, because he had no egocentric wish to rise on institutional ladders; who, in short, fit most of the definitions one can arrive at in describing a good man: Chambers, aware of his lacks and minor indulgences, was dissatisfied with everything about himself.

On a crutch and a leg, he swayed down the steps and across the street to the Faculty Club (administrators could eat there) for lunch; Stella had thought she should pack his lunches while his cast was on, but most mornings she would doubtless forget and besides he felt he ought to be speaking with people. He ordered a mound of lasagna, took it to a distant corner, and nibbled at its lukewarm edges in solitude. His mind, concerned with dissatisfactions, would not let him alone. Whatever the difference in degree, the dissatisfaction he felt lay also within his daughter as well as within black leaders or conservative elderly professors. What release was possible for any of them? Stella had said after reading Mary's letter, "Let her go . . . She has to find her own salvation," echoing Mary's own words. Mary was lucky to be able to go to Europe, lucky to have a friend whom she could help. Mary might be saved from bitterness. Whatever his own love for her, Chambers could resolve

JURY CHARGES BRUTALITY TO PATERSON

her problems no better than he could resolve those of anybody else; and—queer, subjective world that he inhabited—he knew that he had been responding to what had happened to her, what she had said in her letter, all the time he had been talking to Phyllis and Terry about his childhood, his concept of himself.

In the afternoon he talked to a few students about trivial matters and at 3:30 had Phyllis place a call to the dean of the Agriculture School. The dean was busy, but returned the call an hour later.

"Dean Gorham here. Who wants him and why?" He had the impatient voice of a termagent.

"George Chambers. I'm calling about—"

"Who?"

"George Chambers. The office of the Dean of Students. In fact, *I'm* the Dean of Students—"

"I didn't know this number I was supposed to call was a long-distance number."

"It's not, Dean Gorham. It's an extension number in the Administration Building."

"That's what I mean. Up here in Agriculture, we say it's a long-distance call to the Ad Building; you see, we rarely get our messages through."

Chambers made a face at the telephone. "I'm calling about that boy who had his hair cut off."

"He looks much better, thank you for calling."

"I haven't seen him, Dean Gorham, so I can't say; but I wanted to tell you that nothing can be done about the boys who did it if nobody makes a complaint."

"Why should anybody do that?"

"I thought the boy himself might be able to identify them. I thought *he* might want to make a complaint."

"He doesn't want to do that."

"How do you know?"

"I talked to him."

"Could you tell me his name?"

"We can handle our own problems here, thank you. Good day." The telephone clicked.

The weather began to clear as he stood in the driveway loop, waiting for Phyllis. "What kind of car is this?" he asked, climbing into the rear seat.

"Your own car and you don't know yet?" She laughed. "A Chevrolet."

"I can tell Volkswagens, the rest are all alike."

"You're grumpy. Stella said you'd been grumpy at home, but I haven't noticed it at work until today."

"Am not." But he was silent while she drove down the hill. The nursery school was in a two-story frame building on the street that separated the black neighborhood from the Italian. It was neatly painted and surrounded by a new link-chain fence. "Isn't this a nice nursery school?" Phyllis said. "It's about time this town thought of its working mothers. We've got *you* to thank for this, George."

"Why me?"

"Aren't you on the board of Community Action Now? CAN raised the money."

"I just help advise, it's a luxury. I didn't canvass at the supermarkets or go see the manager of the typewriter factory; the college kids did that. Give them the credit."

"OK, George."

Spider came running down the walk and out the open gate, clutching a handful of papers. "Get in front, Spider," Phyllis said, "George's in a bad humor."

"No, I'm *not*," Chambers said. "Sit on my lap, Spider, and let me see what you've been drawing today."

Smiling, Spider climbed over his cast and plumped herself on him, thrusting out her drawings. "Look, a boogeyman," she said about one drawing, "a bird," "an airplane," as he rapidly flipped through the smudged sheets of fingerpainting. They drove down Floral Street and past the house where he and Stella had lived when their children were small; and when they were out in the country, and he could see the sunset from the

ACCORD ON BOMBING HALT . . . GHANA SHUTS

window, he thought of how much the strands of cloud resembled the figures Spider had drawn.

"Look, Spider," he said, "there's your boogeyman—there's your bird."

There was a dark strand near the sun, one that was slender for about half its length and larger and slightly curved for the rest. It reminded him of a rifle. No, of course it didn't, it had nothing to do with Mary (". . . *And I did, I honestly did, feel then this real love for that soldier . . .*"). But he had no business messing up the innocent sky with his obsessions. He would cast out that particular image.

"Stop hugging me so tight," said Spider. "You're hurting me."

7

The Committee on Student Affairs was no more capable than the Student Judicial Board of resolving the issue of the three blacks who had participated in the demonstration, partly because if the issue was beyond George Chambers' abilities as a dean it was also beyond solution by committee; and partly because the committee remained hopelessly divided.

Therefore the committee postponed any action until the spring term by appointing a subcommittee of two to contemplate a suitable posture toward the blacks as well as toward the letter published in the *Sentinel* and read by Collier at the Board hearing. A problem with the subcommittee was that, in the name of fairness, it was composed of two figures who had taken opposing sides—Morris Freedman, the chief author of the Code, and George Chambers. The two members were destined (as the whole committee must have known, voting for the proposal) to fruitless argument. If ensuing events hadn't cut off their deliberations, they would also have been destined to the ultimate presentation of opposing reports.

A further problem was that neither the committee nor its subcommittee had the authority to require witnesses to appear before it. That the subcommittee couldn't demand the black students to come was, Durant said, in its favor: to request informally the three accused students to appear before it and possibly before the larger committee would be to take away the onus of coercion. Since no judicial apparatus would be invoked at that time, the blacks would have an opportunity to engage in a rational debate. Would they appear, if asked? "Of course," said Durant as if there could be no doubt, "when the emotional heat is off—after Christmas, yes."

The committee spent the greatest part of its last scheduled meeting before the holiday arguing the relevancy of the official deposition and of other information possibly gathered by the campus patrol. Chambers, thinking such material of interest at least to the subcommittee, had volunteered to ask Proctor Warren for it; but Durant, on the advice of Morris Freedman, decided that for him to do so—as a member of the Student Affairs Committee though not perhaps in his capacity as Dean of Students—would be to confuse the committee's policy-making function with the operation of the Judicial Board.

"But that's already *happened*, hasn't it?" Lawrence Sanders, the child psychologist, asked, puzzled. "I mean, when the Board turned the case over to us?"

"It's what we can't allow to happen," said Freedman. "If this whole issue turns on the question of whether or not the judicial process can continue—and I think your vote at the last meeting tells us how you feel about *that*, Larry—how can we possibly ask for materials that belong to the judicature? We would be in violation of the Code ourselves. It may shock you to hear me say it, but the actual facts of the case are irrelevant to us—"

"Then why do we want to talk with the blacks?" Chambers asked.

There followed a moment of silence. "I suppose to clarify the issue, Dean Chambers," said Durant. "To let them know why our hands are tied, so to speak; you can't expect a boy from the ghetto to have intimate knowledge of the difference between executive power—policy making, I mean—and the adjudicatory—"

"I think perhaps you can," Chambers said. Though he spoke

BEN HUR STAR RAMON NOVARRO BLUDGEONED

mildly, he found it difficult not to express a certain incredulity.

Durant, who was more emotional than his ally Freedman, colored. "In society, perhaps," he said, "but not in a university. Certainly not in this university."

"I thought," said Tom Phillips, one of the students on the committee, "that the Board had asked us to make the judicial decision for them."

"Oh no, no, *no*." Durant rose to his feet. "You students have to be absolutely clear about that. All we can do is examine the options and make a considered recommendation."

"In other words, tell them how to act?" In asking the question, Phillips had kept his eyes on the brief minutes of the previous meeting rather than on Durant or Freedman.

"Oh, *Tom*," said Freedman, exaggerating a sense of personal disappointment.

"But they don't even have a chairman," said Phillips, his head still down.

"The regulations are clear on the method for appointing a new one," said Freedman; he spoke with a self-deprecating irony that took away any irritation his erudition on technical points might provoke: "Roman eight, alpha, arabic two."

"What this discussion means, I suppose," Chambers said, "is that what I learn wearing my hat as dean I can't pass on to myself wearing my hat as a member of the committee or my cap as a member of the subcommittee."

Hat jokes, being a common source of committee humor, were normally received with tolerance; Freedman smiled, the two students laughed, but Durant looked disturbed. After the committee was adjourned, Durant said he wished to have a few words in private with the dean. Holding his crutch and leaning against the wall, Chambers waited for him to speak.

"George," said Durant, looking out the window, "this issue, God knows, is serious enough, though we'll get by if we play our cards properly. I lie awake nights worrying about my responsibility in this committee when I'm not worrying about my responsibility to my own boy. I don't know what you say to

Mark; that's not my concern any more than what I say to Phil
is yours . . . But what you say in committee meetings is very
much of concern to me."

Chambers took a breath. "Do you object to what I say?"

"I had a talk this morning with the president about the need
to preserve the integrity of the judicial system. God knows we'll
have chaos without it. The white radicals, it goes without saying, will want to join the blacks in attacking both the Code and
the Board—anything to bring our house down. I'm surprised
that Morry Freedman can maintain his patience and humor at
our meetings—"

"We still have to face up to the criticism of the Code and the
judicial system, don't you think?"

"The League's letter? That's the same thing the president
said, so I'll tell you what I said to him. The letter was *clever*.
If the Code was passed long before there were more than a
handful of blacks at the university, that doesn't in my mind
make it discriminate against *them*. The law and the judgments
based on it have nothing to do with matters of race, they have to
stand above such concerns. As for blacks on the judicial board,
we would of course have been delighted if they'd volunteered
themselves as candidates. They didn't. Wouldn't it have been
some kind of reverse discrimination if we'd gone out trying to
capture one?"

Chambers shrugged. "What I had in mind was that point in
their letter about trying them all as a political unit, the way
Pan-Hel does with social units that have misbehaved."

"*That* point surprised me. After all, there's not a word about
unit punishment in the new Code, dealing as it does strictly with
individual offenses. You wouldn't think they'd *know* about it:
That's a rule of the Pan-Hel Council and hasn't been openly
invoked in the last five years. It's the sort of thing . . ." Durant
hesitated, turning from the window to look at Chambers. "Well,
it's the sort of thing one might expect *your* office to know about.
There's not a boy in the League who belongs to a fraternity."

Chambers laughed. "You think I helped them with the letter?"

AZORES . . . ISRAEL COMMANDOS HIT NILE

Durant cleared his throat. "I'm glad to know you didn't, George. I hardly know what to expect from this administration. The president agreed that we needed to support the judicial system, but I'm sure he thought me a fool. I did say some foolish things to him. But why wasn't Niemeyer with our committee just now? Was it to demonstrate a kind of presidential disdain for what we're trying to do?"

"Don't start suspecting motives, Phil. Maybe Niemeyer was busy with his decorating projects or maybe he's just losing interest: I hear he's leaving at the end of the year—"

"You ridicule even your administrative associates, George. That's what I object to in our meetings, the maverick tone you set, let me be wholly frank." A red spot throbbed on Durant's neck; it seemed to Chambers he was ready to fly out with his fists, at least to burst with a cry through some curtain of frustration. But he spoke with restraint. "Do you know what I was thinking today? I was thinking that you and I both have boys almost of college age; and I was looking at the students on our committee, at Tom and Jim and at how serious and attentive they were and I was wishing that if Phil ever got to college he would have that kind of social responsibility. And then you tried to ridicule everything we were doing—"

Chambers put his crutch under his arm; he didn't like to stand against the wall and be lectured at like a schoolboy. "Listen, Phil, it's a slow trip back to my office, if you want to walk along and talk—"

"I thought you were rude to Morry; and then you made Tom and Jim laugh at both of us."

Chambers leaned on the crutch, swinging out to pass Durant and reach the door. That he'd had no intention of making a personal attack was clear enough to him, at least he'd felt no vindictive nastiness; what he'd been doing, if anything, was to protest a legalistic conception of problems and their resolutions. Did Durant identify himself wholly with such a conception? But Chambers would not argue. Swaying down the hall, he was surprised to find that Durant remained at his side.

BRIDGES . . . MYOPIA LINKED TO READING . . .

"I didn't mean to attack you just now," Durant said. "What I really wanted to do was to explain something."

"Explain what?"

"I lost my temper with the president. I always do. Morry laughs at the way Doran makes me apoplectic. Don't waste your energy on him, he says. Morry says the thing to do is to organize the faculty. Get them to give him a vote of no confidence and then take it to the trustees. Morry's convinced most of the law faculty, and has a good part of both history and economics on his side. He doesn't have to say a word to the ag faculty, that goes without saying . . . But I can't help telling off a person directly, that's my nature. What I told the president"—Durant waited until two secretaries passed them and then said—"I told him among other things what I thought of him and his whole staff; I was carried away as I always am by that heavy presidential complex of his—'it all depends on how we cut the cake' and all those phrases leading nowhere but into the dark." Durant raised a hand to defend his own words. "Don't say I'm engaged in ridicule: I'm not. It's old-fashioned hatred for everything that's happened to a university I once loved. I was carried away, you see, and when I got to you, I said—I said you smoked marijuana."

Chambers' crutch tip had clumped down on the tile in readiness for his next awkward leap; the accusation was so unexpected he nearly lost balance. "Whatever could make you say—"

"Mark told Phil. It was one of the things Phil held up to me last night. We had a terrible row. I'm not trying to excuse myself; I've already written a note to the president. I doubt if he'll ever mention to you what I said, but I want you to know I'm sorry. Do you need help on the stairs?"

"I can do better on my own."

Durant gave him an embarrassed half-wave and hurried ahead.

It was, for Chambers back in his office, an unusually disturbing encounter. Not that he was concerned with Durant's accusation to the president; that, in itself, was more damaging to

NAKED PAIR DISRUPT GALBRAITH SPEECH . . .

Durant than to him. What was disturbing about it was the
extent of animosity toward him that Durant's irrational act had
demonstrated; and beyond that, the unpleasant sense of half-
guilt he felt for the entanglements of his family with Durant's.
If only there could be a firmer base of shared assumptions from
which human relationships derived! Without such a base, everything became other than it was; resonance gave to the echo a
shock-wave greater than the original sound; as in bad poetry,
the smallest gesture became part of a portentous symbology. His
wife Stella, being an artist, had brought home from God knows
where a little jar smelling of pickles and containing a minute
quantity of a nonhabit-forming drug that, perhaps because of
societal confusion, was illegal. Had he shared a cigarette with
his wife because he was in rebellion toward social institutions
or because he was simply curious? He suspected the latter.
Secretly observing the act, Mark—who was still, after all, an
adolescent—gave it a connotation it didn't possess; Mark, for
God's sake, shouldn't have been *proud* of what his parents had
done. Chambers didn't know Phil; he suspected that his otherwise pointless slogan on the courthouse wall—"Alleluia, I'm a
bum"—was a public rejection of his father. If so, Phil's use of
Mark's confidence was a deplorable exploitation of it. Durant
must worry over Phil as much as Chambers worried over Mark
and Mary.

What had Durant said in his letter? "Dear President Doran:
I'm sorry I told you what I did about Dean Chambers"? There
was a story that Stella had told him about a newly appointed
artist at the university who—receiving one of the lengthy ques-
tionnaires about personal attitudes that graduate students in
sociology send through campus mail as source material for their
doctoral theses—had written across the initial sheet with a felt-
tipped pen, "Fuck you." Shocked or incensed, the doctoral
student, a girl, turned that particular questionnaire over to her
chairman who phoned a complaint to the elderly chairman of
the art department. The latter called in the new instructor and
told him that such reprehensible behavior could be damaging

to a young artist just beginning a career in the academy and
that an apology was required. "Well, if that's how you do
things," the young man said, and scribbled a note with his felt-
tipped pen: "Dear Miss ——: I'm sorry I said fuck you. Sincerely
yours." The artist had resigned his post after a single term to
go to the West Coast. Cecil Maynard had reported seeing him
once on a Los Angeles expressway driving a pink Studebaker
convertible.

Phyllis came into Chambers' office to see if he was ready to
go home. "Why are you smiling to yourself?" she asked.

"Am I?" He wondered at his reason for finding such pleasurable warmth in an obscenity. Did there exist in *him* a growing
antipathy toward the academy that went beyond a simple dis-
trust in institutions? In a way, the committee meetings, which
were part of his job to attend, were narrowing down to a question of choice: "Choose *us*, choose to support the institution and
the integrity of the judicial system," Freedman and Durant were
saying; "Choose us or choose chaos"; while no doubt the blacks
and dissident whites believed that anything but the suspension
or dissolution of judicial processes was an espousal of white
racism.

At supper that night he found himself to his astonishment
making an absolute harangue to Mark on drug abuse that
sounded in his own ears so full of drums and trumpets that he
imagined it the sort of thing Durant would say to Phil.

"I wouldn't touch the stuff," Mark said angrily.

"Why did you boast to your friend Phil that Stella and I
smoked pot?"

Both Stella and Mark were startled. "I wasn't exactly *boast-
ing*," Mark said. He stammered, trying to find some defense for
a remark which had been, after all, an indication of his fond-
ness for his parents. He admitted saying something off-hand to
Phil about what he'd seen through the hot air grating after Phil
had told him his father was upset by his participation in Information Please. "It's not as if I told Phil my parents were dope
fiends," Mark said.

TO BUY PHANTOMS . . . THIEU SAYS SAIGON

"Phil's father was mad enough to tell the president."

Stella shrieked. She ran into the kitchen. "Where did I put it?" she asked. Pans clattered. She came back with the jar. "Here it is, 'Exotic spices,' " she said, reading the label. "Would the FBI know what it really is?"

"I suppose so," said Chambers.

"Would they make me tell where I got it?"

Chambers found in Stella's drama a release. "Imprisonment and torture," he said; "they'll brainwash you. Poor Maynard."

"It isn't Maynard's, it's Marjory Feidelman's."

"I thought you'd grown it in the garden," Mark said.

Stella shrieked again. "Is that what you told Phil Durant?"

Mark ran his hand through his hair. "It isn't funny," he said. "It's about as serious as it can get. Both of you seem to think it's some goddamned circus or something." He looked at his mother accusingly. "You know how you're acting? Like an acid head, that's how."

Stella looked back at him unhappily. "When your father goes solemn, I go silly," she said, "then he joins me. I guess it's our marital rhythm . . . I'm sorry I shrieked, Markie." She sat next to him, running her fingers like a comb through his disarranged strands, as she had done when he was much younger; he moved his chair away. Stella seemed about to cry. "I'm sorry I shrieked," she said again. "I must want more excitement in life than's there."

Mark remained stern in his detachment. "What I'm trying to tell you both is that I can understand why Phil's father might do something nutty. Phil's been on drugs all term; he must have been high when he did that sign. *We* didn't know. His father's been in to see Ferguson about it; Phil hasn't been in school all week."

Chambers waved a hand helplessly. "I'm sorry," he said.

"Well, so were *we*." Mark's parental expression of disapproval vanished; he turned to his father almost with an appeal. "We tried to help. But a guy like Phil who can't be serious shouldn't have been in Information Please; and now they have *him* to hold up against us. Isn't it a mess?"

They sat in silence. Stella finally went into the living room and scattered the dried leaves of her jar upon the embers in the hearth. Mark, who had watched her without objecting, said, "You must want the whole countryside reeking with pot."

"Will it?" asked Stella in alarm.

"For God's sake, what difference does it make?" But Mark wandered disconsolately outdoors in his shirt sleeves to see if he could smell the marijuana in the woodsmoke; Stella followed him and Chambers hobbled after them both. It was a cold but still night. Above the heat of the chimney the stars swayed and grew large; Orion was perched more solidly on the broken weathervane of the barn they used for a garage.

"I think I can smell it," Stella said.

"If anybody asks," Chambers said, "we can always blame it on the dump"; but as he looked at the stars it seemed astounding to him that any human could find a whiff of marijuana or any other odor of the slightest significance; or that a trivial mischance—such as *this* one over a marijuana cigarette or *that* one over a broken window—could tangle human lives and lead people to consequential misunderstandings. Human emotions went on despite the stars; a sense of wonder at human life, of the emotions that flare in the dark universe of the human skull, moved him in a way that lay beyond communication to his wife and son. He thought of Mary heading for Europe with her invalid friend; of Durant and his son in rooms, metaphorical or not, from which the other was locked; of particular faces in the hospital; of ghetto children much younger than Phil who robbed and pimped to buy narcotics that would release them from self-hatred and dull anger, from fears and discontent and solitude. Dissatisfaction lay in *him* as it lay in Stella, as it lay in Mark and Mary, a family well fed and adequately clothed, a family without serious internal discord. Why should that be? How incredible! In the hospital, carried off by no sounder a justification than he had now for his feelings under the stars, he had thought

ARAB SHOPS IN JERUSALEM . . . POLICE END

of the mindless adaptation of mankind to any situation and had been depressed into emptiness; here, led by the vastness of the night to consider not the species but the fragile, almost miraculous nature of personal identity, he thought of passions and fears. For a moment he loved his chimney, the barn roof, the distant ridge darker than the sky, even the glow of the flames visible above the trees at the dump; he loved everything his limited but unique mind could grasp or want to reach, both people and things.

It passed quickly; an odd feeling of unity more painful and lonely than any despair, it vanished with the appearance of Hayden Wilcox on the road before the house, Hayden Wilcox leading a cow with a softly clanging bell, both of them smelling so heavily of manure that no evanescent wisp of marijuana or transcendence had a chance. To Hayden, weary after a long day and leading an escaped cow that perhaps bore the name of one of the constellations (all of the Wilcox cows being named for figures in classical mythology), there was nothing strange in three people standing in the cold dark without coats and staring up. "Lovely night," he said, tipping his shapeless hat as he came into the faint glow of the porch light; "Lovely night," the three of them echoed as he ambled on, the bell tinkling and the cow's angular hindquarters a pale and fading apparition in the dark.

"I sometimes wish I could live like that," Chambers said; and his wistfulness, which they understood and shared at that moment, made both Stella and Mark laugh.

8

In the morning he woke thinking of Fred Henry; it had something to do with a suspicion that had come to him while listening to Durant that Fred had written the letter for the Black Students League; and, in a more important but less tangible way, with his feelings of the night before. He hadn't seen Fred since his stay in the hospital; that visit, made in friendship, had been incomplete and unsatisfactory. Racial tensions might continue to grow, but Chambers saw no reason for passively sitting back and letting them devour his relation with Fred. Still, he didn't think he ought to ask Fred by phone or note to stop by; it might sound too much like an official request no matter how friendly his voice, Fred might think he was trying to pump him for information, Fred might take offense for some reason that Chambers hadn't the slightest knowledge of. It was odd how difficult it had suddenly become for him, a university official and a member of the Committee on Student Affairs, to return a gesture of friendship without making it appear something other than it was. Perhaps he was being unduly sensitive about Fred's sensitivity; he simply couldn't tell, and that in itself was a barrier.

When Phyllis brought in the campus mail, he asked her to go have some coffee in the Student Union. If Fred was there (the black students often sat in long debate with one another in a far corner of the cafeteria), she could mention, in passing, that Chambers had been thinking of him and would like a chance to wish him a happy holiday before Fred went home. Phyllis left; Chambers looked at the pile of brown envelopes, most of them filled with chaff from the administrative mills. One envelope, tightly sealed with Scotch tape and marked CONFIDENTIAL in red ink, had Durant's name in the sender's column. Chambers opened it to find a tissue copy of the typewritten note Durant had sent to the president. Above the letter Durant had written in the impeccable manner of a calligraphist: "Dean Chambers: I thought I owed you this copy. Please keep in strict privacy. P.D." The letter to President Doran read:

DEAR SIR:

I spoke to you this morning of various feelings of mine, most of which were not new to you. In previous meetings as well as in letters and interviews in the student newspaper I have made clear my distaste for those in high administrative office whose actions are inconsistent with their apparent personal convictions. Granted that we are each of us to a greater or lesser degree prisoners in Plato's cave, we should not praise the actual sunlight in private discourse or public lecture while behaving when threatened by shadows as if they possessed the higher reality: which is to say, Sir, that the president of a great university (or at least one with the vestiges of greatness) should "cut the cake" according to consistent principle and not in response to vociferous and changing demand.

I regret not the substance of my remarks but my lack of control in speaking of specific individuals, particularly of the Dean of Students. That I would make an accusation founded on nothing but hearsay seems to me, though undeniable, so improbable a fact I fear that even you may be hesitant to accept now my withdrawal of that accusation. Perhaps you will exonerate the dean without further ado if I say that shortly before our conference I had become aware in the most painful possible way that drugs—hard drugs—are not only in the possession of some of our undergraduates but that these students in order to support their own addiction have stooped to trafficking in them to high school youngsters too inexperienced to realize the bondage that a few experiments may subject them to.

Yours truly,
PHILIP DURANT, SR.
AGNES MERRIVALE PROFESSOR
OF PHILOSOPHY

Copy to: Dean Chambers

That Durant's pride in his integrity was so strong that he had felt it necessary to make a difficult if oblique reference to his own son in order to make his letter convincing and to justify (no: that was unfair, to make more explicable) to himself his aberration—this struck Chambers with greater sadness than did the stiff phraseology of the whole letter. How old was Durant? Five years away from retirement, perhaps? Phil, his only child, must have come to him quite late in life. Chambers thought of a white-haired janitor he had seen earlier in the year leaning on his broom in the basement and listening intently to some boys who were trying to explain to him the degree to which he was being exploited by an institution dedicated to the preservation of a privileged class. "I wish my boy'd had the chance to come to Brangwen," the janitor cried. "By God, I'd of seen that he'd gotten an education instead of trying to tear down the school!" Chambers, gratified on the one hand that the students had been trying so warmly to persuade the janitor, was gratified on the other by the janitor's dogged refusal to enter the new world; there was a quality alike in the janitor and the Agnes Merrivale Professor of Philosophy that he respected, however much both of them could be classified among the forces that resisted change. It was, he supposed, that they were what they were; one would never find them adapting their identities to a particular situation or audience. Which also made Durant so infuriating to work with; but any letter he might write would be preferable to one Chambers had received from a psychiatrist named Howard Bannister who had spoken of daughters—his own and

POLICE IN WEST BERLIN . . . NIXON WINS IN

Chambers'—as if his interest in them lay wholly in the degree to which each was supplying therapy to the other. That letter, sliding down cascades of slippery phrases, becoming immobilized in pools of guarded generalizations, had finally, through some miracle not contained within it, reached a muddied sea of optimism (". . . and had they no anxieties Sylvia and Mary would not have found each other and for that matter would be isolated from their own generation. It now seems to me the sooner they leave for Europe the better.") Chambers could not disagree with what the letter said; he wanted simply to hear in it—dictated to a secretary though it had been—the gurglings of the central spring which produced the flow: some sense, that is, of an individual speaking of other individuals in concern or regret or at least self-justification. Ambling the paths of his own associations, Chambers was sitting back in his chair, hands behind his head, looking at the ceiling, when President Doran came into the office.

"Good morning, Dean," Doran said, smiling but looking around to make sure they were alone. "I came downstairs to see if I could have a drag on one of those whatever you call them—" He perhaps knew the word but was uncomfortable about pronouncing it: the president of Brangwen was always caught between his desire for easy familiarity with staff and faculty and a need to maintain the dignity of a more remote position.

"You call them 'joints,' " Chambers said, sitting more upright.

"Don't get up. I'll sit in one of Marty's monstrosities." He sat down on the divan, crossed his legs, and lit a cigarette which he immediately stubbed out. "I promised Mabel I'd cut down on these things," he said.

"You don't like the new furniture either?"

"Frankly, no, I think Marty's talents lie elsewhere. I don't know what persuaded me he could be an interior decorator. Did you know he's leaving us?"

"I'd heard."

"He's a sharp liberal thinker, a bit too impatient with young people, particularly those on a revolutionary binge; but he'll be missed from the team. We need all the help we can get. My thorns, Dean, are not only certain blacks but some of the more firmly entrenched conservatives." A tall and thin man with graying hair, with a faint Oxford coloration to a Boston accent, he might have been an Episcopalian priest speaking of problems in his urban diocese to a deacon whose alliance he particularly desired. The studied joviality of his entrance and now his reference to an element in the faculty he found a problem had made it clear enough—without mention of a name or an allegation— that Durant's accusation would never have been considered seriously, whether it had been withdrawn or not. No doubt his unusual visit to the dean's office was being made at least partly to make this evident; now that it was accomplished he set off in a new direction, speaking in a friendly, almost intimate manner of the walk around the campus he had made with his predecessor on President Matthews' last day in office. "What I remember most, Dean," said Doran, "was when Bill Matthews put his arm around my shoulder and pointed out to me that little circle in the chapel road. Matthews, you know, once did some important work in the West for the Indians on the reservations; he was given a totem pole in acknowledgment of his services, there was a ceremony soon after he took over the presidency, you must have known about it. The totem pole's in storage down here"—he pointed toward the basement—"because not even the museum or art department would take it. 'During all my administration,' Bill Matthews said to me, 'I wanted to put that totem pole in that little circle on the chapel road where the oak used to be, but I couldn't.' 'Why not?' I asked him. He said the faculty wouldn't have allowed it; they would have laughed him out of office. That struck me as sad, Dean; but I thought that in my administration there would be all sorts of changes, I thought even that I'd have that totem pole put up in his honor. But do you know what I've accomplished so far?"

Chambers smiled sympathetically. "An across-the-board pay raise for the faculty and staff."

. . . POLICE ARREST 100 AT NEW YORK CAMPUS

"I was thinking of the start of the disadvantaged students program. It seemed to me a disgrace that a university such as this one had only a handful of blacks; the faculty approved the whole proposal without dissent, though we had to make alterations in admissions requirements which disturbed some of them. I thought," he said, lighting another cigarette and stubbing it out almost as quickly as he had the previous one, "we had a great thing going."

They chatted on about the program. From the beginning there had been unexpected friction in the living quarters, particularly in the women's dormitories; some white girls had refused black roommates and by so doing had raised almost as much resentment among the blacks as had the eager white integrationists who had surrounded the black girls, wanting to be taught black songs and dances and to speak black phraseology. Joe Collier, now married to one of the girls whose initial roommate had demanded another room, lived in the married students' housing area; after he became president of the League somebody had slashed the tires of his car, and he had found under his door a message printed in block letters, a crude half-jingle:

I'VE GOT MY RIFLE TRAINED ON YOU
EVERY TIME YOU WALK ACROSS THE CAMPUS, NIGGER,
ONE OF THESE DAYS I'LL CLOSE MY EYES
AND SLOWLY PULL THE TRIGGER . . .

an astounding message, even to those faculty members most cynical of the abilities of the student body, to come from a Brangwen undergraduate. But a university as diversified as Brangwen doubtless contained a few psychopaths.

The black movement toward separation, which at first had surprised Doran as well as Chambers and most of the campus liberals, had begun soon after Fred Henry organized the League. Henry—who, as an aide in Chambers' office, had been known even two floors above in the presidential suite as a rational young man with a social awareness that extended beyond

. . . CZECH CROWDS BURN SOVIET FLAGS . . .

the divisions of skin color—had won support for limited separatism simply by pointing out that the black girls were ill at ease and defensive in the dormitories; that, scattered as they were in predominantly white living units, away for the first time in their lives from their homes and neighborhoods, they were unable to concentrate on their studies and thought of themselves as examples chosen by a white institution to prove its open-mindedness. A large frame dwelling just beyond the campus gates was converted at the suggestion of Vice-president Niemeyer into a cultural center for black students, with bedrooms upstairs for fifteen black coeds.

Such a decision had, in Doran's phrase, "interesting ramifications"; it brought up the question not only of reverse, but of sexual, discrimination. Women were required to live in dormitories for at least two years; some of the more politically active of the white girls—unable to protest the special privilege that allowed black girls to leave the dormitories—took out the resentment they nevertheless felt by attacking the regulation that kept women but not men in dormitories. Niemeyer had managed to stop *their* movement for equal rights by pointing out, shrewdly enough, that if all students were permitted to find living quarters in town the effect would be to raise rents and to transform houses for families into apartments for students; in short, to make the housing problem for the poorer black and white families even greater than it was.

In speaking generally of matters known in much greater detail to both of them, Doran, chatty and intimate though he wished to appear, clearly had his own motives; as an experienced administrator, he was capable (as Chambers was uneasily aware) of obtaining in dialogue a series of agreements that could lead his conversational partner to conclusions the partner might not wish to reach. Chambers disliked calculated friendliness as much as he disliked phrases such as "the whole package" or "an entirely new ball game" as well as "how we cut the cake" and such variations of the dessert metaphor as "the kind of frosting we put on it"; but what he *did* like was the way the

POPE ASKS FOR CUTBACK IN CRIME NEWS . . .

president had committed not only his verbal armory but his prestige as president into the battle for the disadvantaged students project. Having accomplished nothing else, Doran was determined to make this project work; it appealed to his liberal instincts and was in keeping with the sort of activity he had successfully managed for the federal government and private foundations. He had reached the decision that some kind of black studies program was a requisite for the success of the project and for anything that the university might do that would be of value for blacks in America.

"A year ago, even six months ago, Dean," he said, rising from the divan and standing by the window, looking out, "I wouldn't have dreamed I would be advocating black studies as a separate program; that I support them now, and have given the League verbal assurance of my support, is a further example I suppose to some of the faculty of my famous lack of principle. But if I have learned something, if I'm not quite so innocent now of the psychological problems the black students face, if I see that the game has to be played with different rules—" He sighed. "I thought at first, 'What a marvelous place Brangwen is for minority groups!' We have a liberal tradition with a radical undercurrent; our government and political science departments are showcases; I thought too that nowhere else could they take a first-rate engineering physics major while electing, say, masonry or carpentry—you know, the practical stuff the Ag College offers that would be of help to them in rebuilding the ghettos even if they didn't do the actual labor—"

"I took the plumbing course," Chambers said; he had done so after buying his farmhouse. He enjoyed working with his hands, making or fixing things and had even managed a number of mechanical repairs on the Volkswagen. "It's true, though, that if you suggest anything like that to a black he's apt to get defensive or angry."

"They don't want any tinge of the laborer—the skill or pay hasn't anything to do with it—they want to use their minds; it's understandable. But then they resent many of our intellectual offerings; not so much in science or mathematics as in the humanities where everything carries a subjective weight. They can't see that Emerson or Edmund Burke has anything to say to them at this particular point; they don't want to be transformed in everything but their skins to fit into a middle-class white America. I'm convinced, Dean, that our offerings have slighted the achievements and culture of black peoples; that before we ever can manage any kind of harmony or good relationship between the races the black man needs to understand his past even as we understand ours, however partial that may be; that he has to be able to find pride in himself as a black who is a man before he can find pride in himself as a man who happens to be black." He turned around suddenly, smiling in a disarming fashion. "I'm giving you the speech I rehearsed for the trustees, I might as well admit it. Why not do as *they* first suggested? Why not just add a dash of black culture and history to our regular courses? Why not give a new flavor to the mix without using a separate kettle? And I argued the point with Joe Collier himself. 'Joe,' I said, 'why do you ask for a separate burner on the stove?' The answer is that finally they need to do these things for themselves. We hire the black professors, we find the facilities, but they—the black teachers and students—do the real work together. When you get one or two blacks in a white class, no matter how sympathetic the lecturer, the blacks are—what's their word? 'uptight'?—the blacks are uptight, they feel they're representing their whole race, it's the dormitory shambles all over again. They need, you see, to get their own show on the road." He paused to light his third cigarette; after a look at the ashtray, he inhaled deeply and kept the cigarette between his fingers. "Tell me, Dean, what's *your* position on the program?"

Chambers disliked the question. For that matter, he disliked the whole discussion, though his feeling had no reasonable basis. It was a subject he had discussed not only with Stella and Mark but with Terry and Phyllis; in these private discussions he invariably had advocated the president's position. He saw the problems: that a black studies program might, and probably would on a *de facto* basis, exclude whites altogether; that it could possibly turn into racial jingoism or at least into a program with exclusively political ends. He was aware of the misuses to which cultural and racial studies could be put. The glorification of one's own genes and history, accompanied by the revilement of other races, was in his mind as close to sinful thinking as one could get in a nonreligious age. He was opposed, as he always had been, to anything that increased the divisions among men; but he believed with the president that pride in their race, in the dignity of their color, was—for reasons that lay more with whites than blacks—a requirement of the blacks before any greater unity could be obtained. "Black is beautiful," however defiant the words, was the cry of a people who didn't yet believe it, who had been forced into acquiescence to an alien standard of beauty; in Chambers' view neither white nor black was beautiful and neither could be until perceived as such in the eyes of the other; at which point it would cease to matter. There was a point at which the planets, while actually following their pre-destined paths to the music of the spheres (Chambers, agnostic and relativist as he was, still held to such ancient metaphors, still believed obscurely in some transcendental truth), seemed to reverse their motion. He could accept the movement of black separatism with that analogy.

"My position—" he began, but hesitated; he would have had difficulty in explaining even to himself his hesitation. A number of conflicting attitudes and ideas, perceived in his mind more as physical sensations, paralyzed his tongue. One of them had to do with his liking for Fred Henry, who, as an assistant to Chambers, had been a sometimes eloquent advocate of Camus' argument in *The Rebel*. Henry had been fond of paraphrasing Camus' distinction between resentment and rebellion. Resentment is an impotent envy for what one does not have and for what one is not; since the person who feels it wishes to be other than he is, the resentment is actually directed at himself. Rebellion, on the other hand, comes from an implicit assumption of equality; the rebel demands recognition of what he is. In a secular age, rebellion asserts the meaning and oneness of man formerly found in the Christian concept of divine grace. A person even with Chambers' emotional hatred of violence could endorse a notion of rebellion.

What was it that held his tongue from an immediate endorsement of a black studies program which, regardless of his own anxieties about it, he firmly advocated in private and which Fred Henry and the other blacks believed was in their best interests? He knew instinctively that the president was leading him into a trap from which he would have difficulty extricating himself: he was going to be offered the vice-presidency and for the best of reasons. But to accept it would be to allow himself to be manipulated, to be fouled up by that administrative language he so thoroughly detested. To accept it would be to help the blacks at the expense of whatever friendship he might have with any of them. To accept it would be to use his own reputation with the faculty—for he knew, without taking pride in it at the moment, that because of his years at Brangwen, because of his integrity, and because of his inability to be anything but himself that he did have a useful reputation—to push through a program stalled both by its problems and by a lack of confidence in the president's leadership. What was so maddening was that despite the limitations of his administration, the president was behaving on this issue in a brave and perhaps (considering his shaky footing) even in a foolhardy manner; Chambers ought to be cheering him on.

Sensations, whatever the length of their verbal transcription, are flashes of feeling; his hesitation was brief. "I suppose," Chambers said mildly, "my position is pretty much the same as yours."

"Would you say it's worth risking my neck for?"

"Mmm, yes."

"You definitely support the program?"

"A lot depends on the spirit with which it's carried out. The faculty will have to give some, and the blacks will need to be responsible—"

DAY OF RIOTING . . . TITO DOUBTS RUSSIAN

"But you think it's possible?"

"First we have to get past this impasse over the Judicial Board."

"Can we do that?"

"Like everything else, like the black studies program itself, it'll turn on the matter of trust, won't it? There's no reason, at least at a university, for people to carry around suspicions and animosities. If we can't break the racial barrier here—" He shrugged.

Doran approached Chambers' desk. He considered for a moment perching on the edge of it (a sign of intimacy), moving some papers aside for that purpose; he reconsidered (a sign of dignity), and returned to the divan. He had just sat down when he saw the ashtray, looked at the length remaining to his cigarette, tapped off the ash and stood up again to come to his original position before the desk. "I suppose you've guessed why I wanted to know your feelings?" he asked almost gaily.

"I suppose I have."

The rest of Chambers' dialogue with the president, having already been given him through the gift of prescience, contained little that was surprising except perhaps for the president's confession of mistakes he thought he had made, an open admission he felt he could make to the dean but not to anybody in his immediate staff—"those bright young men"—or in the faculty. ("Coming from government service as I did, I thought it natural enough to bring along a team. It was one of the conditions I put to the trustees when they were considering me. That was an error. I hadn't realized a move like that would arouse the faculty's suspicions of me from the start, Philippa isn't Washington and Brangwen not HEW or State. No, the team needs some home products . . ." and "When I took the presidency, I was innocent on a number of counts. I've been in administration, but on the high policy level, a good many years. I know how to get along with my immediate staff and my superiors; we all speak the same language. I hadn't realized how much of my effort here would be directed toward winning the vote in both the student and faculty precincts. Frankly, Dean, I haven't been too good at that. The *Sentinel* accuses me of being away too much; when I'm here the blacks get angry, which is terribly ironical to my way of thinking; but *they* think I'm hired to sit in my office to manufacture excuses. For them I'm the bank president who puts off their loan because they're black.")

Chambers, who felt even the president's openness to be aggressive, part of a planned psychological attack, tried to resist the verbal momentum. "You can overestimate the help I or anybody else might give," he said. "I've been pretty ineffectual this year on the Student Affairs Committee."

"You've got two of the toughest opponents possible there; but Marty sings your praises. Marty didn't go to the last meeting because Durant and Morry Freedman are so hostile to him; he didn't want to disturb your style."

"My style?" Chambers was puzzled.

"Oh, your *way*, then, Dean. You and the students are already pretty thick; and Marty's sure that Sanders is swaying toward you. Marty will come in on any vote; you've got the game sewed up there, in our thinking."

"If I'm so handy where I am, maybe I ought to stay there."

"But I need support of the kind you can give on my own staff —I need a man of your reputation in the top-level administration. You may say I'm being egotistic, Dean, but I think if I lost out the program would be gone too. And I don't think even the blacks would be so hostile to me if it was you who ran their black studies through the wringer."

"I don't think they—"

Doran raised a hand. "It's something to talk over with your wife, isn't it? I don't want an off-the-cuff answer because I just might get a refusal. I wish, Dean, you'd think not of yourself or the salary that goes with the job—a considerable boost, of course —but of where you'd fit in best for the sake of both the blacks and Brangwen."

As soon as Doran left, Phyllis entered; she had been listening

TRANSFER LAND TO PEASANTS . . . AMERICANS

to the end of the conversation. "You can't refuse it," she said. "What he said was perfectly true. He needs somebody who can speak English and who really cares. You ought to be glad. Why are you looking so gloomy? I'm going to run out for a bottle of champagne."

"Don't bother. Did you see Fred?"

"Why change the subject?" Phyllis frowned. "I don't think Fred'll stop by before Christmas."

"Why not?"

"He was deep in some political strategy with Joe Collier and some of the other League members. When I gave him your message I thought he was embarrassed. One of the blacks laughed . . . I think Fred resented me stopping like that; the whites usually make a wide detour around their table."

"I thought Fred was on the outs with the League."

"Well, he must be back in . . . Listen, George, when you look so silly and sad when you ought to be—well, at least *excited*, I want to scream and pull your hair."

"Pull it, if it makes you feel better."

"Would it make *you* feel better?"

"It might."

"Then I won't," Phyllis said.

She left him to his misery, which was intense.

KILL 70 IN DELTA . . . SATELLITE SAVES

9

Stella expressed shock upon learning that her husband was seriously considering the vice-presidency. "There's one thing, George, I absolutely refuse to be," she said as they lay in bed that night. "I absolutely refuse to be married to a character in a novel by C. P. Snow. 'George Chambers and his wife pondered the dinner invitation from Sir Percy. One of the most influential of the group in opposition to the headmaster Eric Brooke, Sir Percy was known as a staunch supporter of traditional educational policy as well as of the cricket team; he was a friend of that other distinguished alumnus of St. Michael's, the Secretary of the Exchequer, who once had come to verbal blows with Chambers over the headmaster's radicalism in doing away with the gazebo by the goldfish pond. "Sir Percy has his cruder moments," said Chambers reflectively, putting the note beside his *Guardian* and reaching for a muffin. "Do you suppose in inviting us he has in mind—" ' "

"What in heaven's name is that parody for?" Chambers asked. In bed he enjoyed reading published letters—he was in the midst tonight of the letters Chekhov had written while sloshing through Siberia to the penal colony at Sahalin. Stella was desultorily turning the pages not of a Snow novel but of Berenson's *Italian Painters of the Renaissance,* a book she didn't like and which she often skimmed through when something else was vexing her. But tonight not even tactile values had channeled off her disturbance. She closed her book and he closed his, and they looked at each other unhappily.

"What I don't like about modern novels about political leaders in Washington or successful lawyers in New England or corporation executives in Manhattan or educational administrators in England," Stella said, "is—is—" She paused. "I don't know what it is. They just depress me. In Berenson you can at least look at the pictures."

"It would depress you in the same way, if I became a vice-president at Brangwen? God knows it depresses me enough, just thinking about it; I don't want to get involved in campus politics any more than I have to . . ."

"Why is it, George, that it's always depressing to see people *simply* in their political and social contexts? Is it because these contexts aren't satisfactory, never have been satisfactory, and really—if you're honest about it—never *can* be satisfactory in telling you what people are like inside and what they're happy or unhappy over? Those books that I don't like—I don't like them because they see the social context as the implicit standard or value against which the character is judged, and it's the context which finally gives him his label and decides whether he's a success or a failure. Actually, it's truer to think of the context as an enemy, something you have to resist if you want to be yourself."

Chambers flipped through his book. "There's something here somewhere," he said. "You know nobody has ever been able to say exactly *why* Chekhov so suddenly decided to make that wild trip across Siberia . . . He had consumption, he went alone, he had to wade streams, sleep in filthy beds and sometimes in the mud waiting for a ferry to take him across some flood. I don't know what a verst is, but it sounds more difficult than a mile; he had to go thousands of versts. Why? Well, I'm no artist like you or Chekhov, but I do know because in a way we're all like that, or most of us, only maybe it's more apparent to people

MOVES TO MONTREAL . . . COMMISSION CALLS

who want to write or paint . . . There's a letter here he wrote
the year before the trip, before I guess he even thought about
going to Sahalin; here, listen to this," and he propped himself
up against his pillow and began to read aloud those lines which
had touched him when he had first read them: " '. . . I am not
a liberal, not a conservative, not a believer in gradual progress,
not a monk, not an indifferentist. I should like to be a free
artist and nothing more, and I regret that God has not given
me the power to be one. I hate lying and violence in all their
forms, and am equally repelled by the secretaries of consis-
tories—' "

"What's a consistory?"

"It sounds like a religious institution of some sort. Do you
want me to get out of bed and look it up in the dictionary? The
floor's too cold . . . 'equally repelled by the secretaries of consis-
tories and by Notovich and Gradovsky—' "

"I don't care much for *them*, either."

"They sound mean, don't they? 'Pharisaism, stupidity and
despotism reign not in merchants' houses and prisons alone. I
see them in science, in literature, in the younger generation . . .
That is why I have no preference either for gendarmes, or for
butchers, or for scientists, or for writers, or for the younger generation. I regard trade-marks and labels as a superstition. My
holy of holies is the human body, health, intelligence, talent,
inspiration, love, and the most absolute freedom—freedom from
violence and lying, whatever forms they may take. This is the
program I would follow if I were a great artist.' Stella?"

But Stella had fallen asleep. She always fell asleep when he
read to her in bed; when he read to her, she said, it reminded
her of her childhood and of her father's voice reading yet another chapter of *Little Women*. Thinking of Chekhov's journey,
thinking of that impossible question "Where does human meaning come from?" he was filled with tenderness toward his wife.
Chekhov had been impelled to take that trip across Siberia for
two motives which were absolutely contradictory: on the one
hand—where was the letter that said this?—because prisons had

CHICAGO VIOLENCE "A POLICE RIOT" . . .

destroyed millions of men and it was "not the superintendents of the prisons who are to blame but all of us"—the Russian society of which he was a part; and on the other hand simply out of the desire to escape that society, to be as free as he could be. He could have gone by ship—as he did on his return—saving himself from solitude and misery and peril. On the ship he engaged in that other singular activity of his life, the action which helped cast light on the reason for the journey by land. He dived from the prow of the ship (that man who was anything but an athlete) while it was under full steam, grasping as it came by a rope dangling from the stern; a shark came close to him as well as the pilot fish that depended on the shark for their food . . .

What Stella had said about politics and social institutions wasn't wholly true, at least not for all men. There *were* people, he was sure, who did find fulfillment enough in the labels and structures—though those who strove mightily for the furnishings and the power doubtless trusted to some kind of reverse transubstantiation, their imaginations strong enough for them to believe in the miracle that would somehow transform the body and the blood into the bread and wine beneath their glittering chandeliers. As for artists, they were never happy with politics or political structures not because "bohemians are like that" but because a true artist (as well as he could understand it) was in pursuit of uniqueness. Uniqueness was not idiosyncrasy; uniqueness implied a connection somewhere, somehow, with everything else that was unique. For uniqueness was a value, and for it to be a value there had to be a point at which everything that was unique merged with everything else that was unique. If Chekhov was disturbed that he met not people but gendarmes and censors and merchants and poets and despots and all the other classifications including no doubt university bureaucrats, if he was disturbed by the selfishness and stupidity and lying and violence about him, if he felt he must give some of his limited energies to the building of schools for uneducated peasants, to the caring for their diseases, to the amelioration of the lot of convicts: what was all this but a social awareness that was the counterpart of his artistic awareness, a conviction that man was unique and that his uniqueness implied a merging into something beyond him, something unknown and with a principle of order or beauty doubtless utterly indifferent to that precious uniqueness which it paradoxically provided?

Chambers felt himself getting beyond his depth; what he was trying to grasp was some sense, so necessary to himself, to anyone who believed in something so abstract as the brotherhood of man at a point in history where such a belief was at odds with the actuality, some sense that the old humanistic impulse for unity still lay at the basis of art and life; that now as always man was caught between the conflicting demands of personal freedom and societal pressures and that the conflict was not so much mutually destructive as salutary, a necessary tension to prevent a willful self-annihilation (which the pursuit of personal freedom eventually amounted to) or the construction of the perfectly efficient beehive society (in which the honeycomb counted, but not its swarming inhabitants as individual creatures). Seemingly preposterous and absurd because of the contradictory impulses he read into it, Chekhov's Sahalin expedition was for Chambers actually a perfect analogy of those tensions within which human meaning had at least once been found . . . The bedlamp burning against the outer dark, Chekhov's *Letters* on his chest, he fell asleep, dreaming of vast Siberian skies, of flooded streams, of limitless oceans and their predatory life; beside him Stella slept, her hand open in Berenson on that colorful detail, Crivelli's "Still Life with Peacock."

In the morning Stella told him that she had been depressed for *his* sake at the thought of Doran conning him into a vice-presidency but that if he was going to be as unhappy in rejecting the offer as he would be in accepting it he might as well accept it for the salary increase, although she would have difficulty in explaining her husband to her friends. No doubt she was teasing him, but he was glad, really, that she saw no particular honor in the prospective promotion.

Somehow (Phyllis?) the word had gotten around the Ad

NEWARK PANTHER HQ . . . GREECE REJECTS

Building and among his faculty acquaintances that he had been offered the position and that nothing but his scrupulous lack of professional ambition was standing in his way; he saw with annoyance not only that Terry treated him with the reserve of greater respect but that even Morris Freedman, who came to his office on the last day of classes before the holiday, had taken a new attitude toward him. It struck Chambers that in the past he had been the sort of person whose "goodness" allowed others to view themselves with a certain self-indulgence even as they dismissed as impractical whatever he might have to say; now Freedman, who had come to open their discussions for their subcommittee report on the response to the matter of the judicial system and the three recalcitrant blacks, listened carefully to him. Chambers had no reason, for God's sake, to be annoyed that his word would be listened to; it was simply unfortunate that to be heard one had to be in a position of possible influence. It surprised him that Freedman was willing to forego—was this in deference to him?—Code details and legalistic interpretations for a general discussion of the growing difficulties between the races at Brangwen. Freedman was in agreement with the president and with Chambers that the black studies program was both valid and necessary; he also understood the reasons for the establishment of the residential unit for those black girls unable to adjust to dormitory life . . . They spoke of the fear of some faculty members that the blacks, in refusing to acquiesce to the judicial system, were in the process of destroying academic freedom. Freedman said reports were coming to him from instructors who were beginning to feel a certain constraint on what they were able to say in class. Much was now being made, Freedman said, of an incident of the previous year in which a visiting professor had aroused the anger of black students in a large lecture course by repeated references to the ineptitude of African political leaders; refused the opportunity to refute the professor, the blacks had taken over the class to read Leroi Jones while the instructor, pushed to the back of the room, shouted

TORTURE CHARGES . . . LODGE TO REPLACE

at the class at large not to listen to the obscenities but to join him in singing "The Star-Spangled Banner."

"It's usually the absurdities that get us into trouble," Freedman said, "but the point is that what happened in that class happened, just as what happened in the men's room of Old Dent happened; and there has to be a way—doesn't there?—to allow the university to keep operating."

"When I was in graduate school," Chambers said, "I had two or three perfectly dreadful instructors. I had one course in which the professor spent all his time baiting four Jesuit students instead of teaching sociology. He used to give that old argument that if God was omniscient He couldn't be omnipotent; you know, that if He foreknew what was to happen, why then He was powerless to alter it . . . He was a perfect little tyrant in class, he took pride in himself as a sort of antichrist. The Jesuits were unable to do anything but pray and prepare mimeographed statements. They would hand out their mimeographed statements at the door of the classroom; the instructor finally stopped *that* by saying it was a violation of some regulation or other. I thought then—and I think now—that students who feel a lecturer is wrongheaded or unfair should have a chance to have *their* positions heard."

"Wouldn't that just turn the classroom—at least in these uncertain times—into political warfare?"

"It might prevent that from happening instead. Thanks to you, Morry, we have a revised Student Code, one that treats students as if they were responsible and mature; why shouldn't that Code include all of us, as members of the same community? There could be a system of redress for anybody who had a complaint—"

Freedman smiled. "I don't hold the present Code sacrosanct, whatever the blacks or anybody else might think. That's the sort of reform we might hold out to the League as a real possibility, once those three boys accept the principle of a continuing system of justice." He rose abruptly. "I've been at odds with Doran over most of his appointments, but I do think, George, he

couldn't have done better than to ask you to take Marty Niemeyer's place . . . Listen, you accept that offer now and let the
president make a public statement about it; he can't keep
Marty's departure a secret much longer, anyhow. Then you'll be
in the position to bargain with the blacks—"

"Bargain?"

"You find that word offensive? Then don't bargain. Just tell
them (they'll meet with *you*, I'm certain) what they stand to
lose—the support of the faculty and their whole black studies
program—if they refuse to let the boys appear before the Board.
You can be pretty definite too in telling them the Board won't
inflict anything but the most trivial of penalties. Tell them to let
the system operate for their own sake and show them your ideas
for reform and listen to theirs."

At what psychological point does a person make a decision,
particularly such an uncomfortable decision as the one that
faced George Chambers? In a sense, the decision he made was
(granted his nature) an inevitable one, and yet if the president
had asked him for an immediate response he most likely would
have said no, that it was beyond his abilities or inclinations, his
negative reply really a consequence of resentment at the president's bizarre combination of liberal ideology, craftiness, and
verbal insensitivity; in bed with Stella, reading Chekhov's
Letters late at night, able to consider the problems of society and
the individual in isolation from that society, he had felt convinced that he would not only accept the offer but conceivably
would find personal meaning in the tension it provided; talking
with Freedman, feeling unpleasantly as if Freedman saw in him
not a person but an influence, that Freedman like the president
wanted to *use* him (the president to maintain his position and
to bring his liberal project to fruition, Freedman to maintain the
integrity of the Code and judicial structure), he wanted simply
to beg the question, to flee back to his farmhouse. He would
have been happier had he been a farmer, a carpenter, a mechanic . . .

He made his decision at an odd moment, immediately after

PARLEY . . . NEGROES INVADE FORDHAM DEAN'S

returning from the hearing at the courthouse dealing with his accident. He had thought from the beginning that the county officials—the officiating judge was Horace Casey, and Sheriff Delaney was present to give evidence about skid marks—were antagonistic to him. They didn't like university people, for one thing. And wasn't it quite possible that for them he was a disreputable character, a pernicious influence on the young? They might know (though how they would know it didn't occur to him) that he had supported both his daughter and son in their plans for Information Please. Perhaps they disliked him too for his support of such causes as CAN, that community action group that was making itself a nuisance to the County Board of Supervisors over welfare issues and to the local realtors over discriminatory housing policies.

Possibly, of course, they were antagonistic to him because he felt antagonistic to them. His leg was shriveled and hot in the cast, which he had been wearing already for a month longer than he had first expected to; he was irritable at his own indecision about the president's offer, concerned too about his children, and of course still felt in his mind the bruise inflicted upon Mary by the soldier at the Pentagon. At any rate, when Judge Casey began, "What I don't understand, Dean Chambers, is why somebody at your age, and in your position, would be driving like a college kid—" he replied brusquely, "My mind was on the town dump."

"The dump?"

"The Fitzwater Road dump. I was upset by the conditions there."

"I can't see why that—"

"No, you probably can't see. You ignore it; you officials always have. You'd penalize me for an accident, but how about enforcing the law where it really needs to be enforced?" His voice began to shake, which was stupid of him. "My dump—I mean, the Fitzwater dump—is in violation of every *conceivable* state law. There's no attendant—"

OFFICE IN PROTEST . . . POWER FAILS IN FOUR

Sheriff Delaney became aroused. "We're not here to talk about garbage. Let's not drag any red herrings—"

"If I had one, I could let it rot at my dump and nobody would do a damn thing about the stink," Chambers said. "Who buries garbage there? Nobody. You should see the rats. And people burn tires . . . You county officials allow such a condition to exist," he cried, quite beside himself, "and then have the temerity to accuse *me*—"

At this point Phyllis, who had driven him to the courthouse, took over the defense. "You accuse him when as a matter of fact he should be instituting a suit against you. I mean for not having a sign that a school bus stop was ahead, in a dangerous location just over that crest—"

"I'll be goddamned," Sheriff Delaney said, pointing a finger at her.

"That'll do," Judge Casey said. "You two have said more than enough," and he fined Chambers fifty dollars and suspended his license for six months.

Climbing into the car, Chambers said to Phyllis, "Am I beginning to suffer from paranoia? You know, we brought a lot of that on ourselves—"

"He didn't like Stella's nude on your cast," Phyllis said. "You can't get anywhere with imbeciles like them. But I don't mind." She laughed. "I really don't mind driving you home for six more months, George."

Back in his office he wrote, almost without thinking, a note of acceptance to the president. Why did he make up his mind at such a moment? Chambers himself didn't know; but had he tried to answer the question he would have found no greater purity or singleness of purpose than he had found for Chekhov's trip across Siberia, and probably considerably less human significance. He was ashamed of his irrational behavior in a drab courtroom beneath a face of George Washington supported in the painting by what looked like a wad of cotton, for his act of hostility against two minor officials of the county government. If *he* felt that kind of antagonism to society, who could blame the black race for *their* hatred? In accepting the post at that moment doubtless he was atoning for his hostility, punishing himself, even perhaps—in violation of everything he felt about titles, positions, honors—finding a solace for a wounded self-esteem. And of course he knew that Phyllis wanted him to accept it.

That afternoon she bought a bottle of champagne and they drank toasts after the office closed at five o'clock. The brightness in her eyes, the happiness with which she talked and tossed her head, would have seemed to him excessive had he not been able to see that the champagne had made her quite giddy.

FINDS SANCTUARY AT BRANDEIS . . . BRUSSELS

10

The party at Cecil Maynard's house, which had begun early with drinks and dinner in the large room with the Thermopanes overlooking the lake, was nearing its expected midnight climax with the celebration of the New Year. Already the guests had drunk to any number of occasions: to the New Year as it moved across the ocean, to George Chambers' forthcoming promotion, to the commission Cecil Maynard had received from the state of Nebraska (the real purpose of the party, but long since drowned by later toasts, by the awesome amplified beat and wails of the student quartet, and by the semicoherent cosmological conversations shouted out above, and abetting, the general noise by groups sitting on the floor or in the conversation pit or moving toward or away from the bar tended by Maynard's Japanese houseboy).

President Doran and his wife Mabel had arrived and departed early, their departure occasioned perhaps by some unpleasantness at the buffet dinner between Mabel Doran and David Garmonsway, the SDS adviser and mathematician from Oxford. They sat on the floor separated only by their plates. The president's wife, a thin and nervous woman whose face became flushed after a glass or two of wine, had started the quarrel by accusing Garmonsway of making an already complex racial issue more complex in his efforts to involve the blacks with SDS through the latter group's attack on the university's investments in banks which in turn had investments in South Africa. Garmonsway replied that certainly if there was a single institution in America which should not support the subjugation of a race, financially or otherwise, it was the American university; Mabel Doran said that if he wished logically to press his point he would have to demand that Brangwen withdraw its investments everywhere, since nearly all stocks were connected in one way or another with what was socially reprehensible as well as with what was socially beneficial.

"Now, Mrs. Doran, you're getting the point," Garmonsway said; other guests had moved their plates nearby, and he looked at them in triumph. "I wish you'd pass on that insight to your husband."

"Would you have him try to convince the trustees to sell all the university's investments?" she asked. "And if they were mad enough to agree, where would your next salary check come from? You'd have to take the next boat back to England."

"Which, from your point of view, wouldn't be such a bad idea?"

"I'd hate to sacrifice a university even for *that*," Mabel Doran said.

After the Dorans had left, Doris Banks asked Maynard—who had effusively expressed his gratitude to the president and his wife for stopping by and had gone outside into the snow without an overcoat to help them back their car around the other cars in the driveway—why he had invited them to his party. "For kicks," Maynard said laconically, turning his back to her to adjust one of his paintings which had slipped slightly on its cord.

"Cecil," said Doris to everybody near enough to hear her voice, including Maynard himself, "is a status-mad existentialist. That's what makes him so interesting."

Maynard took Chambers by the arm. "An idea just occurred

to me," he said. "You've got to be in Stella's next show at the museum."

Chambers was startled. "I'm not an art object—" he began.

"The painting on your cast," Maynard said. "It's the best thing she's ever done; she thinks so herself. We could have you in a chair on a pedestal in the main hall, with the lights just so. You'd be the first thing people would see. It would be even more effective if you'd stand, leaning on your crutch, though I imagine you'd find that tiresome after an hour or so."

"The doctor says he'll have the cast off next week."

"For shame," said Maynard. "That's a decision for artists, not laymen." He led Chambers around the few pairs of gyrating dancers to the center of the room. "Stop the music," he cried, raising his hands; an electric guitar twanged on for a moment and then ceased, as did even the voices from the conversation pit where Marjorie Feidelman, who had disentangled a strand of ivy from a stake implanted with the roots in a ceramic pot to wrap it around her head, was reciting a poem in praise of perverts and drug-takers and others deserving of the laurel. "Look, all you people, look at this painting," Maynard shouted hoarsely. He dipped the musicians' torchère like a flashlight at Chambers' cast; the colors seemed phosphorescent in the glow. "What chiaroscuro," Maynard cried. "Does a doctor have the right to demolish that?"

There were cries of "No, no," laughter, and applause. A drunken art historian, the only member of the history of art department on amiable terms with the artists, crawled up to examine the painting more closely. His heavy black beard gave him the look of an eager poodle. "Not properly cared for. Smudged. A blow—some sharp object—has damaged the plaster here." He pointed with a finger. "Hmm. My verdict is that we can save it," he said judiciously, turning his head to look up at Maynard. "There are methods of removing frescoes from church walls; you can make the plaster so pliable you can roll it like paper, it's amazing, an art in itself; there's a man in Venice—"

"Could we get him to come to Philippa?" Maynard asked.

"Oh no, he's much too busy trying to save the frescoes there," the art historian said. "We'll have to ship George to Venice."

"I can't go," Chambers said.

"Barbarian," said the art historian.

There was a crash from the conversation pit. Forgetting she was tethered by the vine to the ceramic pot, Marjorie Feidelman had sent it crashing to the tiled floor; she collapsed next to the shards and spilled earth, either sobbing or laughing hysterically. "Oh, damn," said Maynard, who was keeping a sharp eye on all his artifacts and other possessions.

The student quartet resumed, as did the separate discussions. The Japanese houseboy cleaned away the dirt and broken pieces of the vase in the conversation pit; meanwhile, Chambers, who felt unhappy at this party, who wished only to go home, hobbled over to the untended bar and poured himself a full glass of Scotch. Out of some perversity, perhaps to show his dislike for Maynard and his extravagant house built on stilts over the cliff, he hadn't been drinking, but now he decided to catch up. He looked for Stella, and saw her dancing with the art historian; then the two of them walked off toward Maynard's studio, where he had some of the designs for the Nebraska project tacked up on a cork board. David Garmonsway joined Chambers at the bar. "I hear you've lost a friend," he said.

"Who's that?"

"Fred Henry."

"He thinks I've sold out, I suppose."

"Well, yes."

Chambers took a deep drink.

Garmonsway went on, almost confidentially, "You can't imagine the pressures a boy like Fred is under. He started the League, but actually he's no organization man—or at least he *wasn't*. I mean, he never believed in violent action—"

"I know," said Chambers.

"He was brought up, actually, on a college campus. His father's president of a black—no, a *Negro* college in Georgia, and his mother teaches English there."

. . . *POLICE USE MACE TO PROTECT SAN*

"He wrote the letter for the League, I suppose," Chambers said.

"Well, he's been off and on with them ever since Collier took over the leadership . . . But wasn't that a damned fine letter? Would you tell me how the faculty and administration can deny the validity—"

"I'm sorry he's lost trust in me."

"The point is, George, he admired you as a man who made your own decisions and wouldn't ever sell out . . . You might even say he modeled himself after you; I mean he would stand up against the League or anything or anybody if he thought an action or idea stupid or wrong. That demonstration for black studies is an example. He thought it an adolescent trick that might hurt more than help the implementation of the program. Fred's really a loner. Actually what got him in trouble with the League was an argument he had with Collier; Fred said the League shut out the rest of the world too much and refused to admit the possibility of good anywhere but in their own souls . . . You know, after they have a conference with the president or any other white official they meet together to ridicule everything he said, they mimic his actions, and everything about him makes them simply explode with laughter—"

"That sounds the way servants or people still aware of their social inferiority would act," Chambers said. "I thought they had enough pride now to be beyond that." He was surprised to see his glass was empty. He filled it again, feeling pleasantly giddy. "You've been invited to their meetings, then?"

"I've been once, to try to get them to work with SDS on this university investment business. Maybe they were putting on a show for me, but I don't think so; and they probably ridiculed *me* after I left. Fred was the only one I seemed to be getting through to. I suppose if they tolerated me at all it was because I had British citizenship, I don't know; actually they don't want to think *any* white can be an individual, a person."

"Of course that's understandable enough. They're responding now the way the white world has usually treated them." Chambers sighed. "Maybe it would be a good thing for the university if you *could* manage to get the League to work with SDS on something."

"A good thing for the *university?*" Garmonsway was suddenly chagrined. "If you would say a good thing for *mankind,* George—"

"Are the two that distinct?"

"Oh, come now, George," Garmonsway said impatiently, and began to talk about a friend, a mathematician at MIT who argued that the Columbia riots had been socially beneficial, that the sooner the university was demolished the sooner a better one might be built. His friend said that education at Columbia was simply a front for military research and real estate, classes for Columbia were what a candy store or a pool room might be for the Mafia. "All you need to do is look at the bloody financial records," Garmonsway said.

"But that's not really fair, is it? No university I ever heard of wants to make a profit from teaching; of course Columbia loses money on its students—"

"Education is an infinitesimal part of what goes on there or what goes on here, for that matter . . . For God's sake you're actually talking like a vice-president already. Listen, George, if you really want to help—" But his voice was drowned out by the quartet.

Garmonsway's face was flushed from shouting; Chambers realized that he too had been shouting, and he suddenly felt dispirited and tired. He took his glass and left Garmonsway to the Japanese houseboy. He made his way to the conversation pit, where there seemed to be room for one more on the leather cushions. When he stumbled on the step, Jimmy Bolgano took his crutch and helped him to a seat next to Phyllis. He hadn't known Phyllis was at the party.

"Terry's baby-sitting with Spider," she said. "I came in just as Maynard was making such a *spectacle* of you. George, I'm so furious with him I could cry. And why didn't at least Stella—"

"Hush," said Bolgano, for Marjorie Feidelman, a piece of ivy still dangling from her hair, was standing before the hearth around which the pit made a semicircle and talking. "And what I'm *saying*," Marjorie said, "is that though I believe neither in Jehovah nor Christ, though I've given up even on the Unitarians, my disbelief is part of my personal damnation. I was born a Christian and married a Jew and we both said to hell with the New Testament as well as the Old; but I *know* man is a sinful creature, that his concerns are wholly selfish, that he murders and devours and justifies his bestial rapacity with words like democracy and communism and capitalism; and other words like order and synthesis—"

"My senior English paper at Bennington was a synthesizing thesis on the myths of Sisyphus," said a girl who taught in the comparative literature department. She was at the party because she was working on a novel. She giggled nervously. "We're teaching *Paradise Lost*—"

"—like order and synthesis and sweet reason and progress and technological advancement and the good of all; and above all by words like love . . . As for love, sexual love, did you know, Jimmy, that that apostle of it, D. H. Lawrence, used to get his hands around his wife's neck and demand she admit his mastery? So if you want to know why my oil paintings are all blacks and reds, well, that's the reason: I refuse to lie about what we are or where we're heading. Armageddon is coming, Jimmy boy, it was prophesied in the Bible and we're making it come true even faster than my granddaddy thought when he shouted at me for going to the movies on Sunday."

"I worked in West Virginia on Project Ozma," the young man who had accompanied the girl who had written the thesis on Sisyphus said; he was a graduate student in astrophysics.

"Was that one of those Vista projects in Appalachia?" Jimmy Bolgano asked. "By God, I respect the way the kids these days get out and try to help. Their compassion and social commitment is the answer to your gloom, Marjorie."

"Project Ozma tried to contact superior beings on another planet," the young man said, embarrassed. "We had a couple of questions we wanted them to answer. One was how they cured cancer—"

"We'll get that one licked without any help," Bolgano said.

"—and the other was, how did they end war."

Marjorie Feidelman asked grimly, "And did you get an answer?"

"No."

"Only silence then? Guess what must have happened to your superior beings. Boom! Boom is what happened to them."

"Oh, they're still out there all right, Mrs. Feidelman," the young man said confidently. "It's just a matter of time. Myself, I've gotten more interested in quasars. Can you imagine something off at the edge of the universe, something with a principle of energy that makes our sun no more than a spark at the end of that log behind you?"

"*Paradise Lost* was written to justify the ways of God to man. I've been petrified that one of my students might ask me if I could justify the three weeks we've been spending on it—"

"Aren't quasars the door to the next universe? I think I read that somewhere."

"That was in *2001*."

"No, in the movie it was a slab, a concrete tombstone or something, first on the moon and then floating in space—"

"What's that line in Cummings about the blue-eyed boy fed up with all the militarism? 'There's a hell of a good universe next door'?"

"That was a movie you had to be stoned, I mean absolutely stoned, to enjoy. I sat out in my car and smoked my last joint before I—"

"What do you make of the sociologists' terms? People who are chronic smokers of pot are 'non-naïve,' those who smoke occasionally are 'semi-naïve,' and those who don't smoke at all are of course simply 'naïve.' They say the 'non-naïve' suffer an intellectual loss—"

"But of course. One has to be naïve to be reasonable. It's reason that made the bomb and developed our foreign policy.

DEBATED AT PARIS TALKS . . . U.S. DESTROYERS

It's reason that makes us deny God. It's reason, nothing but human reason, that will bring our total destruction—"

"We'll get to the end even quicker without it."

"I heard that business about intellectual loss was a typographical error."

Chambers was bewildered. He didn't know who was talking. Phyllis was wearing a very short skirt made of some shiny material. She caught him looking at it. "Are you scandalized?" she said. "It's vinyl—feel it." He touched it gingerly. "I should think you'd be cold," he said. "Short skirts and bright stockings always make me feel sad somehow." "Why?" "It seems like such an attempt to be happy." The Japanese houseboy refilled everybody's glass. "Cheers," said Marjorie Feidelman, seated on the other side of him, where Bolgano had been, and clinking her glass against his. Bolgano was on his feet and pointing a finger at Marjorie. "What I want you to realize, Marjorie, is what an extraordinary period we're living in, and what extraordinary power we have."

"I'm listening," Marjorie said. Everybody had suddenly stopped talking to listen to Bolgano and the student quartet was taking a break; the silence rattled him and for a moment he forgot what he was going to say. It had something to do with his living in the country. Chambers, who also lived in the country, tried to listen intently. Living in the country meant you collected animals, Bolgano said. Word must have gotten around that he was a soft touch, because people were always dropping off kittens and puppies in front of his house at night. And Marlene and Sandra, his teen-aged daughters, both had horses, though they were both at the age now where the horses were being neglected for boys with Mustangs. A few weeks before, one of the older strays, an arthritic and deaf hunting dog, had been hit by a car; the vet told Bolgano to keep him confined in a small room. Bolgano left him overnight in his study; during the night the dog had a bowel movement on the carpet. Bolgano lit his pipe and turned on his FM radio as distractions while he began to clean up the mess—

The story was hardly an extraordinary one, Marjorie Feidelman said, and began a similar one, but Bolgano waved his hand and insisted on being heard to the conclusion. He had just commenced to clean the rug when one of the cats darted into the room, jumped on the Victorian chaise with the silk covering and retched all over it. It was Sunday morning; Bolgano had been to a party the night before, his wife felt ill and was still in bed, and he didn't feel too good himself. The combination of vomit and feces being too much for him, he had gone down to the stable to talk to the horses. *There* he discovered the neighbor's children had been playing in the barn; they had broken a window and turned the neatly piled bales of hay into a maze of tunnels. To get to the stalls, he had to crawl on his hands and knees through a tunnel. Upon reaching the stalls, he saw that the tails of both of the horses were heavy with burrs and that his daughters hadn't been removing the manure. It had reached such a level that the horses were rubbing their heads against a ceiling beam. In wrath he returned to the house to discover everybody awake and screaming; another cat had caught a mouse and his daughters had discovered her in the act of chewing it. The cat had scratched first Marlene and then Sandra; and the mouse, still alive, was bleeding under a radiator. His wife was having hysterics in the bathroom. He took the mouse outside, cradling it in his hands, feeling it twitch; it was injured so badly he knew he had to kill it. He left the door open, thinking only about the mouse; but outside in the snow he heard music from his radio. All this time the FM station had been playing a recording of his favorite opera—

"*La Bohème?*" Marjorie Feidelman asked indulgently. "You're a sucker for schmaltz, Jimmy."

"*La Bohème*," Bolgano said. "What else do you expect from a guy half Italian and half French whose best friends are artists? And when I dropped the stone on the mouse the tenor was singing his love for his mistress dying of consumption. But you know what? I didn't kill just the mouse. I killed the lovers and I killed the aria and I killed Puccini. All at the same time, by

STUDENTS DISRUPT REGENTS, CALL FOR BLACK

God I did." In his intoxication and excitement, his eyes seemed to bulge.

"How did you kill Puccini?" asked Marjorie with incredulity.

"An act of will," Bolgano cried. "A simple goddamn act of will. I couldn't stand that kind of gorgeous torment anymore. 'Puccini, old boy, you're dead,' I said, 'dead forever, Giacomo.' Of course I was talking to the dead mouse, but it was true just the same, there I was standing out in the snow with tears running down my face. And it was then that I thought, 'What a perfectly incredible thing it is to be alive today!' Because today we know that by this simple act of will we can kill everything that ever was alive! That old sawing—saying, saw, whatever the hell it is—about God being dead isn't even half the story! The past is vulnerable in a way it never used to be! By an act of will we can kill Aristotle and Shakespeare and Homer and Beethoven—"

A composer who worked with an electronic synthesizer and random sound effects said from the pit railing above, "You can't kill Beethoven, Bolgano."

"Why not?"

"He dead already."

Chambers felt moved to protest. "No, he's not dead; he's not dead at all. It's just the very endings that are dead, that wind-up at the end."

"Teleology is dead," the composer insisted. "Beethoven was a teleologist of the worst sort."

Most of the party had come to the vicinity of the conversation pit, drawn in the respite from the music to Bolgano's impassioned words and histrionics.

"I think the 'Ode to Joy' simply marvelous, but of course I've been a subscriber to the music series from the beginning."

"Composers by definition stay away from musical performances."

"Gangrene touches the ends first. For George, Beethoven is just beginning to die, but for me his compositions have already decomposed."

REINSTATEMENTS . . . HUAC HEAD SAYS REDS

"Remember that character in *Point Counterpoint* who said the third movement of the fifteenth quartet proved the existence of God? Well, you can listen to it and be just as convinced it's a requiem for Him. What makes Beethoven a genius and as relevant today as the day he was born is his ambivalence."

Bolgano banged the hearth poker so vigorously on the empty copper kettle used for logs that it reverberated like a gong.

"Don't do that, Jimmy, for God's sake," said Maynard.

"*Silence*," roared Bolgano. He paced back and forth in the pit, hands behind his back, looking solemnly at the people seated on the cushions and those crowded behind the railing. He declared that from his point of view the issue was resolved, his argument proved by those who had just volunteered as witnesses: "That there is such disparity in response *proves* my case," he said. "Some of you have already committed the murder, some of you stand with knives in your hand, some of you will defend Beethoven with your lives. It hence follows that each of you has the power of life and death over him and the entire human past; and if this is so"—he stopped, raised a finger, and slowly waved it so that it pointed from one face to the next—"if this is so, ladies and gentlemen, why not try your power to kill not on Beethoven or so tender a figure as St. Francis of Assisi, but rather on Tamburlaine, who made pyramids from the skulls of those he slaughtered and carried vanquished kings about in cages? Why not on those in the past who are a living reproach to all of us? Why kill Jesus when you can kill the first slave trader to bring the black man in chains to America? Why kill Socrates when you can kill Hitler? The confessed murderer of Puccini, I stand before you and ask you to join with me in a mutual act of will to destroy the man who annihilated six million Jews."

"Is he serious?" Phyllis whispered; she was frightened, and reached for Chambers' hand.

"I—" Chambers was silenced by a finger pointing imperiously at him; what he would have said was that Bolgano, a lawyer who defended only that in which he could believe, had trans-

INVOLVED IN CONVENTION VIOLENCE . . .

ported himself to the courtroom, the scene for him of one personal triumph after another, so persuasive was he in vindicating the innocent and the just; and that what had started out as the lugubrious account of a Sunday morning was ending up as yes, as an emotional but a sincere mass incantation to destroy the evil and let the good survive. Chambers was in as good a humor and as intoxicated as the next to see if the thing wouldn't work . . . For a minute or so the room was wholly silent. The quartet had been out in the kitchen; now a bearded guitarist returned and, seeing the party had turned into some kind of prayer or mystical rite, plucked softly on his strings. "*Tuck-a-tee, tuck-a-toe,*" the guitar sang. Tears streamed down Marjorie Feidelman's cheeks. Bolgano's eyes were peacefully closed. For a moment Chambers, concentrating not so much on killing Hitler as on expunging greed and cruelty throughout time, felt rapture: his tightly shut eyes saw crystalline shapes, patterns of soft greens and yellows. "*Tuck-a-tee, tuck-a-toe,*" the guitar sang quietly over and over.

Then a voice whispered hoarsely, "Have you killed him yet?" Doris Banks giggled, and the effect was lost. Guests opened their eyes to blink at the firelight and to laugh self-consciously at their own and their neighbor's folly; the quartet, their amplification at full peak, their voices refreshed and their fingers renimbled, began something by Paul McCartney. "We've missed midnight," cried Cecil Maynard in despair. "Play 'Auld Lang Syne,' for chrissakes," but the quartet, refusing on professional grounds, went, though somewhat reluctantly at that, into "We Shall Overcome." Couples kissed. Chambers kissed Phyllis. He looked for Stella, but she was nowhere to be seen.

Maynard rushed to the terrace door, opening it to let in a blast of the snowy wind sweeping across the lake. "Pour on the kerosene," he yelled out into the dark. "Are the Roman candles ready? Is the soup hot? For chrissakes, fellows, it's a quarter before two. Why didn't somebody tell me?" He slammed the door. "Into your coats, everybody. The party's moving down to the beach."

MARINE INDICTED UNDER OPEN-HOUSING LAW

"Why, that's a crazy thing to be saying," Phyllis said. "What a crazy thing, to go down to the beach. This is a crazy party, George; everybody's crazy here."

"No, that's Maynard being careful of his reputation," Chambers said. "Cold air and hot soup." He hiccoughed. "He doesn't want anybody going home from his party drunk and getting into an accident." He found his crutch and slowly lifted himself from the cushion. Phyllis, who was not steady at all, tried to help him and they both nearly fell.

Bolgano stood in the middle of the now almost empty conversation pit talking with the graduate student in astrophysics. "It didn't work, so help me it didn't work," Bolgano was saying earnestly. "Can you tell me why I can destroy Puccini but I can't destroy Hitler?" "Well, as I see it," said the graduate student, "it's like this: it's a matter of yeses and noes. A no can cancel a yes every time, but a yes can't ever cancel a no any more than another no can. Yeses, you see—" "Stop spitting on me," Bolgano said irritably. The graduate student said with patience, "Yeses are vulnerable, open as the first letter y is typographically; noes are closed, witness the final letter o. A fine mnemonic system for remembering, in case you forget." "But why should it be like that?" asked Bolgano in anger. "That means we inevitably have to kill off everything good and noble and are left holding on to negation, cruelty, evil." "Well, as I see it," the graduate student said, "God, being simply the repository of all our yeses, in fact the leader of all yesdom from, say, Jesus to Puccini, God toppled down with the first no (which I suppose was Satan) and took down with Him all the yeses, even the yeses to be, but it's taken us all this time to find that out. What we need to discover and worship now is some new principle, the principle of Yo, something that holds within it all the yeses and noes and hence is both open and closed, vulnerable and invulnerable . . . You will note," he added in sudden excitement, "that the o is as much a sexual symbol as the y, so here we have in the principle of Yo a love beyond death and corruption—" "That's Hin*doo* thinking. Christ, man, that's not new." "Well, I first

. . . *ISRAEL RESTRICTS ARAB TRAVEL IN*

started thinking about it when I started thinking about quasars," the graduate student said.

Their coats on, walking toward a door that led to the terrace and the inclined elevator, a sort of small funicular that Maynard had installed the previous summer and was very proud of, Chambers said to Phyllis, "Just ten years ago we used to play charades at these New Year's Eve parties. 'Intimations of Immortality from Recollections of Early Childhood' and things of that sort." They stood in line on the redwood terrace overlooking the lake. Snow touched Chambers' eyelashes, blurring what he saw until it melted. On the beach below a large fire blazed, illuminating the boathouse and dock and the crust of ice by the shore. The funicular held two people; Maynard handed each passenger a long Roman candle, touching the wicks with a piece of punk as the funicular began its descent; the little colored balls arched up and down like Gothic vaultings on each side as the passengers were lowered.

"Maynard wouldn't have a party if he couldn't dream up some new gimmick," David Garmonsway said. He was standing behind Chambers and Phyllis with the girl who had been with the graduate student in astrophysics; farther back in the line, Bolgano and the graduate student were still arguing. "Listen, George," Garmonsway said, "what I wanted to ask you when you left me at the bar—"

"What I don't want you to think is that I'm some blind defender of capitalism, somebody who can't see that democracy is a political concept and capitalism is an economic concept," Chambers said; he felt as if he had to be defending himself, against what he hardly knew. "I've never thought a system that espouses personal gain—you know, selfish interest—should ever be treated as if it were a goddamn spiritual value."

"That's precisely our—"

"Do you know what the first movie I ever saw was? It was Edna Ferber's *Cimarron*. I was only five or so and can't remember anything about it, and I only remember seeing it because after it they showed a documentary, a short film on Russia's first Five-Year Plan."

"What's happened in Russia hasn't got much to do with spiritual values, either. What's happened in Russia is really no different—"

"But the *ideal* of communism is Christ-like, isn't it? I was brought up to be a good little Christian; and what I remember is oil refineries and locomotives and factories on the screen and how noble and brotherly it all seemed, and then this deep voice from the March of Time or The Eyes and Ears of the World or some other sepulcher saying, 'But of course it is a plan doomed to failure, for it doesn't take into account private initiative and individual interest—' "

"How old did you say you were?"

"Maybe he didn't use those exact words, but anyway I got the point; and what I remember it for isn't that I *disagreed* with him—how could such a young boy disagree?—but because it just made me feel terribly sad for all those busy doomed Russians." Remembering the boy of five he felt the man of forty-five, the next Vice-president for Student Affairs, justified, ennobled . . .

Garmonsway said, "What this university lacks is the personal touch. Doran is isolated in his self-image and can't give a coherent speech unless it's written down for him; he's Eisenhower without the smile; everything's too big and bureaucratic. What SDS is planning for the spring term under the general rubric of 'Capitalism in Crisis' is a series of little talks every noon in the Student Union to be followed by a general discussion. We're asking for volunteers from the liberal faculty and the administration, and of course there will be selected students. The League won't join in, but Fred Henry thinks some of them will come. What we're trying to prove is that there does exist at Brangwen a community of interest that goes beyond race or class."

"I could talk about my town dump."

"So you'd be willing to join us?" Garmonsway patted him on

SOCIETY ON TENTH BIRTHDAY VOWS DEFEAT

the shoulder. "Fred said you might be getting too cautious, a VP has to look out for his image . . . Actually, I don't suppose your town dump would be terribly appropriate, though of course we'd be pleased to have you talk about anything that holds your attention and is related to economics."

"How about something on the relationship of economics to white antagonism to blacks coming into white neighborhoods? For that matter, I have a plan—"

"That would be just fine, George. In fact we'll make you our lead-off speaker."

Maynard thrust a Roman candle at Chambers and another at Phyllis. "Step in for chrissakes before we all freeze to death," he said. "We're running more than an hour and a half late." He helped Chambers into the seat. "Oh, George, Stella called while you were having that death mass for Hitler—"

"*Called?* Where is she?"

"She went off into a snow bank with Harrison—you know, the art historian. They weren't hurt, she said not to worry—or wait."

"What was she doing? I mean, driving off with *him?*"

Maynard rolled his eyes and shrugged, to show his helplessness before such a naïve question. His beaver-skin cap was covered with snow. "It's time for some soup, Georgie." He touched the punk to their Roman candles.

The funicular started smoothly down its rail. Phyllis was pressed tightly against him in the little seat. Pouf, pouf, went the Roman candles. "Oh, the Fates, we're fated for each other on New Year's Eve, George," Phyllis said. "I'll take you home."

"But isn't Terry baby-sitting?"

"He won't mind. We'll call him from your house."

"But it's far out in the country, the roads are slippery. You'll have to stay the night."

"Terry's quite understanding . . . Anyway, I've already made up my mind to it if it's all right with you. I heard about Stella going off with Harrison when I was waiting in line for the bathroom."

"So everybody knows?"

OF REDS . . . SAIGON DELEGATES PLAN LONG

"I'm sorry, George." She pressed her wool mitten against his glove.

It surprised him how Phyllis—who not long before had been frightened by Bolgano's incantations, who protected her child even to a greater degree than he ever had Mary and Mark, who wore clothing like the vinyl skirt more as a wish than as a statement of what she actually dared to be (or so he had thought)—it surprised him, and it gratified him, at how willing she now was to trust blindly the Fates; at how openly, even, she embraced them. The house would be empty: Mark was spending the night with an Information Please crony, doubtless planning strategy and programs for the year ahead . . .

Pouf, pouf, went the Roman candles.

"Did you read in the paper that article they were talking about in the house—about the pot smokers, I mean?" His voice was husky in the cold.

"No."

"It said the habitual smokers were faithful to their loved ones to an extraordinary degree. Pot smokers are said to be excessively dependent because of their insecurity—"

"I don't smoke pot." She spoke in wonder, as though he had been criticizing her. A veil of snow was heavy on her hair and lashes but delicate on her skin.

"I didn't say you did." He hadn't been thinking of her. Though Stella's behavior tonight gave him all the justification for license any man would need, what he had been trying to point out to Phyllis was that the article on pot, a summary of a social scientist's research, tacitly assumed fidelity to be a weakness, the symptom of a neurosis. He was in that state of partial intoxication in which it seemed completely normal to be descending a funicular at two o'clock of a wintry morning with his secretary, speaking to her of a newspaper article while small glowing balls exploded from tubes which they clutched. His was that willing suspension of disbelief which enabled him to accept the dubious truths of journalism, the meaning behind a shrug and the rolling of the eyes, the inevitable death of Beethoven and all other yeses. Granted Stella's frivolous infidelity, wouldn't it be better for *her* if he behaved likewise? Hadn't he in his earlier and more generous thoughts wished Stella as free and happy as possible, and hadn't he believed his own desire for marital loyalty one of his generation's hang-ups? He refused to acknowledge that he was full of the bitter jealousy of all men who would make their homes a bastion.

"All I want is to be of help to you, George." A simpler appeal could hardly be imagined. Phyllis, this aggressive champion of his professional career, this bulldog for his rights, this young woman who knew herself more loyal and helpful to him by far than was his wife—*she* was dependent upon him. Of course. He had always known it. Stimulated earlier by a kiss, now by the youthful body pressed against him and by the knowledge of her dependence, he felt the tenderness he had as a humane person enveloping her like the snow. Granted this night, this party, this violent and shifting world in which all men are lost, who was there who could possibly blame him?

The funicular was slowing to a stop, the last colored balls shooting up and away into the blowing snow; they were coming into port, his crutch, pressed between his thighs, erect like a mast and his plaster-stiffened leg thrust forward over the protective bar. The whole effect was even more like the *Pequod* than his wheelchair voyages past Geriatrics had been. He was drunk and swollen larger than life. Still talking to Phyllis, of what he couldn't later remember any more than he could remember talking to Garmonsway either of the documentary he had seen when he was five or of his promise to speak in public, he forgot that they had reached the bottom; and so intent was she on his words, so much was she a woman listening to a husband who had a brilliant career before him, who wouldn't inexplicably and without warning be taken from her, that she too was unaware. They were extracted from the funicular by guests already on the terrace, guests whose laughter showed that the obliviousness of Chambers and Phyllis was amusing, touching, preposterous, ridiculous, extraordinary.

IN WIDE CLASS PURGE . . . BIAFRA CALLS FOR

PART II

. . . OVER FORTY THOUSAND DEER IN MAINE

Wednesday, January 1, 1969

New Year's Eve was extraordinary in other ways, some of them related. Inspired, perhaps, by the departure of Stella Chambers and the art historian Harrison, some of the guests had paired off in an unexpected manner. Not only had Chambers gone to bed with Phyllis; Garmonsway, a widower, had gone to bed with the girl novelist brought by the student astrophysicist. Maynard had gone to bed with Doris Banks; Marjorie Feidelman, perhaps to prove her damnation, had elected the composer who made random music with the electronic synthesizer. Doris Banks was unmarried; Marjorie's husband, an accountant, had sat quietly sipping orange juice and reading the same page of an old copy of *Art News*, and had slipped out of the house alone. The Japanese houseboy had departed with one of the girls brought by the student quartet, leaving the house in a shambles for which Maynard, waking at noon, forgave him. For it had been a fine party and only his ceramic pot was broken. Jimmy Bolgano had come to the party without his wife. He and the student astrophysicist, having found they had much in common, returned from the beach to resume their argument. They had fallen asleep in half-moon postures at opposite ends of the conversation pit; they ate scrambled eggs and toast with

KILLED . . . U.S. BUSINESS SLOWDOWN IS

Doris and Maynard at a one P.M. breakfast at which nobody but Maynard felt like talking.

As for Stella, she had left shortly before midnight with the black-bearded bachelor Harrison in order to look with him in his campus office for a book which, he insisted, had all the information an amateur would need—if he was careful—to peel off the painting from her husband's leg. It had been a whim on Stella's part; earlier, when she had taken Harrison to Maynard's studio to see the plans for the Nebraska project, he had praised her drawings while looking contemptuously at Maynard's and Doris Banks'. Marjorie's he had liked but had felt their rigorous gloom hardly the thing for a rehabilitation center for disturbed youngsters. Harrison had said that doubtless Maynard's contract was a consequence of her genius. Talented she was, but hardly a genius; she denied his praises but showed her pleasure by blushing and laughing. Harrison, who was drunker than she had imagined (that she hadn't realized his condition suggested something of her own), had plowed his car into the snow bank while attempting to navigate between the Scylla and Charybdis of the campus gate. They had trudged to his building through the snow, pounding loudly on the door until the janitor, a long dustcloth trailing from his hip pocket, came from an upper floor to unlock the door. "Damn fool," the janitor said indulgently, as if he were on some familiar footing with Harrison, who promptly gave him some money from his billfold. "I don't—" began Stella, but Harrison held a finger to her lips. "Hush," he said, leading her to his office suite in the half-basement. There were plaster statues in his front office, a Venus, an Artemis, a Mercury, and a Pan, rows of shiny plastic chairs in reds and yellows and greens, a wall of books, a projector, and a screen. She waited in a chair, slipping out of her wet shoes (she had neglected to wear her snow boots); but Harrison found, instead of the book, a tray of slides of erotic Hindu sculpture which he demanded that she see for their superb integration of kinetic and potential energies. The warmth of the room, the humming of the projector, the fuzziness already in her head, made her doze off; she woke, to her fright, lying on the couch in the inner office just as Harrison was dimming the desk lamp—an Oriental artifact of bronze, originally for oil but modernized with an electric bulb and a rheostat. The couch cover had a print of bleeding Madras. He attempted to kiss her. His wiry beard made her think (unoriginal thought) of a goat. She came to a sitting position like a corpse which, while being trundled along some subterranean hospital passageway, suddenly rises stiffly at the waist; her finger pointed to the door. "Get the book," she cried. Momentarily panicked, he backed into the other room. Stella locked the door. "I've got it," he said immediately, pounding on the wood. But she was dialing Maynard's number. Maynard responded to her explanation and plea for help by whispering that everybody at the party was engaged in something that demanded absolute silence and concentration. "George of course can't drive," she said, not comprehending, "but I don't see why you can't come, Cecil." "And leave my own party? Aren't you quite safe?" "Well, yes—" "I'll tell George you're quite safe then," and Maynard, with a barely audible giggle, hung up. Which was inexcusably irresponsible and self-centered and contained perhaps a twinge of animosity (she *was* the better painter)—in short, it was precisely what she might have expected. Harrison beat against the door. "Don't you want to save your painting?" he begged. In a town like Philippa, she supposed, middle-aged bachelors like Harrison often had to resort to desperate expedients; but his heavy breathing and the eye perhaps at crack or keyhole gave her a sense of her own impurity. She had, had she not?, unfairly encouraged him. Her damnable vanity had gotten her into this mess. Why had she never been satisfied with what she was and what she had? She sat at Harrison's desk, the lamp glowing as brightly as she could make it. She thought of the fine figure she had managed on George's cast. She had done it quickly, something to amuse her husband; at the moment of its execution she had been happy, pleased simply that he was alive. Could she possibly take similar advantage of her feelings tonight? Of her guilt at having de-

INCREASE BOMBING IN LAOS . . . KY IN PARIS,

serted George? Of her loneliness and wish that they were safely home? She couldn't really blame him if— In a drawer she found India ink, a pen, and paper. Rapidly Stella began to sketch out something she was beginning to see in her head. It was quite rough, only a visual idea, but perhaps— On the other side of the door, Harrison slowly slithered down to a sitting position; his back against the door, Stella's damp shoes clasped firmly in his hands, he began to snore. Shortly before dawn, Stella started to sob: it was the depression that always came after she had drunk too much. Her life was devoid of meaning, she couldn't say why; she had no talent, but talent, a relative quality prescribed by ever-changing tastes, itself had no meaning. The greatest art she knew of was impersonal art, made in skull crucibles so hot that all human impurities were burned away. Great artists never even thought about words like talent. "Oh, my God," she said, not understanding her despair, thinking to herself she ought to devote herself wholly to her husband and children but knowing that she had to go to Nebraska to paint better murals on the walls than Maynard at his fastidious best ever could, murals so strong in their beauty they would by their very force support and give longer life to shoddy masonry walls. Then she too fell into a deep slumber, her head cradled on her arm in a litter of crumpled paper balls.

There were two other extraordinary—at least for Philippa— events that night. Sam Duncan, a member of the Black Students League who had gone home to Harlem for Christmas only to return to Philippa because of some bitter altercation with his mother, was caught by the local police as he was coming out of the window of a discount sporting goods store, a new shotgun in his hand; and later, at almost the moment that Stella was falling asleep, an unknown person or persons—a white student who hadn't gone home? an incensed bigot from town?—took a kerosene flare from a road barrier and threw it on the wooden porch of the black girls' co-op, empty because of the holiday. A night watchman saw the blaze and called the fire department before it got out of control; the damage was negligible. But briefly, in the gray before dawn of a winter's morning on the first day of the year, sirens wailed in the vacant streets and echoed against the hills.

LEADS TO CRISIS IN NEW JERSEY TOWN . . .

Friday, January 10

Fred Henry sat at a desk by a window in the study room of the undergraduate library, trying to complete research for his term paper on Attitudes to Blacks in Selected English Novels; it was for an honors seminar on the novel, and the research should have been completed before Christmas. He had dropped out of the honors program—it had seemed inappropriate for him to want such academic distinction—but continued to enroll in its seminars; his performance in them in his junior year had been OK but erratic, though in the present term—the fall term of his senior year—he was doing miserably. Why had he selected such a topic for a paper? To justify taking the course by proving that white hostility to, and ignorance of, his race extended beyond geographical barriers? Well, yes: part of him wanted to reject these books, and it gave him a reason if he needed one if somebody like Joe Collier were to ask him what for Christ's sake was he doing in such a course? On the other hand they were novels that anybody who wished to write novels himself whether he was black or white probably *ought* to read—for the technique if nothing else. And it pleased his mother that he was reading these books; they were the ones she taught and admired.

For example, this exceptionally long novel he had been reading, Mrs. Gaskell's *Wives and Daughters.* His mother had told him *Wives and Daughters* was of nearly the same stature as George Eliot's *Middlemarch.* His mother had conservative tastes; while she taught *Invisible Man* she refused to discuss or even to read the more current black literature. He'd read *Middlemarch* last summer, sitting—just as if he were a child again—under the big oak on the campus and surrounded by all those acres of sweet-smelling grass. What it seemed to prove, at least to him, was that man never could realize in any real measure the fulfillment of his passionate dreams for change. George Eliot wished for a better and more generous world and the novel had a strong social sense, at least so far as whites were concerned; but there were these accents of resignation in her voice. He found the same sound in other books his mother liked, in late Jane Austen and *A Passage to India.* To be compassionate, to pity and love mankind, one apparently had to feel this quality; and yet to feel it was to admit impotence, to deny present possibility, to avoid specific action (which might hurt somebody). Reading some middle-aged or older white authors, he could believe in humanity, much as he was able to believe—or anyway had once been able to believe—in the truth of Camus' argument in *The Rebel,* which, whatever its advocacy of rebellion, depended pretty much on the same kind of unifying vision.

Camus was the bridge which had enabled him not to feel guilty about liking the same books his mother did while still wanting to start something like the Black Students League. But what he often did, after reading a book, was to call up his mother and argue with her about it. He would tell her that what she was really doing by living in an old-fashioned fictional world was to bypass terrible social wrongs in order to concentrate not on black spirit but on human spirit. He would point out to her examples of racial intolerance in these so-called compassionate books. Maybe that was how he'd gotten the idea for his paper. The book he was finishing had some examples he wanted one of these days to call to her attention. On a large index card he had written in a small but tidy script,

Wives and Daughters, Mrs. Gaskell. Leipzig: Bernhard Tauchnitz, 1866. Author, the wife of a clergyman, was noted for her concern for underprivileged—working class, etc.—during Indust. Revol.; see *Mary Barton.*

Squire Hamley, who opposes engagement bet. his son Roger & Cynthia Kirkpatrick on class & economic grounds, says to her stepfather, Mr. Gibson, about Roger, "Two years among the black folks will have put more sense in him." [Roger has left for Africa for scientific research.] "Possible, but not probable, I should say," replied Mr. Gibson. "Black folk are not remarkable for their powers of reasoning, I believe, so that they haven't much chance of altering his opinion by argument, even if they understood each other's language; and certainly if he shares my taste, their peculiarity of complexion will only make him appreciate white skins the more." (Vol. II, p. 249) Later, (Vol. III, pp. 219–20), after Roger comes back from Africa, Mr. G. reports on his appearance ("caught a little of the negro tinge") but says of his conversation: "I didn't catch any Hottentot twang, if that's what you mean. Nor did he say 'Caesar and Pompey berry much alike, 'specially Pompey,' which is the only specimen of negro language I can remember at this moment."

He finished the novel; there were no further references. At the bottom of the card he wrote, "No indication that author finds fault with these judgments of the kindly and loving doctor!!!"

He turned to the cards—there were four of them—containing quotations from *Heart of Darkness.* Conrad used "black" and "blackness" in such an ambiguous way that it was much more difficult to pin him down than it was to pin Mrs. Gaskell. Conrad had doubts about civilization and progress, and "white," as an opposition to "black," seemed to refer primarily to illusions, perhaps necessary ones, but illusions just the same. Conrad was not altogether clear about his response to capitalism, though he hated the greed and hypocrisy that accompanied it to Africa. It seemed to Henry that Conrad even treated with irony his own doctrine of salvation (a Victorian carryover and hang-up), Work and Duty. Conrad deeply interested Henry; he seemed to be fighting for his own sanity (hadn't he once tried to commit suicide?) in a world that had no meaning. Conrad's confusions were those of somebody trying to find meaning, he took his own confusions and resolutely made them into art, which was the value that saved him. Which was what Fred wanted to do, if he ever could.

Not quite knowing what his response to *Heart of Darkness* was, he had turned to another book of Conrad's not because it was about blacks or blackness or Africa but because it dealt (so the anthology of summaries said) with revolutionaries in London. The book was *The Secret Agent*. Conrad, a Pole, must have had sympathies with the attempts of a conquered people to free themselves. But the book was not about that; it was about a cowardly professional revolutionary who kept a sordid shop in the London slums. This man, Mr. Verloc, was ordered to get the Greenwich observatory blown up; he mismanaged the whole affair, and ended up blowing up not the observatory but a half-wit child, the young brother of his wife. The senselessness of violence was what horrified Conrad: explosives, the dismemberment of a person (the book was based on a news account Conrad had read in the London paper), were added threats to a man who wanted to find human meaning and didn't really know where to look. In a way, the book was concerned more with Mrs. Verloc's love for her younger brother than it was with the activities of a revolutionary; the boy himself, like Conrad, wanted to resist brutality and injustice. The boy Stevie was a half-wit perhaps because he believed in love and mercy but lived in a world which, except for his sister, was devoid of either. Stevie, on a cab trip through the slums with his mother and grandmother, saw the crippled cab driver beat his emaciated horse, understood the motives for it, but couldn't stand the physical fact. His only comment was, "Bad world for poor people." In her own insanity upon discovering her brother had been dismembered by the bomb, Mrs. Verloc murdered her husband, stabbing him with a knife. The novel was claustrophobic; Conrad, seeing the misery and oppression of the poor, having nothing really to oppose to it in his story but a sense of love between two of the oppressed, a love which—granted the nature of the world he was describing—could only intensify the sense of cruelty and outrage, which in fact turned his characters into ciphers, had lingered in an almost obsessive way upon Stevie's dismemberment, upon the details leading to Mrs. Verloc's killing of her husband and to her ultimate suicide. A strange and imperfect book: novels might, and often did, deal with problems for which they had no solutions, but this novel went further than that, it dealt with problems that were beyond the author's imaginative ability to encompass, so that even his irony went sour.

Fred had read it twice, not skimming but word for word, and had been left simply with a severe headache and depression and a dream of Stevie's body in bloody pieces. He had copied on an index card the following authorial comment about Stevie: "Like the rest of mankind, perplexed by the mystery of the universe, he had his moments of consoling trust in the organized powers of the earth," one of the rare occasions in which illusions seemed to benefit the characters; he had added to it a postscript: "For my next letter home," thinking that perhaps it partly explained both his parents, but mostly his father. He had not yet written his parents, and couldn't bring himself to the task. He had a further quotation from the same portion of the book:

> [Stevie to his sister upon seeing policemen in the street]: "What for are they, Winn? What are they for? Tell me."
>
> Winnie disliked controversy. Guiltless of all irony, she answered yet in a form which was not perhaps unnatural in the wife of Mr. Verloc, Delegate of the Central Red Committee, personal friend of certain anarchists, and a votary of social revolution. "Don't you know what the police are for, Stevie? They are there so them as have nothing shouldn't take anything away from them who have."

. . . *SOVIET INCREASES MILITARY BUDGET BY*

Fred stared at the quotation. What was Conrad's own position? Was he separating himself wholly from Verloc's position, here assumed by his wife? Was he able here to possess the irony he wouldn't grant her? He was trying to, but it hardly worked: the remark, at least from Fred's point of view, had too clearly the ring of absolute truth. But why worry about *The Secret Agent?* His mother dismissed it as the work of a writer who was fatigued. He didn't like the book either but had read it as obsessively as Conrad had written it. It couldn't possibly enter into his paper except as a footnote suggesting the spiritual bankruptcy of white culture. But then his paper would never be written anyhow. He had no clear conclusions to draw from what he had read, no simple line of argument. He had spent too many days simply engrossed in his reading, feeling himself justified in not thinking about problems like the one, say, Sam Duncan raised.

At the president's party so long ago, it had been Sam's silence—the way he had of looking a person in the face—that had rattled President Doran into that phony good fellowship act. It had been that look more than the knife Sam had dropped. Silence can seem dangerous, as if the person had something on his mind so big there aren't any words he can use to talk about it. Fred could understand that: sometimes you can only take out your feelings with your body, with moving around restlessly. Sam moved restlessly all the time.

Sam wasn't particularly friendly with anybody in the League, though at first he had talked some with the brothers, if only to ridicule them. A place like Brangwen was for nigger ass-lickers who wanted to make it big in the white world, Sam had said. Blacks who went to white prestige colleges know they had already sold out. They resented having sold out that way, and this was the reason they playacted at making trouble. For some reason, Sam never thought that any of this applied to *him*. It was as if his hatred of the white world, its cops as well as its colleges, gave him a purity of motive beyond anybody else's. What he was going to do some day was really blow up the whole goddamn university: he'd see to it that Brangwen was just a memory. The only reason he was in school at all was that he was humoring his mother.

Joe Collier had looked up Sam's mother once. Her husband had deserted the family years ago. She had four children. There was a son older than Sam who was in prison for armed robbery, and two younger daughters. The mother supported her family through a combination of welfare checks and work as a chambermaid in a Manhattan hotel. She dreamed of Sam as a brilliant student, one singled out for praise by President Doran and the entire Board of Trustees, one destined to honor as a doctor or a lawyer. That was, at least in part, what Sam was carrying around inside him—this was what Joe Collier thought—these great expectations of a mother who had sacrificed everything for him. Whatever his talents, Sam had no particular aptitude for academic work; he disliked Joe for being such a brain. He despised Fred for wanting to be a writer and reading books from the other culture. He was full of contempt for Brangwen and the hicks of Philippa. His closest friends weren't students. They were a boy from his Harlem neighborhod who had never finished high school and who sometimes came up to Philippa to see him and another boy, one from Philippa, who had worked at the typewriter plant until he had been fired or laid off: the union, being of course racist, hadn't given a damn. His friends were like him in being nervous and quick as cats and silent.

According to Joe Collier, what kept Sam from being a valuable revolutionary, a leader, went beyond his contempt for so many of his own race. The trouble with Sam was that he bungled things: like (Fred thought of this) that knife-dropping so long ago. His bungling was part of some contradiction in himself. Hating Philippa, he still had come back before anybody else, before the Christmas vacation ended. And you wouldn't expect somebody who could vanish so easily into the shadows to let himself get caught stealing a gun. Why had Sam been so dumb to try to break into a sporting goods store on the main street in town when, if he had really wanted a gun, he could have found so many safer places to rob? In Joe's mind, it was a way of course of getting back at his mother. Fred could understand that: his own parents, having achieved their professional ambitions, had no need to depend so overwhelmingly on one son, and yet they wanted to see themselves in him. Sam's bail fund had been raised by CAN, a local group of do-gooders, the sort of whites Sam mocked above all others. Fred wondered what the moment had been like when his mother (her bus fare paid by the same group) arrived at the jail with the chairman of CAN to greet her son and take him home. Fred didn't know Sam well enough to understand all the intricacies of his mind, but he understood him well enough from what Joe Collier said to believe he suffered from what Fred fought against in himself, an impotent self-hatred. Sam was the sort of person you could write a novel about, if you had a solid position yourself to look at him from.

Sam of course had been part of the subject at the Monday meeting of the League. What Joe Collier had been angry about was not that Sam had tried to steal a gun (the police had guns, probably every white bigot in the county had one, and for that matter there was said to be a regular arsenal at one of the fraternities) but that he had been caught. The League was, in fact, slowly collecting its own weapons, and had been doing so ever since Joe, the day after his election to the presidency, had received his first threatening note. Unlike so many of the rest of them, Joe had been able to concentrate on his studies— he was in engineering—despite all conflicts. Maybe marriage and the thought that he would soon be a father kept him level-headed about League objectives; maybe too his studies—being chiefly factual or dealing with mathematical abstractions— didn't mess up his mind. The point was, he could be almost frighteningly clear. The Black League at Brangwen was composed of eighty members out of a black enrollment of little more than a hundred. There were six thousand whites on campus. In the town of forty thousand, there were maybe five hundred blacks, all of them dependent upon whites for their jobs. The League, in doing *anything*, would inevitably arouse the fear and hostility of many of the whites, maybe even of the other blacks. The attempted arson at the black girls' co-op proved the danger. For the blacks to deny themselves guns was to acquiesce in the white man's historical emasculation of the black man, to admit the blacks' helplessness before white rapacity.

But there was a point at which Fred—who willingly would have given his life for a cause larger than himself—could not accept either rationally or emotionally what Joe Collier said. Joe had quoted with clear approval a story which Malcolm X in a speech had himself quoted with the same approval, the story of how somebody had once asked a gathering of three hundred people how many of them desired freedom. They all did. Then the man wanted to know how many of them were willing to kill anybody who stood in the way of that desire. Fifty or so were willing. He separated the fifty from the rest and told them that the two hundred and fifty, made up maybe of their own families, stood in their way to freedom and were obviously the first ones for them to get.

Now, he knew that Joe, like Malcolm X, was trying with a story like that to get through to people like Fred himself, to get people like Fred to see that they were, at some crucial juncture, standing in the way. They were as dangerous to the cause as a fucked-up Sam Duncan was. In Malcolm X's speech, which Fred had looked up in the library, he had been criticizing the Uncle Toms, those who "want that good image." Nobody, said Malcolm X, who wanted that kind of image would ever be free. The general argument so disturbed Fred that listening to Joe he was almost willing to acknowledge his own cowardice; he could only think with clarity about it when he was off by himself. Personally, he wasn't looking for any kind of image, he hated the word, it belonged to white business and Madison Avenue; he wanted only to be himself. And the argument worked only if "freedom" was taken to be some kind of abstraction, like a mathematical symbol. For example, if he were to kill his father (whatever the confused feelings with which he viewed his father, the hostility his father sometimes raised in him: for his father was somebody who really *did* want that good image), he would certainly not be free. To kill his father or anybody else he could think of would put him in bondage to the abstraction of freedom, and make him other than himself. His head ached terribly, just thinking about such a choice; for a moment his vision blurred.

He knew all the arguments for blacks to work as a single group, not as individuals: after all, *he* had been the major force behind the organization of the Black Students League. Yet didn't a writer, if he was to have any kind of understanding, need to be an individual as well? Fred had other cards, as useless to his paper as his notations from *The Secret Agent;* but they contained quotations from other blacks who had become successful writers. These cards were soiled, for he had thumbed through them many times:

Richard Wright ("How Bigger Was Born," *Native Son*) on Bigger:

I made the discovery that Bigger Thomas was not black all the time; he was white, too, and there were literally millions of him, everywhere.

James Baldwin, "Notes of a Native Son":

I hated and feared white people. This did not mean that I loved black people; on the contrary, I despised them, possibly because they failed to produce Rembrandt.

Ralph Ellison, *Shadow and Act:*

He [Wright] was as much a product of his reading as of his painful experiences and he made himself a writer by subjecting himself to the writer's discipline—as he understood it. The same is true of James Baldwin, who is not the product of a Negro store-front church but of the library, and the same is true of me.

"BLACK BOOK" DISCLOSES ROLE OF POLICE

As he looked at these cards, his eyesight was still blurred; he saw fuzzy lines, knowing by memory what the cards contained. They didn't make his headache go away, whatever his concentration. Maybe these writers already belonged to another time. The anger he felt inside himself was unfocused. But somebody had drawn up a chair opposite him, and was sitting. Looking up from his cards helped his vision become clearer. It was Dean Chambers, who was smiling self-consciously, attempting to radiate good cheer and brotherhood.

"Phyllis said I'd find you here, Fred," Chambers said. "And see"—he waved a cane and reached down to pat a trouser leg— "at last I'm able to go out in search of you myself. I'd hoped you would stop by the office—"

The intrusion of an actual person, a white man, was, given his thoughts, almost too much at first; he turned hostile. "If I'd wanted to see you, man," Fred said, making his words drawl the way he had when he'd left Chambers in the hospital, "I would've come . . . You see, man, I've got all this work, all this *ree*-search," and he pointed at his books and his index cards. "I've been the good little black boy, reading the white man's *edifying* words, but I tell you it's mighty heavy going—"

"For Christ's sake—"

"No, man, I wasn't really doing *ree*-search, that was a lie: what I was doing was thinking about my parents. You know, my mother went to this little Negro college in Columbia, South Carolina. She used to have to walk down Queen Street, past these fancy white houses, carrying her books; and the white ladies having tea on their verandas would just *look* at her, you know? fascinated-like; and they would talk about her in the loudest and most *genteel* voices. 'Why, look, Mrs. Bourdine,' they'd say. 'There goes that precious little nigger girl carrying that passel of books! Why, I declare! She'll get herself a college education, and you know what she'll do with it? I'll tell you what she'll do with it, Mrs. Bourdine. She'll come around to this very back door with her diploma just a-begging me to take her on as a maid, that's what she'll do.' But do you know,

Mr. Chambers, my mother fooled those white ladies on Queen Street. She got herself that degree and then another one and then she got herself to be a professor so that she could teach new precious little nigger girls those same books she used to lug under her arm—books by Jane Austen, you know, Mr. Chambers; and George Eliot and Mrs. Gaskell and Ralph Waldo Emerson and other fine white writers like them, both in England and America—" Fred was horrified at his own voice going on like that. He was praising his mother for being so much smarter and better than those white ladies in their wicker chairs, those white ladies on Queen Street he had despised ever since his mother, without rancor, had first told him that story: what then accounted for the terrible mockery in his voice? Dean Chambers must believe him crazy. But what he really was thinking was that the whole culture bit, this thing about humanism, this belief in man which his mother honored despite the evidence, this belief which had sucked him in and kept him irresolute, which had sent him off to see Chambers in the hospital instead of participating in a demonstration for which (of this he had no doubt) three of his brothers were being treated unjustly, this belief which Chambers had always seemed to him to represent (and for a black man to believe in it, in something that was not his own invention, he had to believe in the integrity and selflessness of at least *one* white man)—this whole thing was one lie after another, lies intended to sugar over the greed of those in power and to placate those in servitude. What the mockery was about was Dean Chambers, who had always put his feelings for anybody black or white above personal gain, who believed in all that high-minded shit, but who yet had jumped at the first chance to be Johnny Doran's well-paid boy; what the mockery was about was that he had caught in those eyes, just at the moment he had been able to focus his own upon them, the furtiveness he knew so well from his own father's eyes. Over the holiday he had learned that his father had awarded a graduate fellowship in drama offered without strings by Cornell or Yale or some place like that, a more prestigious Brangwen, not to one of the black girls at his college but to a white girl from the town, a girl from "good white society" who had promised to come back to teach drama at the college. His father thought it better to get in with the white elite than to give the scholarship to any number of talented black girls. When he had accosted his father with *that*, his father's eyes had showed his father up for what he was—cardboard, a stereotype, empty.

"What I wanted to find out," said Chambers with formality, "was whether or not you could arrange for a meeting in my office with some of the blacks to talk over the whole problem, nothing official of course; just something to see if we couldn't find—"

"Go see Joe Collier," Fred said brusquely; it was clear enough, wasn't it?, that Chambers wasn't interested in him as a person, but simply wanted to use a friendship. And Fred turned back to his books and index cards.

Chambers got up to go. "Good-bye, Fred," he said.

Looking up quickly, Fred saw that he looked pale and unhappy and that he used the cane like an old man. "Will you always have that limp?" he asked, not wanting him to go off looking like that. If what Garmonsway had said was true, Chambers had agreed to attack the capitalistic system at the first SDS noon session.

"I hope not," said Chambers, already moving away.

They had always gotten on together when the subject was a literary one. "Oh, hey, Mr. Chambers," Fred said, fumbling through his cards. "There's something you might want to see before you go," and he handed Chambers, without looking at him, a card with a quotation from *Tristram Shandy*; it was the only one of its sort his hours of research had uncovered. The quotation was a dialogue between Uncle Toby and his white servant Corporal Trim as reported by the narrator Tristram; Corporal Trim was in the midst of telling Uncle Toby a story about his brother Tom:

. . . ENEMY REPORTED ENGAGING IN SOUTH

When Tom, an' please your honour, got to the shop, there was nobody in it but a poor negro girl, with a bunch of white feathers tied to the end of a long cane, flapping away flies,—not killing them. —'T is a pretty picture! said my uncle Toby;—she had suffered persecution, Trim, and had learned mercy.

—She was good, an' please your honour, from nature as well as from hardships; and there are circumstances in the story of that poor friendless slut, that would melt a heart of stone, said Trim; and some dismal winter's evening, when your honour is in the humour, they shall be told you with the rest of Tom's story, for it makes a part of it.

—Then do not forget, Trim, said my uncle Toby.

—A negro has a soul, an' please your honour, said the Corporal (doubtingly).

—I am not much versed, Corporal, quote my Uncle Toby, in things of that kind; but I suppose, God would not leave him without one, any more than thee or me.

—It would be putting one sadly over the head of another, quoth the Corporal.

—It would be so, said my Uncle Toby. —Why then, an' please your honour, is a black wench to be used worse than a white one?

—I can give no reason, said my uncle Toby.

—Only, cried the Corporal, shaking his head, because she has no one to stand up for her.

—'T is that very thing, Trim, quoth my uncle Toby,—which recommends her to protection,—and her brethren with her; 't is the fortune of war which has put the whip in our hands *now*;— where it may be hereafter, Heaven knows!—but be it where it will, the brave, Trim, will not use it unkindly.

After a few moments Fred looked up from his books and cards; Chambers was reading the quotation with what seemed to him an unnecessary deliberation. When Chambers had finally finished it and handed it back, he said uncertainly, "You know, Fred, that's not really poking fun at Toby or Trim; it's a serious quotation, and a fine one, though I suppose to a black these days that line about a negro having a soul which Trim says—what's that word in brackets?—'doubtingly'—"

"Don't you suppose I know that?" Fred suddenly cried. "For

God's sake, man, how dumb do you take me to be?" His en-
raged voice echoed in the quiet library, and he half-rose, almost as if he would strike the older man. At the other desks
students looked up in surprise.

"I'm sorry," said Chambers.

After Chambers had limped out of the room, Fred stared at
the quotation himself, and at another one from the same book,
one which—like the quotations from *The Secret Agent*—he had
carefully copied down for his own sake, not for the paper he
would never finish for English Honors 421; this one he had
copied because he had the urge to be a writer and it was
Tristram on the art of writing:

> . . . For my own part, I am but just set up in the business of
> writing so know little about it;—but, in my opinion, to write a
> book is for all the world like humming a song;—be but in tune
> with yourself, Madam, 't is no matter how high or low you
> take it.

"Oh, shit," said Fred, putting his head on his arm and trying
not to think about anything.

PROPOSE   NEW   SEATING   ARRANGEMENT   IN

Saturday, January 11

Lago di Pergusa, lying ten kilometers south of Enna on the road to Piazza Armerina, is nearly in the geographical center of the island of Sicily. The Michelin Green Guide to Italy says of it, "A mysterious atmosphere broods over this oval lake, which is fringed with eucalyptus and aquatic plants. On its shores, according to legend, Pluto carried off the youthful Prosperine, daughter of Ceres and future Queen of the Infernal Regions. A speed-track for racing cars has been laid out in this once sacred spot."

Seated on a rock in the sun just beyond the oval, Mary Chambers sucked an orange and read these words in her tattered guide, some of whose pages had fluttered out of the convertible on the Milano-Venezia autostrada, others somewhere on the twisting mountain roads between San Marino and Urbino; and, looking over the lake, she tried to imagine Pluto—had he risen from the waters?—bearing off his bride to the Infernal Regions. But what had Pluto been doing here? Hadn't her guidebook located the entrance to the Infernal Regions in the Campi Flegrei north of Napoli? She and Sylvia had visited Cumae, paying the man at the gate the required lire to see the cave where the famous Sibyl was said to have dwelt, and had watched the mud bubble in the sulfur stench at Solfatara. At Solfatara, if you

pound your heel sharply against the earth, the packed dirt re-
sounds, telling you all is hollow underneath, the arch of earth
held up by the steam of the fires. Factories and a military installation are nearby, all perhaps floating over the caverns of Hades.

Around and around the racetrack buzzed Sylvia's red Triumph
Mark II. Sylvia wasn't driving: Gian was at the wheel, his teeth
flashing, his arm waving idiotically (he ought to keep both
hands on the wheel) every time the car sped by Mary. Next to
him Sylvia was laughing, her long blond hair blowing back and
shining in the sun. An hour ago Gian had been a strange boy
standing disconsolately beside a broken-down Fiat 500: Sylvia,
caught by his wistful smile and half-raised arm, had slammed on
the brakes. Gian had a rope; they had towed the tiny car (he
could have pushed it, really) up a gentle slope and down to a
garage, and from the garage they had seen the glittering waters
of the lake. It had been Sylvia's idea to try her car on the racetrack and then have a picnic by the lake. A few thousand lire,
and the chain across the entrance to the track clattered to the
asphalt. "*Va bene? Va bene?*" asked Gian excitedly, standing
beside the car, pointing from herself to the driver's seat. "*Va
bene,*" said Sylvia happily, though all she knew about him was
what his gestures and bits of English told them: he played calcio
on Sundays for the team in Taormina, which was the most important thing apparently to know, and worked as a clerk or
waiter or something in a nearby hotel which was run by an
uncle or a family friend or somebody who took an interest in
him. He was learning the hotel business; he needed to know
more English to be successful.

And now Sylvia and Gian whirled about the asphalt oval in
this former haunt of Pluto while Mary (the car being a two-
seater) sat with the wine and fruit and bread and cheese, reading first the guidebook and then some more of Plumb's *Penguin
History of the Renaissance.* "*Va bene,*" according to Sylvia, was
really the only phrase one had to know, at least in the South,
where the sun was warm in winter and ripe oranges everywhere, not only in the trees but in baskets before store fronts,

and spilled from overloaded trucks into roads and gutters; and where the dark-skinned young men were shy of foreign girls at first but never lost their grace and charm even when they were encouraged to grow bolder. Unlike Sylvia, Mary had not reached the euphoria of acceptance. The thing was (she thought) that she was just beginning to find herself, a process that for her required looking and talking and then thinking and reading: any kind of psychic alteration was for her an effort that took both activity and contemplation. And the trip had been a series of surprises. Sylvia had surprised her from the start. Sylvia at first had wanted simply to drive furiously here and there, she wouldn't give Mary (who had thought she would be serving Sylvia, so passive in Manhattan, not only by driving in Europe but by planning routes and finding hotels) a chance at the wheel. Out of London, to the Channel, to Paris and beyond: Mary had believed they were on their way to a psychiatrist in Switzerland, but Switzerland was a small country lost in clouds and with roads tunneled beneath the rocks and snow and when the clouds were gone and the tunnels behind them they were in northern Italy. "I thought we were to stop off at a clinic in Zurich or somewhere," Mary said; but Sylvia had said oh no, that had been simply something to protect her father's reputation and absolve his conscience before her mother in case anything serious happened to them. Mary couldn't see how that could be; Sylvia replied that it had been clearly understood when he had given her the letter of credit: for if he *really* had wanted her to stop off in Zurich, he would have given her only enough money to get to his psychiatrist friend and would have made arrangements with him for her to get more money only after she had completed her consultations and treatment or whatever. "He knows, you see, that money is his only control over me," said Sylvia. "It makes a relationship clearer when you know precisely what it's based on. My father is, you have to say this, a clear-headed businessman."

"But he's a psychiatrist—"

"When his patients object to his fee, he tells them the size of it is part of the therapy. Oh, honey, you've got a lot to learn about the world," said Sylvia; and Mary was inclined to agree. One of the things she had already learned was that Sylvia was not so ill as Mary had imagined. That drugs had deranged her in college was true enough, but the taking of drugs, even the way she had allowed herself to be used by a fraternity in a—what was that dreadful term which made a prank of bestial behavior?—a gang-bang: it was all part of an objective decision to experience whatever was available to her. Sylvia was after sensations: mystic visions like God in onion cells, bodily debasement for the masochistic kick, lesbian relationships to see whether they gave you something that men couldn't (Mary had fended her off in a Belfort hotel), as well as smaller pleasures such as eating squid and octopus and other aquatic oddities, deliberately going the wrong way on a one-way street in Bologna in front of a traffic officer to see if she could win him over with a lovely smile (she could) and confuse him by showing him the page in Chinese in her international driving permit (she also could). In Florence, Sylvia had deserted her for a week, going off somewhere with a young anarchist, a student at the university; on her return she told Mary she had so exhausted him that he had been converted to the monarchists and was well on the road to fascism. English novelists had convinced her that Italians were wholly instinctive, charming, and healthy animals—a view that Mary thought was composed of equal parts of Anglo-Saxon repression (a negative quality which Mary herself doubtless had too much of) and British condescension—but one could usually find whatever one was looking for. In Sicily, where there was greater poverty than was to be found in the north, as well as a warm intuitive response totally inimical to urban sophistication, Sylvia—off on her healthy animal kick—was having a glorious time of it.

The car whirled on the track, Sylvia now driving. It didn't seem blasphemous or even odd to *her* to skid a Triumph Mark II around a lake once sacred to the gods. Mary wished she might be that free. Why couldn't *she* enjoy herself? Why

HAZARDS ADMITS SAFETY FAILURES . . .

couldn't she respond so eagerly to what was available to her young life? She was losing weight, a good thing, by staying off those heavy Sicilian dishes (only the fruit in Sicily appealed to her, and an occasional fish), her body responded to the warmth of the sun, the vistas of orange trees and sea and sky, but she worried, she continually worried. She saw the natural beauty and wondered how long it would endure. From the distance Sicilian cities like Agrigento were new and fanciful spires perched on cliffs: the apartment buildings, cheaply constructed of tiles and concrete slabs, were occupied even before the workmen were finished. Those better off were crowding into the new buildings; the poorer were burgeoning in the quaint older structures on the tiny streets. A photograph of the Pope decorated the windows of many of the little gas stations, not a pyramid of Esso oil cans; *il papa* was beloved, he was a good man. But the Pope's attitude toward birth control made no sense unless he was looking forward to a revitalized Church in the Dark Ages to come. And the poorer people saw in the brood of children that kept them impoverished not only the blessing of God but the hope for the son who would be successful in life and support them in their advanced years. How long could the process continue?

Mary was bewildered and disturbed beyond that, and in a more profound way. Throughout Italy she had marveled at the cultural riches of the Renaissance in the manner of any sensitive and intelligent young American who has seen examples of those riches only on slides in school lectures or in photographs and reproductions in the extravagant books exchanged at Christmas time; she had marveled at the palaces and churches and paintings and sculpture, thinking that she—this girl born and reared in Philippa, New York, a town in a region of lakes and hills but devoid even in its campus buildings of any answering human aesthetic appeal—was, in spite of all, a child, at least a survivor, of such a period, the modern period: that whatever she aspired to be as an individual (for wasn't this the period that *said* the individual was freed from fetters, from feudal bondage to Church and baron, that affirmed the importance of individuality on an Earth that itself was a value?) must have its roots here, in Venice and Florence and Perugia and Bologna and Pisa and Rome. And she had bought not only guidebooks to cities and museums but whatever history books she could get hold of that were in English and in paperback, and she had read them carefully; and though they contained nothing that she had not studied at some time in high school or at college, it was as if she were reading them for the first time, even as she saw paintings she had seen on slides or had pasted as stamps into books in a grammar school unit on art appreciation and still was seeing *them* for the first time. She read the words, and she was as horrified by them as she was gratified by, say, the Masaccio frescoes in the Brancacci Chapel in the Church of Carmine in Florence. What she couldn't resolve was a dreadful dichotomy characterized for her most clearly by this example: in the Bargello Museum in Florence is a statue by Giambologna, that specialist in sensuous female nudes, in which a graceful and serene lady has caused a bearded male to bow beneath her knee. It was not her favorite statue, nor her favorite Giambologna for that matter; but it was nevertheless a considerable achievement. The statue represented Victorious Florence over Pisa. She hadn't read of the battle strategy used by the Florentines in that specific struggle, but she had read on the day she had visited the Bargello of the means used by the Florentines in their attempt to defeat Siena, their rival to the south: the Florentines, in the first example of biological warfare that she knew of, had thrown dead donkeys and human excrement over the walls with the intention of infecting the populace with the plague. The vileness that accompanied the triumphant rebirth of Individual Man appalled her; for several days she had been obsessed by images of excrement and thought herself unclean, and the pain that had once been in her stomach like an ulcer had returned. She believed herself unworthy of the love of the generous father whom in her own thoughts she always called George, not knowing of course that her father, on the day of his accident, had been obsessed with the same image.

But she *was* beginning to find herself; Sylvia as well as her own knowledge of her past naïveté was a help. On the shore of the little ex-sacred lake in central Sicily, beneath the radiant sun, Mary sucked at her orange with juice running down her chin; around the lake the Triumph Mark II whirled and whirled.

Tuesday, January 14

George Chambers was waiting in his office for Joe Collier. On the previous day Collier had telephoned that Fred Henry had asked him to stop by; they had arranged for a ten A.M. meeting. Chambers was glad that Fred had thought to say something to Collier; he hadn't expected it. It was now a few minutes after ten. He could hear Phyllis in the outer office, talking to somebody and then typing.

He opened the top drawer of his desk and began making a chain of the paper clips he found in the tray, wanting simply to occupy his hands. What he was thinking was that what had happened between himself and Phyllis on New Year's Eve was meaningless. He wanted to believe that. People were always going to bed with people they weren't married to. He loved Stella. That he had gone to bed with Phyllis that crazy night only made him love his wife the more, though that was probably guilt. There was, of course, no reason for being guilty, because Stella and Harrison had almost made his own response, his assertion of masculinity, necessary. He could almost convince himself that he had done what he had done so that Stella, whom he loved, wouldn't feel remorse.

On the other hand, he didn't believe that his wife suspected anything. Stella of course knew that Phyllis had driven him home and stayed the night. What Chambers told himself was that Stella thought they had slept in separate rooms and that after Phyllis rose in the morning—from, say, Mary's old bed—she had made up the covers, as a considerate guest would be expected to do. Like Philip Durant, Chambers had so much difficulty in believing he had committed an act in violation of his personal code that he also felt nobody else could possibly believe it: he saw the connection, was disturbed by it, and told himself it wasn't true. Stella would never be suspicious of him.

Both Stella and Mark, however, were behaving oddly toward him, as if some new territory, some reach of desert, separated him from them, as if he, or they, were unsubstantial, were mirages floating on the horizon. He assumed this oddness was a consequence of some oddness in himself that he ought, but couldn't, correct. He thought Stella undoubtedly saw this oddness in him as a consequence of *her* betrayal, about which she had said nothing. He was, after all, justified in being strange with her, whatever his wishes that she be as free as she wanted to be. But of course he couldn't be angry; he couldn't play the role of the jilted husband. As for Mark, it was possible he might have noticed a certain queerness in the car on the days Phyllis drove him home. For example, when Mark was in the car Phyllis and Chambers were usually silent, a silence which somehow made Chambers a conspirator with Phyllis, though as a matter of fact even when Mark was not in the car she didn't talk to him as much as once she had, not feeling the need perhaps, being able to communicate with a look of affection or sudden tenderness. And when Mark was in the car Chambers felt awkward in his relationship with Spider, not knowing whether he should sit her on his lap or not and wondering what it meant to Mark to see his father playing the role of father to Phyllis' child. Still, if Chambers seemed constrained in the car, Mark probably saw it as a consequence of the tensions at the university. Probably those tensions *did* account for some of the oddness in the car and at home, even when he was doing something for Stella he liked doing, such as zipping up her dress or fastening the catch of the neck-

MUST AID CITIES AND STATES TO MEET URBAN

lace he had bought for her ten years ago and which she sometimes still wore at parties. She had worn it on New Year's Eve.
Chambers felt empty.

He knew that he was deceiving himself.

He had not gone to bed with Phyllis again since that night,
but neither had he repudiated the act. There were good reasons
he had not told Phyllis it was a mistake, but they were beyond
his ability at the present time to cope with or even to think
about. But it bothered him, it had been bothering him these past
two weeks even when his mind was on other things, that he had
given in to a passion for a younger woman. Though such a surrender was no longer a violation of what they had called in his
sociology classes the mores of his peer group, it *was* a violation
of his personal conviction. He kept coming back to that. The
fact that he was still secretive about it made him think of himself as some stereotype: happily married middle-aged men
were supposed to run after the first younger woman who showed
she was interested. He couldn't stand the thought of himself as
a stereotype.

The sense of strangeness stayed with him during the interview with Collier, who arrived, no doubt purposely, half an hour
late; coming late to appointments was a League tactic. Morris
Freedman had once said of Collier that he was a football type
masquerading in a tribal outfit. Though he was a burly young
man whose hair was cropped to resemble a large helmet, the
description was unfair. He clearly had confidence in his intellectual abilities, and he wore his African shirt and his necklace
of tusks as if they were part of a nature he had been born with.
He sprawled on the plastic divan with the chrome arms, fully at
ease in it; and what he said, when Chambers began to speak of
judicial reforms as Freedman had asked him to do, was that the
League could not possibly begin to discuss reform until the case
against the three blacks was dropped. The reasons he gave were
the ones that had been given several months ago, in the letter in
the *Daily Sentinel;* but Collier restated them patiently as if
Chambers had never heard of them.

CRISIS, PANEL REPORTS . . . THREATEN

"And Mr. Chambers," Collier said, "you ought to see that we can't discuss reform while the sword of Damocles, so to speak, hangs over the heads of three of our brothers."

"It's a pretty harmless sword, I would think," Chambers said. "It's no threat to their lives. I don't really see why we have to talk like rival ambassadors at the United Nations. I mean, there's no need for propaganda—"

"Well, excuse me, but I thought *you* were being the ambassador." Collier smiled at him; it was a polite smile, the kind that carries with it no possibility of intimacy. "You know that we consider the case unfair. You shouldn't single out three people for an event planned by us all."

"The charges were made in accordance with the Student Code. No code I know of can take into account whole organizations; what's always at issue is what individuals do, or get caught doing."

"The Student Code was designed with neither our advice nor —how does it go?—our consent."

"Why should it have been? The Code was in operation at Brangwen long before there was a Black Students League."

"Or even black students. Which proves how racist it is."

"That doesn't necessarily follow," Chambers said. "If you begin to talk like that, I can only respond by telling you what certain members of the faculty feel about the refusal of the blacks to appear. To them—"

"You mean Professor Freedman?"

"Professor Freedman isn't alone, you must know that. He may even represent a majority of the faculty. To them, the refusal of the blacks to appear is not only a strategy to destroy a judicial system but perhaps part of some larger tactic to destroy a university. That might very well be a consequence—"

"Isn't that the UN ambassador for the white principality of Brangwen talking? Listen, Mr. Chambers, you tell all your Professor Freedmans that the blacks aren't the political action arm of SDS. You tell them to keep in mind that the BSL and SDS at this particular moment in time have opposing concerns. I'll tell you about SDS. They're well-to-do whites and full of guilt; to them the university is the place to go to make it big in the world of their fathers. To them the quote idealism unquote of the university is the hypocrisy of their fathers. So they want to destroy it. Or some of them do. Nobody likes to believe he's eating shit . . ." Collier readjusted himself on the cushion, leaning forward so that the tusks dangled away from his chest. "Now, I frankly admit that *we* sometimes feel guilt too, about being here at this great white institution. But still we can look at our presence here in a less hysterical way. I mean, we've made our calculations. We want to use the university if we can. That was what the demonstration was all about, to make it useful to our needs. You've got services and facts and resources—money —that we can use. All we're asking, since after all you *invited* us here, is for you to let all that stuff work for us." He paused; the smile briefly reappeared. "We want this to be our home too, you know?"

"You know better than I do," Chambers said, "that some blacks must hate us enough to want—"

"And some whites feel the same about us. But you've got the university to control them—"

"Not, perhaps, if the judicial system is destroyed."

"—and we've got the League. The judicial machinery never should have been cranked up for a paper towel dispenser. If you'd indicted us all instead—"

"How could we have done that? Haven't we been through all this before? To indict a group is to deny personal responsibility."

"You do it all the time with the fraternities."

"But this was a political act, I suppose that's the difference. Judicial systems in this country don't know yet how to respond to political actions . . ." Chambers sighed. The tangles oppressed him. His own sense of strangeness appalled him. He wanted to get back to some personal relationship, to some belief that one person could trust another. He said what he felt. "I sometimes think," he said, "that you want to keep people like me guessing,

off balance. Wasn't that what you were doing last fall, saying
people like me have a generational hang-up on guns? I'd like to
believe in everything you say, and I'd like you to be able to
believe in me . . . I'd like to believe in that business about your
wanting the university to be your home—"

"Why can't you?"

"You sounded at least half ironic."

"Isn't the half that isn't ironic, isn't that good enough for
you?" Collier stood up. "Your side has always had the advantage, we have to be careful about giving ourselves away . . .
Why don't you level with me first, so that I know where *you*
are, Mr. Chambers? Why give me what Professor Freedman
thinks? You've got a reputation for saying what's on your mind.
Now you tell me this: Do you think those boys should be tried?"

For a moment the smile lost its conscious politeness, it seemed
to be inviting Chambers into friendship. He wanted to say what
he said in committee meetings, what everybody really admitted,
"The boys never should have been tried; I was in an accident
you see, and my assistant was inexperienced." He wanted to say
what he felt as overwhelmingly true as he looked at that face
inviting him to be truthful, "If I were one of the accused students, if I were black, I too would refuse to come." Especially
would he be unable to come now, after all the furor, after the
symbolic intensifications attached to an inept act. From the beginning he had been opposed to a trial. And yet Collier's smile
held on too long. Collier wished simply to exploit him. When
was it, he wondered, that people had ceased being humans to
other people, becoming instead objects to be used? The smile
was Machiavellian. If he gave Collier his genuine response, he
could expect to find his remarks in the next day's *Sentinel,* and
the case (doubtless Collier's intention) would be mired even
more deeply in confusion. At that moment Chambers was envious of a man who could believe so singlemindedly in his cause
that he had no compunctions about a ruthless exploitation of one
who stood outside it.

He avoided a direct answer, and the conversation soon came

. . . SOLDIERS IN SAIGON ON NIGHT ALERT

to an end; nothing could be accomplished between ambassadors. Collier bowed in a ceremonious but ironic farewell, his
tusks swinging. Chambers, alone in his office, fiddling with his
chain of paper clips, thought that what he had said was probably the correct thing for a man in his position to have said.
Certainly anybody shrewd and practical would have applauded
his reticence; but then neither shrewdness nor practicality had
ever in his mind counted among the shining virtues. And he had
difficulty in knowing whether he had judged Collier properly.
Had he really been so ruthless as he for one moment appeared?
All that Chambers could say with certainty was that his own
continuing sense of strangeness was a consequence of his becoming a stranger to himself.

Phyllis came into the room smiling, to hear from his own lips
what he had said to the leader of the Black Students League.

Friday, January 17

THE PHILIPPA WEEKLY ADVERTISER

FROM THE EDITOR'S DESK

There are issues which are difficult to speak about because they reflect upon our community, our children, and ourselves, and touch upon conflicting opinions of Town and Gown. Neither our daily newspaper or the student-run daily on Campus Hill has wished to face up to these issues for fear of offending those leftists who constitute the majority of the "intelligentsia" on the Hill, the increasingly militant student Negro organization "The Black Students League," the radicals of SDS, or even certain "liberal" elements in the town itself (we are thinking of certain prominent attorneys, etc.).

But there are times when voices must speak out clearly. Your editor has long been known to step where radicals fear to tread (for fear of stepping on their own kind), and so we were the one to be called these past few weeks by a number of our concerned citizenry, including various officials of our watchdog Taxpayer's League, the American Legion, the Volunteer Fireman's Association, etc.

The shocking story, as brought to the attention of your editor particularly by Doris Gibbs of the League, is composed of these elements:

1. A group of rabble-rousing kids at the high school, in most cases children of the university "intelligentsia," have organized under the title of Information Please (!!!), an underground organization aimed at overthrowing the traditional curriculum and establishing a series of revolutionary-type courses. (They are aided of course by the Supreme Court, those "interpreters" of the "law" of the land, in their pronouncements about prayers in the schools, *de facto* segregation, etc., but that is a different story.) Their affiliation with the radicals of the university is only too clear, since

. . . BIRTH CONTROL ADVOCATE SAYS FAMINE

they have distributed and even put on bulletin boards articles furnished by the national SDS organization on such topics as "Apartheid in South Africa." Denied use of high school facilities, they have brazenly sponsored lectures on the high school lawn and in the shelter house of Lakeside State Park by convicted Catholic "priests" and other members of the radical movement at the University and are now engaged in attempts to get Negro students at the high school to join them in their subversive activities.

2. Past activities of the university chapter of SDS are known too well by the readers of the *Weekly Advertiser* for us to refer to them again. We are grateful to Doris Gibbs for giving us a report on the next phase of their strategy. They are attempting to curry favor among militant Negroes by sponsoring early next month a series of talks by the University "intelligentsia"—faculty and administrators and others—attacking the Free Enterprise system. Capitalism is to be blamed for our struggle to defend democracy in Vietnam, for poverty in minority groups, and for the support of apartheid in South Africa. A full-fledged assault is to be made on the investment policies of the university.

These are the FACTS. What we can only wonder about is the degree to which we have here an organized Communist conspiracy, part of the worldwide Communist conspiracy, depending on agitators

in the national SDS movement or elsewhere, who are intent on using Philippa as an entering wedge of an attack upon the smaller centers of America which are at the heart of this nation's stability. We wonder why groups both in the high school and the university have become so intensely interested *at the same moment* in apartheid. Are they trying to arouse our minority groups against us? Philippa has had a proud tradition of peaceful relations with its Negroes.

Although the citizenry of Philippa has no control over the university (and cannot for that matter even get taxes from that huge "educational" factory overlooking our houses and small businesses), we DO have a say about our local schools. We don't want SDS and radical Negro groups to get a toehold in our schools, preaching anti-Americanism, trying to divide us for the sake of a foreign ideology. The school board must meet this impending crisis head on. If they don't, an informed citizenry knows how to take action not only against the school board and its appointed lackeys but against that insolent group of young rabble-rousers who are only too typical of the cancer spreading throughout our society today.

What do you think? Phone or write us. Mrs. Powell will answer the telephone during Elsie's lunch break.

GRANT POWELL
Editor and Publisher

Monday, January 20

THE PHILLIPA DAILY EXPRESS

A brick was thrown through the plate glass window of the *Weekly Advertiser*, Third St. at Merwin Ave., sometime during last night, according to Police Chief Merrick. The vandalism was reported at 8:30 A.M. by *Advertiser* editor Grant Powell, who said the damage was covered by insurance. He could give no motive for the vandalism other than possible retaliation for what he termed an "outspoken" editorial in the current issue of the *Weekly Advertiser*. Police are continuing their investigation.

Thursday, January 23

Phil Durant had been locked in his own bedroom by his father. That he had obeyed his father by going to the bedroom bothered him; but it had seemed almost beyond his endurance when he'd heard the key turn in the lock. He could of course jump out the window and escape by killing himself that way. "Oh, hey," he yelled at the door, "I can always jump out the window, you know."

His father had locked him in his room because Phil had told him he had thrown the brick through the *Advertiser* window. This was what happened when you told the truth: Your father got furious and locked you up as if he were the sheriff. Phil had been wholly justified in throwing the brick through the window. He had thrown the brick through the window because he wanted to scare that reactionary idiot Grant Powell into thinking that Philippa, New York, really was the center of the worldwide Communist conspiracy. No doubt Powell thought the brick was thrown through his window on direct orders from the Kremlin to get the fearless editor. No, really, it was beyond Phil's powers to know what went on in that dumb-shit Powell's mind. He hadn't thrown the brick because of Powell, but because he was almost certain it had been his father who had telephoned Doris Gibbs of the Taxpayer's League to complain

RETAIN HOOVER AND HELMS . . . WINDS DELAY

about the meeting at the State Park with the priest under sentence for destroying draft records and to call to her attention the SDS series. Phil was almost certain about that because he himself had told his father about them and Phil had caught his father speaking softly into the telephone and had gone to the extension upstairs to listen. His father had heard the click and had tried to disguise the fact that he was talking to such a person as Mrs. Gibbs (whom even his father disliked) by not mentioning her name or saying anything more of consequence; but when the woman's voice said, "Is that all, Professor?" he thought he had recognized the voice. You can always tell the Mrs. Gibbses of the world.

He had told his father about the meeting with the priest to explain to his father about how stupid and suspicious the country had become, for here the priest was simply talking in a quiet and even shy way about the reasons that had impelled him to burn the records, talking to Mark Chambers who had arranged the talk and maybe a dozen other high school kids, and here was this FBI or CIA agent with his dumb bucket of water and synthetic sponge with the price tag still on it (no towels or chamois or anything like that) trying to clean the windows up high that hadn't been cleaned since the shelter house was built, which was during the Depression, by the Civilian Conservation Corps, according to the sign. They didn't teach in the FBI academy or wherever the CIA agents got their training about cleaning windows or even for that matter about how to fish: at a meeting in the park in October there had been this fellow beyond the bush with his line in the canal that didn't have a hook on it. Probably he didn't have a hook because of the NO FISHING sign, maybe CIA agents weren't supposed to break the small laws.

No, he really had told his father about this last meeting in the park because his father said that since he wasn't going to school, since he was suspended until he was cured of his bad habits (meaning acid), he had to stay away from Information Please, too. He had wanted his father to know he'd damn well do what he wanted to. It was a pretty fucked-up world when a father got

BIG UNDERGROUND NUCLEAR TEST IN NEVADA

mad because his only son wanted to hear a priest talk who was opposed to killing and was behaving like Christ Himself. As for the SDS meetings at Brangwen, they were no secret and no doubt posters would be up soon about them and the papers would carry the stories, and if he had mentioned the meetings to his father it was only because at the park he had heard from Stephanie Garmonsway that Mark Chambers' father was going to give the lead-off talk, which was something that had surprised even Mark. There was something fishy going on in that family. Phil didn't know what it was, but Mark, ever since his father had become a vice-president-to-be, didn't talk about his father so much; something must have cooled *their* relationship. But Phil hadn't told his father that; he had told him about the SDS meetings to show his father what the difference was between him and Mark's father.

Throwing the brick through the window after that attack by asshole Powell on Information Please no doubt would get Information Please in trouble just the way Phil's drug taking had done: which was too goddamn bad. But if the truth were known, he didn't really care if he got Mark Chambers into trouble; that kid had always had too much working in his favor. It was pretty goddamned easy for *him* to be the great liberal champion what with his family tradition, not only his father but his older sister Mary, who was spoken of in the group as if she were some goddamned founding saint or something. Maybe if he'd thought before throwing the brick that Mark and his father were finally having some sort of feud, he wouldn't have thrown it.

But he had thrown the brick, really, to disgrace his father. He knew how shook up his father had been after the business about the sign and then the acid. He had thought his law-abiding father, that strict constructionist of Plato, would have just about had it: his father had let him go off to jail once, but his father would feel the necessity *now* to help his son evade the law, his father wouldn't be able to stand the thought of the publicity upon himself and his son or the kind of stiff penalty

. . . *U.S. SUPPLY CONVOY AMBUSHED IN*

that would now be imposed upon his son, who had become when you thought of it what was called a habitual offender in the papers. Phil had thrown the brick to make his father choose between law and order on the one hand and his son on the other. It was a personal disgrace to his father whichever decision he made, but of course to join with Phil in hiding the crime and protecting the criminal was to elect love over justice. He had thrown the brick to make his father love him.

Wasn't it clear to his father that this was so? And if it wasn't clear, then his father had no understanding of him, no sympathy, nothing approaching any kind of insight. And yet his father had made his decision; he had sent Phil to his room and locked his door from the outside and told him he was to stay there until Phil of his own volition called the reactionary idiot who with his wife and Elsie (the underpaid black secretary and telephone operator and scrubwoman, the *Advertiser* being an "equal opportunity employer") ran the newspaper; Phil was to be jailed by his father until he called Elsie—for whose race he had, if but in an oblique way, thrown the brick—and asked for her employer to whom he was supposed to confess his sin and then doubtless wait for the police.

Phil put his ear against the door. He heard his mother crying like mad in the kitchen. It hurt him terribly to hear his mother cry like that: he had been doing that to her all this year. Yet in a way you could say that his father had been doing it to her. If his father could only love the prisoners in the cave as he loved the sun of his shit-ass allegory, if he could put sinners you might say above principle, his mother would not be crying. His mother was crying because she loved *him*. He listened, fascinated, to her sobs.

When a person reaches the point that Phil had reached there was only one thing to do. He had been planning it for months, just waiting for the right psychological moment. Under his mattress was the money he had been saving. There were fifty-eight dollars under that mattress. He had been working on that pile for some time; and when his father, thinking he spent his every cent on narcotics, had cut off his allowance, he had begun to take small amounts from his mother's purse. It was of course really his father's money, so that was all right. He'd never taken more than what he would have got from his allowance, or not much more. He counted the fifty-eight dollars to make sure he had the amount right, put the money in his billfold, and put the billfold as far down in his jeans pocket as he could get it; he got his old Scout knapsack out of the closet and put in it a change of underwear and the Brangwen sweatshirt and socks. Did his father really think he could lock him in a bedroom? Deep in his closet, beneath all the old Bingo and Monopoly games, dart boards, college pennants and the like, was the big tin box with the remnants of his Erector set. There was a screwdriver in that box—small, but strong enough. He found it, and went to work on the hinge pins. The door practically fell into his hands. He leaned it against the wall, looked down the stairs (nobody was there) and stealthily went into the bathroom. For what? For his toothbrush and soap and washrag, for Christ's sake. But his mother would be glad.

Then he finished packing. His heart was beating hard. He sat down on the edge of the bed. But it wouldn't be good to be found sitting like that. He remembered his dark glasses in his dresser drawer; he opened the drawer, put on the shades, picked up his khaki knapsack, and, whistling, went down the stairs.

"Good-bye, Mom," he called from the doorway; he was afraid to go into the kitchen, and anyway he'd write her a letter. It was her crying after all that had made him realize he couldn't hang around home any longer making her miserable. His father came rushing out of his study so rapidly he nearly tripped on the hall carpet. Phil couldn't tell the color of his face; it was green through the glasses. He thought his father looked scared. "Where—" his father began.

"I'm leaving," Phil said. He just wished his father would try to stop him. He just wished his father would put his arms around him. What he would do, of course, if his father did that would be to push his father away. At seventeen he was bigger and stronger than his father. But he just wished his father would try. But what did his father do? "Those goddamned glasses," his father said, not knowing how else to respond.

"Fuck you," said Phil, which were after all the appropriate words, at least the ones his father would expect him to make. He slammed the door behind him so hard that the glass in one of the little lights shattered. "You set the police after me and you know what?" he screamed through the broken pane. "When I get out of jail I'll come home and cut your throat." It was one of the shards of glass that made him think of that.

He set off down the street, knowing he had worn the shades because he had guessed he would be crying himself; but tight against his rear he felt the comfort of his billfold with its fifty-eight dollars. It was a pity he was only seventeen and without a draft card, because right on the front walk would have been a good place to burn it.

SMUGGLING RING SMASHED ON WEST COAST

Monday, January 27

9:30 A.M.

There had been a serious beating of a student on the campus the night before. As soon as Morris Freedman read the news story in the morning *Sentinel*, he wanted to talk with George Chambers about it. The account to him proved beyond doubt the validity of his own position, and his anger was directed as much at people like Chambers as it was at the perpetrator of such an act. Bearing the newspaper like a bludgeon, he appeared at Chambers' office.

"You've got to admit, George, that *this* puts a more serious light on the whole matter," he said, pointing to the *Sentinel*, which of course Chambers had already read; and he sat down on the divan, waiting with what he knew was a look of accusation for the dean's response.

"Well, it's serious enough, God knows," Chambers said. "There's never been such a brutal attack on anybody here as far back as either you or I go, Morry."

"Look, the boy was so badly beaten that, do you know? he was almost *unrecognizable*. It's almost beyond belief that a boy, a sophomore in architecture from Scarsdale for God's sake, a boy who to nobody's knowledge ever hurt a single soul or had an enemy, who was up late doing a project the way architecture

. . . *"NO MORE APPEASEMENT," REAGAN TELLS*

students have done for years, would get waylaid on a campus walk at midnight or whenever it was and be beat so viciously that his face was pulp, his teeth knocked out; that he would be, I mean, knocked unconscious for God knows how long, that he would be so near death that Hauser who was on emergency at the clinic would think it already too late . . ." Freedman, who had wanted to stress these points in logical order, had started to count them on his fingers; but he had such difficulty in controlling his muscles and nerves that he dropped his hands back limply into his lap.

"They say he's going to live," Chambers said. "We mustn't act as if a murder's taken place when luckily it hasn't. And Morry, for God's sake, you can't assume a black did it—"

"What else but racial hostility can be at the base of it? His wallet wasn't touched. I'm doing my best to be sane. God knows I wouldn't make a public statement accusing the blacks, I wouldn't say a word without evidence, but in my own mind I have to allow for the possibility that a black or a group of blacks—"

"But isn't it wrong somehow—I mean intellectually and emotionally wrong—to jump to any kind of conclusion about 'the blacks'—I mean, even suppose it turned out to be a person of black skin who made that kind of vicious attack, wouldn't you want to think of him not by his color but as an individual? I mean, it's wrong to think of the perpetrator of this particular act as a 'black,' because that makes what he did—and whoever he was, he was clearly crazy, a man—"

"Or men."

"—a man demented, out of his mind, nobody carrying out the orders of the League—because that makes what he did part of some kind of racial conspiracy. It's doing on the racial level exactly what we did on the political level when we took a national leader like Ho Chi Minh, and turned his every word and action into part of the worldwide Communist—"

"For God's sake, keep your opinions about Vietnam out of

this. What we've got here is awful enough and sufficiently complicated—"

"All right," said Chambers. "All I'm saying is that you've got to make a clear distinction between the isolated act of a madman and a demonstration such as the one the League put on."

"Whole peoples, whole races, can get demented, and I'm not just thinking of the Winnebago Indians."

"Do you think of the demonstration as part of the same dementia that produced this brutality? I must say, Morry—"

"Their whole attempt—isn't it?—is to make us think of them as black. They're after separate courses, separate living quarters, a separate culture. I'm in favor of that up to a point. But what I would ask you is this: Can you argue with Joe Collier as a person, as one man to another? Oh, come now, George: when you talk with him, you're addressing the League. And more than that: he wants you to see him as the embodiment of four hundred years of white injustice. In his own mind he's a symbol of blackness pressing for a redress of grievances, and what he and the League both want is to have that kind of solidarity—black solidarity—against us, against us not as individuals (for there we might turn out to be surprisingly like them) but as people with a disgustingly pinkish complexion. If they want us to see them like that, can you blame *me* for thinking of any one of them, whether he's an isolated case, mad or not, in just precisely the way they want me to?" Freedman suddenly smiled. He had regained his committee room balance. "But of course, George, you're right," he said, bending forward and pointing a steady finger at Chambers. "You're right all the way—I *was* guilty in my mind of making the racial connection, of thinking that his was a 'black' act and not the work of some berserk Sam Duncan—"

"Is he the one you have in mind?"

"He's back on campus, isn't he? Allowed to return because our Code refuses to put him in double jeopardy: Isn't that right? His trial comes up week after next. I'm not accusing him; his name is just an example. I've been wrong in thinking of a 'black' hoodlum when I should be thinking of an American citizen who might or might not be black. If he turns out to be black, which is what my hunch tells me, they—the other blacks—will want me to make the racial connection, of course. They will want me to say a black committed this atrocity, not a citizen named Sam Duncan. And after I say it, they will turn around and accuse me, and with justice, of racism, and see me as the bigot behind the institutional racism they see reflected in our Code. I confess my thoughts had been taken in so much by their propaganda that I was ready to fall into a trap."

"Mmmm."

"What any act of violence on this campus suggests is simply the need of upholding not only respect for the institution as such but the integrity of a judicial structure which acts impartially, in reference always to its student citizens and never to the judicial irrelevances of skin color. What this most recent barbarous act suggests more strongly than ever is that those three campus citizens have to appear for their trial before the Judicial Board or be suspended immediately."

Chambers began: "But really you've got to keep those two acts separate; you can't confuse a controlled political demonstration with a criminal act or use the latter to strengthen your position in regard to the first . . . Oh, my God, Morry," he said, and became silent. They looked at each other then, saying nothing. There were emotional divisions which no words could possibly cross, no logical arguments bridge.

7:30 P.M.

President John Doran, having gone through the cafeteria line and eaten his pork chop, apple sauce, and green salad, engaging, as he ate, in pleasant small talk with the group of respectful students at his table, had then stood by the coffee urn and presented an informal summary not only of what had already been accomplished for minority groups at Brangwen but of his own reasons—they were the good, liberal reasons—for continuing to push for the establishment of a semiautonomous black studies program. He had accepted—Marty Niemeyer had made it clear to the Macs in advance that he would be happy to accept—a dinner invitation from McIntyre House. McIntyre House was supported by its own endowment and traditionally was composed of unusually bright young men brought to it and the university through the scouting efforts of its own alumni; Doran, who in several public addresses had praised the intellectual and cultural environment of the House as an ideal toward which the whole university should strive, felt more at home here than he would have in a typical fraternity. He had chosen McIntyre House as the logical place to begin the difficult task of repairing his own, alas, battered image. If it had occurred to him when he had accepted the presidency that he would have to seek out a supporting bloc, he would have assumed such a bloc would come from within the faculty; but now it appeared that he needed strong student support to withstand the assaults of such faculty members as Durant and Freedman.

Doran, really, was shy when it came to talking with students, particularly the forthright and sometimes arrogant students of the present generation; he knew they in turn thought of him as aloof and proud. In speaking before this group, he was conscious of the heat from the urn. The dining room was in the basement, the air hot from overhead pipes, but one couldn't open a window because of the winter winds. Perspiration stood out on his face. It was unfortunate that he perspired so easily, the beads on his cheeks probably made an unpleasant impression. Most of the boys were receptive enough to his remarks, although the applause he got upon getting to the end was moderate.

They were worried (as was *he*, of course) by that mindless act of terrorism over the weekend. A Jewish boy asked what he was doing about security on the campus; the boy who had been attacked was Jewish, black militants throughout the country were increasing in hostility toward Jews. Doran replied carefully and sensibly to the question. The campus patrol had been put on overtime duty, the campus—particularly the quadrangle—

was being patrolled all night, the buildings and grounds department was investigating the feasibility of floodlighting the buildings (which had an aesthetic as well as a practical justification). He went on to say that of course it was highly improper to impute this particular act of terror to a black student. The boy retorted that a band of blacks—by this, he said upon questioning, he meant three—had been reported by other architecture students to have been standing near the building on the night of the attack, and to have made threatening gestures. Doran said that even if that were the case, it provided no evidence; and that even if one wanted to conjecture that a black or a group of blacks had attacked the architecture student, one could still not assume that such individuals were Brangwen students. He read again from one of his note cards the statistics demonstrating that the black students at Brangwen were performing (despite an often inadequate high school education, despite the lack of cultural advantages in their homes) at least as creditably as the whites, and suggested, as sternly as he could, that for the sake of the whole Brangwen community no racial allegations should be made at the present moment of heightened tensions.

But the boy was not to be silenced. He had been sitting, but now he rose to his feet and came to Doran's side to speak to the other students. He was agitated enough, he said, to stand before his own fellows and perhaps make himself unpopular with them and perhaps even be considered a racist, since that was the condemnation currently being made against anyone who disagreed with either the president or the blacks; but nevertheless he had reached a position in which he was beginning to question the wisdom of Doran's particular efforts to help the blacks. They were being brought into an almost rural, overwhelmingly white region and were forced by that fact alone to form themselves into a tight political as well as racial faction. Far from the ghettos, far from their parents, they could easily feed on one another's paranoia. Furthermore, in the establishment of a black studies program, the president would be giving the university's approval to what inevitably must be a politically oriented course of studies that would make difficult any resistance to the establishment of, say, a study center representing the views of the extreme right. He spoke of the refusal by the blacks to appear before the Judicial Board and quoted Professor Freedman's remarks in support of the judicial system; and from his pocket he took a clipping from the *Daily Sentinel* and read it—a letter from Professor Durant attacking the lack of leadership that was leading to the politicization of what should be purely objective academic studies. Then he returned to his seat. The other students gave him a much greater ovation than they had given Doran.

Doran wiped his face with his handkerchief. For the moment, it gave him something to do with his hands: he had given up cigarettes completely the week before. He really didn't know, despite the applause for the boy, what the opinion of the majority of these bright students was. Their applause was, he thought, a response to the boy's personal sincerity and audacity of expression. Doran wanted desperately to reach them, not simply because he had to gain a bloc and this was the first test of his ability; he wanted trust, he wanted understanding. The black students at Brangwen were not the only ones to feel the isolation of their position; never in his previous experience as an administrator had *he* ever been so far removed from confidants, from close friends who could slip into his office or come uninvited into his home and with whom he could talk in the fullest of confidence about his wishes as well as his frustrations and anxieties. Here he had his young "team," but a team was an administrative unit trained to compliance. God knew what they said when he wasn't around. Desiring intimacy, desiring to win the Macs over, Doran spoke of what was on his mind as frankly as had the boy. What was on his mind was his private response to Freedman and Durant, and what he said of Freedman was, "What you've got to remember is that the Code is Freedman's baby, and when you've invested as much time and effort as he has in something like that you're bound to be prejudiced in favor of your child"; and what he said of Durant was, "I have the greatest respect for his integrity. But it's as true of him as it is of any of us that personal problems can upset the judgment. I don't want to engage in innuendo. Still, you boys who are leaning to the far left in your political opinions or are wearing your hair too long—you know the effect that can make on your father's actions. He's apt to say something he'll regret." And Doran said all this with a smile which was supposed to draw them toward him and in a manner designed to make him one of them; but he knew, even as he was speaking, that his words, whatever intimacy they were intended to promote, had sent him further into isolation than he had been before. He was as shocked as they by his violation of what a president should be, of what a president should say, and he thought that the smile still affixed to his lips must seem to them to be nothing more than a clumsy leer.

"Let me take that back, for a moment your hospitality made me think I was back in the frat, arguing things the way we used to when I was your age," he said. And he said, "My words were ill-chosen and off the record. Please excuse them," and a few minutes later he left.

Tuesday, February 4

Coming early to the SDS meeting at the Student Union, Phyllis Christy looked like a Greek warrior in her pleated vinyl miniskirt and white turtleneck sweater; around her neck was a chain from which dangled a heavy medallion. What was she thinking, as the people slowly filed into the Union lounge, sitting on all sides of her in the little folding chairs? She was thinking of how well Spider had taken to the Suzuki violin class. She was thinking of the adorable chickens Spider had drawn in nursery school. She was thinking of what Terry O'Brien, who was really still a fraternity adolescent and was terribly jealous of her attachment to George Chambers, had said. Terry O'Brien had said she was infatuated with George Chambers because, if she wanted to know the truth, she finally couldn't have him. Terry O'Brien said that as far as he could tell the shock of her husband's death had made her afraid to seek somebody whom she might really be able to get.

Which was false.

Seated there and waiting for George Chambers to begin to talk, Phyllis Christy smiled to herself. George sat in an upholstered chair while David Garmonsway stood behind the lectern and said some good things about the need for a sense of community at Brangwen and some nice things about George, about his long dedication to Brangwen students. Garmonsway said he supposed everybody knew that George Chambers would be a vice-president in the fall. There was applause, and George was at the lectern and beginning to talk without notes of any kind. She could listen to him and still have her private thoughts. He was talking quite earnestly of how a few years ago he had watched a television news program in which Martin Luther King was leading black marchers through the streets of Cicero, Illinois, in an attempt to bring housing integration to that community, and how dismayed he—George—had been by the hostility and rage on the faces of the whites who were on the sidewalks. What she was thinking was that when George had brought his cast to the office—his doctor had managed to saw it neatly, so that the front half, with his wife's painting on it, was undamaged—he had told Phyllis he had promised Stella he'd get the janitor to find a hook for it so he could hang it on the wall. Phyllis had found it significant that he hadn't said he personally *wanted* it to be on his office wall. To Phyllis the painted cast had been something that had been used by Stella and her self-centered friends to suggest their own advanced ideas and their wholly unwarranted condescension to George. It was like an iron collar worn by somebody who was so far above those who kept him in bondage that he wasn't even aware of it as a mark of servitude. He had left the half-tube of plaster overnight on his desk, standing precariously on end. Before his arrival the next morning, Phyllis, arranging his desk as she always did, sent it to the floor with one angry, but you could almost say unpremeditated, swipe of her dustcloth. When George saw the pieces and the plaster dust on the floor, he asked what had happened and she told the truth. She said it had toppled by accident while she was dusting. He hadn't been mad. He had looked so understanding that she had immediately become so remorseful she had started to cry; but then, she cried only when she was extremely happy. Terry O'Brien had said she would end up destroying George Chambers and maybe herself.

Which was as false as everything else Terry had said.

CAMBODIA RELEASES 12 U.S. SOLDIERS . . .

George was telling his audience how, on that news program, they had shown pictures of the neat bungalows of Cicero and of the shrubs in front and little gardens in back. Cicero was a lower-middle-class town, most of the men were blue-collar workers. In interviews with the TV commentator they said what they were defending when they tried to break up the march, when they shook their fists at Martin Luther King and looked so hostile, was the investment they had in their homes. Their houses were for most of them the only investments they had. Several people were interviewed who said they personally didn't have anything against Negroes, but it was just a fact of life that when a family of them moved into a white neighborhood the price of houses plummeted. There was always a scare, everybody trying to sell while he could still get something, and pretty soon the whites all had to leave and the Negroes came in. Let one Negro family in, you had a neighborhood of Negroes. The Negroes often paid pretty stiff prices for what the whites had sold for practically nothing. The only people who profited were unscrupulous realtors who used the racial scare to fatten their bank accounts.

George was handsome, standing up there in the brown suit he knew Phyllis liked best. Everybody was listening intently to find out what he would say next. Phyllis turned around to see if the lounge was full (it nearly was). With that strange and secretive smile on her lips, people thought she was smiling at them. Anne Kovalsky, Marty Niemeyer's secretary, thought Phyllis was smiling at her and smiled back. The graduate student in astrophysics she had met at the New Year's Eve party smiled back. Several undergraduate boys of the bearded and tattered-jeans kind (there were many of them in the room) smiled back; they must have found her smile odd and appealing. Fred Henry, sitting with a small group of blacks, saw her smile and positively scowled at her, as if he saw something in that smile he didn't like. What Phyllis was thinking, and what Fred Henry couldn't possibly know, was something explicitly sexual and wholly private. What she was thinking was that of all the people in this room only she had seen the undressed body of the man they were listening to. They couldn't guess that he was more muscular than he seemed and that his pubic hair reached to his navel and was a sort of brownish gold, unusual considering the darkness of the hair on his head (except for the touch of white at the temples). Nobody else could guess that she had fondled his testicles and penis, that she had rubbed her own soft pelvic hair up and down his legs and chest and across his mouth. Nobody else could guess that she, Phyllis Christy, on the morning of the New Year had gently taken his erect penis into her own eager mouth or could even begin to imagine the rapture she had felt to hear his deep breathing or his sigh of gratification. Nobody else could know—as she had known, intuitively—that she had given him the deepest sexual pleasure of his life and had explored with him regions so buried from the rest of the world that one could do nothing but smile as mysteriously as no doubt she was smiling. Sitting here among his admirers, people who waited to hear from his lips the simple solution to a puzzling American problem, was more than *déjà vu* for Phyllis, it was as if there were nothing but continuity in her life. She was safe.

What George was proposing was this: Since the economic factor did apparently play such a major role in white resentment to neighborhood integration, it ought to be possible to meet such a problem with an economic solution. In fact, the precedent for such a solution already existed. Ever since the Depression, the federal government had insured, simply for psychological reasons, individual bank deposits up to a specified maximum. The equity that lower-middle-class whites had in their homes was the equivalent of such deposits and constituted for most of them the only savings they had. Granted the history of housing prices since at least the Depression, houses that were properly maintained, houses in neighborhoods that had suffered no mass emigration of their owners into the suburbs, could be counted on to keep or even increase their market value. It seemed to George that if the government could provide for lower-middle-class homeowners the same kind of psychological protection it pro-

WORKERS PROTEST U.S. NUCLEAR SUB . . .

vided for those usually better-off people who actually had money in the bank, that there would be no panic selling when a black family moved into the neighborhood. There might be a considerable slowing down of the process that sent whites farther and farther into the suburbs and turned the cities themselves into larger and larger ghettos. Such a program of insurance, which would cost the government nothing beyond its administrative costs (and there were ways in which even those costs might be met through the program itself), could be a beginning in the attempt to reverse the ever-increasing fragmentation of American society.

His proposal was met, after some initial applause, with silence. The audience at first had no questions. George himself, who had sat down, rose again to point out certain technical problems which he thought could be resolved. Fred Henry rose to ask if the speaker wasn't really making his proposal too late in the day. It seemed to Fred Henry that a great many blacks themselves were no longer in favor of integration. One of the blacks with him laughed. George replied that he realized his proposal was by itself a small one, that much more was urgently needed, and that he could only hope it wasn't too late in the day. While he was answering Fred Henry, the other blacks left the room. One of the SDS members wondered if maybe there wasn't an implication in the dean's talk that the dean had missed, that implication being that the very possession of property was an evil and that if the people of Cicero, Illinois, had owned no property in the first place they never would have tried to spit on Martin Luther King. Thinking the comment naïve, Phyllis smiled at George; she thought he saw the smile and was disconcerted by it, because for a moment he had difficulty answering the boy. What he said was that he agreed there was too much self-interest in America, too great a concern with property, but that, speaking as a man who loved his own old country house, he would be a hypocrite to advise the complete abolition of private property. Oh, God, he said, and was silent a moment. He said he thought it would be unbearable to live in one of a series of pre-

KIDNAPPED GIRL FOUND, BURIED BUT ALIVE

fabricated houses all belonging to some abstraction known as "the people." Perhaps if a nation, or a world, could ever reach the condition of real brotherhood—that is, the condition in which all people knew themselves as members of the same family—a person like himself wouldn't want to hold on to his own house so possessively. But as things were, the sense of "family" was limited to one's own spouse and children. He was willing to admit, he said carefully, that the institution of marriage, which made of the house the citadel of the family, was, like all other institutions, undergoing change: all the social and political institutions which he as a child had considered as immutable as they were familiar sometimes now struck him as ephemeral and strange. But no, as yet he couldn't give up on private ownership of houses. The universe, he said, was itself a strange and inexplicable affair, people were pretty much lost in it, families still constituted a kind of separate identity, and as long as this remained the case he thought a small house and a garden owned by the family was a help. It was an unusually long and involved answer containing both sincerity of emotion and self-doubt, and was met with scattered applause as well as hisses. Phyllis listened to it chiefly for its effect on the audience; the mixture of approval and disdain made her heart beat violently.

David Garmonsway asked him if he would briefly comment on the capitalistic system. George said a brief comment would be impossible. Garmonsway said what he really had in mind was something the dean had said to him in private, but that possibly the dean wouldn't remember it since it was at the same time that the dean had agreed to speak at the lead-off SDS session and what with the troubles at the university the dean had had to be reminded even of that. (This was said affectionately.) There was something the vice-president-to-be had said about the difference between capitalism and democracy that Garmonsway had thought worth repeating here. George replied that he had always thought capitalism was an economic concept and democracy a political concept, that one was material and the other spiritual, was this what Garmonsway had in mind? Garmonsway said yes.

An SDS boy asked him for his opinion on the stock market. George replied he was no expert, for he owned no stocks or bonds himself. The boy said the university, which paid him his salary, owned stocks. George agreed. The boy wanted to know if the stock market, in which the university participated, was a good thing or a bad thing; that is, did the dean think it compatible with his notion, or dream, of the family of mankind? George said that of course it wasn't compatible; he was prevented from saying anything more by another SDS boy who asked him what he thought of apartheid. George said he thought nothing good of it. The boy asked him if he thought the university should invest its funds in banks that themselves had stocks in South African businesses. George replied that as far as he knew the university had only a small share of its endowment in such banks, so the problem, like so many problems these days, like, for example, the problem with the campus judicial system, was essentially symbolic, with the symbols of greater emotional consequence than the facts warranted. The boy said this very well might be true, but what did he *think?* George said he could answer this only as an individual, not as a representative of the university administration; but that as an individual, as a member of the community which these noon meetings were to celebrate, why yes, he wished the university would withdraw its investments from any source that could conceivably abet racial injustice.

He was vigorously applauded by the SDS contingent; Garmonsway thanked him for so successfully inaugurating the series, and the meeting broke up into little groups. Fred Henry walked out alone. Phyllis made her way into the group around George to congratulate him; but he was talking with some boys and a reporter from the Philippa *Daily Express* and seemed too distraught and fatigued to respond to her pride in his performance. He was still upset when she drove him home, though he smiled when she squeezed his hand before he got out of the car.

POLITICS . . . HIGHWAY PATROLMEN ACCUSED

That night, when Phyllis read the newspaper story, she saw that the reporter had found George's remarks about the stock market and the university's investment policies to be the crucial point of the meeting and had given only passing mention to the housing insurance proposal. It seemed to her that newspapers were as unreliable as the world itself was; if it weren't for George and people like him, Phyllis thought, life would be so vicious and so beyond control that only a dictatorship would be feasible. It was not really surprising that Phyllis, whatever the enthusiasm of her support of noble and democratic causes, could think of a dictatorship as a possible solution to human discord. The fearful ones who fervently worship (a man, an abstraction, a nation) can accept such a restriction more readily than those who love.

Thursday, February 6

President Doran, his immediate staff, and various members of the faculty chosen by him for their campus influence and/or their public criticisms of the administration (it was better to get them in on this) sat in the board room at eleven P.M. still discussing possible options.

What had happened before noon was this: an SDS force led by David Garmonsway and including three blacks had entered the Ad Building and locked itself along with an official of the Chase Manhattan Bank and his student interviewees into the suite of offices used for recruitment by business concerns. Conscious of the criticisms against him for his lack of forthright response in the past, Doran had called upon the proctor to stand outside the locked door and to announce, using a bullhorn, that the intruders were in violation not only of the Code but of state and possibly federal law. (Didn't the Lindbergh law make kidnapping a federal offense? He couldn't exactly remember: a university president these days needed as much legal expertise as he did administrative, and all that the university's legal counsel could urge was that for court action it would help to have photographs of the offenders.) He further instructed the proctor to warn them that if they did not immediately release their prisoners and peacefully disperse, they would be ejected by the campus patrol and charged for their offenses in the proper courts. Garmonsway had replied that they would remain within until the university agreed to (1) a general reappraisal of its investment policies, for the purpose of using its endowment in a way that would be mutually beneficial to the university and a just society; and (2) an immediate withdrawal of its investments from the bank whose official they had just captured. There followed a half hour of stalemate and confusion; Doran had summoned the photographer from the News Bureau but had forgotten to mobilize his police. Finally, when all was ready, the proctor repeated his warning. Using a beam from a nearby construction site (a new building for the social sciences), the campus patrol battered down the door. Some of the students escaped through windows; and since a considerable crowd of sympathizers had collected both outside and within the building, still others were able to mingle with the bystanders in the hall. The photographer had snapped and immediately developed his pictures, but they turned out primarily to be shots of the black students and of Garmonsway, who, standing with his arm upraised, looked like some justifiably outraged Cambridge don. Not even the proctor, who had stood in the corridor with pad and pencil, had been able in the confusion (the pad being twice deliberately knocked to the floor by unknown assailants) to get the identity of more than three whites. The problem was that as a consequence of the racial unrest, both the News Bureau photographer and the proctor were aware of the faces and names of individual black agitators and were, consciously or unconsciously, seeking them out. And Garmonsway, to prove that the blacks were supporting SDS had shoved them at the photographer. Though Joe Collier had not been present (so in a way the League was not officially represented), Fred Henry had been; and so had Henry Osgood and Thomas Potter. Most of the whites involved had been unknown, SDS at Brangwen having been that year at least up to that moment, more conciliatory than many other chapters in the nation.

The question of course was, What to do? To press charges

ASTRONAUTS ABOARD HEADS FOR MOON . . .

against the blacks, two of whom were already named in the charges resulting from the League demonstration, would prove to the world the validity of the claim of institutional racism. To forget the violation, particularly after the proctor's repeated warning with the bullhorn, would add not only to the disrepute of the administration but to the general drift toward disregard of the law and the judicial processes.

And the men gathered together in the board room were not men of goodwill attempting to help one another help the administration or even to resolve reasonably the dilemma. They distrusted one another; they were ill-tempered. Professor Durant suspected that Dean Chambers had been in on the plot, at least the edges of it, for why else would he have engaged in inflammatory radical rhetoric about the stock market and the university's investment policies before an SDS-black group two days before the Chase man was scheduled to come to campus? Professor Freedman suspected that the dean had been duped, and was perhaps no better than the earlier selections on the presidential team. The president felt that Chambers probably had been misrepresented in the press, and, having had similar problems with a man from the New York *Times,* was inclined to be sympathetic, though he felt the dean had probably gone too far. Chambers was irritated with both Freedman and Durant. Vice-President Niemeyer knew that both Freedman and Durant detested him. Since he was leaving at the end of the term anyway, he either baited them or was lost in private thoughts. Doran was aware through the increased rudeness to him displayed by both Freedman and Durant that they knew about his remarks about them at McIntyre House. More than once since the discussion had begun, Durant had insinuated that since the administration was engaged in attempts to discredit its faculty as well as its judicial processes, there was no wonder that the whole institution was cracking apart. Other faculty members, like Simpson in government, nodded in sympathy at such allegations. The president, thinking of Durant's personal attacks

ISRAEL AND ARAB COMMANDERS BOTH DIE IN

on him in the student newspaper, felt his own indiscretions to
be almost justified.

When Dean Chambers suggested that they had no recourse
other than to forget the incident, Professor Freedman accused
him of deviousness. Why? Chambers wanted to know. Because,
said Freedman, the incident was of a much more serious nature
than the breaking of a window with a Scott towel dispenser,
and if the administration simply forgot it, any insistence on
pressing the other charge would *appear* more discriminatory
than ever. Chambers thought it a sensible way, then, of getting
rid of both problems at once. At this point, Freedman changed
his mind about the dean being a dupe: he began to see, and to
comment upon, the Machiavellianism of Chambers' strategy
beginning with his SDS talk.

"For Christ's sake, Morry," said Chambers angrily.

"Gentlemen, gentlemen," said Doran.

"What we *can* do," said Durant, "is fire that quixotic hothead
Garmonsway. We have *his* photograph, and by God he's white."

Doran momentarily looked optimistic, but the response of the
faculty present showed this to be an ill-conceived option. However much he was disliked by the men in the room, Garmonsway had tenure. They knew Garmonsway would be smart
enough to see that such a move would bring a good many of the
faculty to his defense if he chose to fight it. To try to fire him
would be to play into the hands of SDS by uniting the whole
student body and half the faculty in a protest movement.

"The only other solution I can think of," said Freedman, "is
for the present administration to resign."

Doran looked at him quizzically. It seemed to the president
that Freedman might, after all, be a racist without knowing it.
It would be difficult for a Jew, even a liberal Jew, not to resent
the attacks being made by prominent radical blacks on Israel.
Perhaps unconsciously Freedman wanted to do in the black
studies program. "I'm still fighting, Professor," Doran said. He
wanted to keep the rancor out of his voice and managed to
respond in an unemotional way. But he had recently started to

JERICHO BATTLE . . . U.S. HOLDS LEAD IN

chew gum, and would put one stick after another into his mouth without thinking about it. He had a large wad in his mouth now, and after he had finished his dignified little phrase began smacking on it audibly.

While the bickering continued in the board room, Sam Duncan and two other blacks were in the process of holding up a white pedestrian, the owner of a package liquor store patronized by students. Two members of the campus patrol who had been secluded in nearby bushes just beyond the campus gate, came out of hiding and demanded that the blacks put their hands up. Two of them ran; Patrolman Johnson fired a warning shot into the air, and then pursued them unsuccessfully; Sam Duncan, having made no attempt to escape, was apprehended by Patrolman Schorer. In his hand was a cheap pistol which later was discovered to have been stolen from the house of one of the city's volunteer firemen. Patrolmen Johnson and Schorer took him to the downtown police station. In a fruitless attempt to get him to name his accomplices, Duncan was roughed up by one of the city policemen. "Pigs," he screamed. His lips were bleeding when they put him in a cell. They wouldn't even let him phone his mother in Harlem. Within the hour, the news of course was out in the bars and eating spots open at night. Three drunk whites attacked Arnie Jones, a black freshman, outside a bar on Grady Street; he managed to break away, ramming one of them in the stomach with his head.

The board room had long since been dark by this time. Everybody who had been there had left feeling disillusioned and betrayed by the behavior of nearly everybody else.

CHURCH ATTENDANCE DESPITE DROP . . .

Friday, February 7

In the early hours of the morning Fred Henry, who had gone to bed fatigued at ten in the apartment he shared with Henry Osgood and Thomas Potter, woke from a dream in which he had been engaged in some violent act that left him perspiring and with a heavy sense of depression and guilt. His headache was severe. He sat on the edge of his bed. He hated waking at two or three A.M.: it was the stagnant interval of night when the air seemed too thick for breathing, when the only sound you heard was the ticking of a cheap alarm clock with a phosphorescent face that let you know how eerie and senseless the perpetual passing away of life was.

Because he didn't want to recollect his dream, he thought of something else. He thought of the SDS action, which had been pretty much of a farce. It had been stupid of him to get taken in by that egoist Garmonsway, who apparently all his life had wanted to direct a big kidnapping operation. You could tell, when the campus patrol broke through the door, that it was a great moment for Garmonsway: his eyes were as shining and as dazed as if he had changed his sex and was getting an orgasm from that battering ram. He'd made sure he got himself in a picture. And he had shoved Fred and Oz and Tommy almost into the camera. He had thought the photographer was from the

New York *Times* or *Newsweek,* not somebody ordered there for discipline purposes by the president or the proctor. Garmonsway wanted to be the big white leader of the oppressed.

And Fred thought of Dean Chambers, who had talked so uncertainly of the universal family of man at the noon meeting. That talk had bugged him even more than Garmonsway's moment of glory in getting caught for holding a Chase man for ransom. How could you believe in old Fat Cat Chambers purring away about integration in blue-collar neighborhoods while up his sleeve was a contract for a vice-presidency and a healthy salary increase and who lived so far out in the country he had no problems except how to buy some more acres? The whites really knew how to make the population explosion pay off: there was no investment better than land, the newspapers said. Then there had been that awful smile of Phyllis Christy when she was surveying the room to see how they were all taking it in. Why had that smile upset him so much? It was as if it were saying, This is mine: what you're listening to is mine; and meanwhile the dean was talking away out of one side of his mouth about a Communistic ideal while out of the other he was advocating private ownership. Just to think of that smug Mona Lisa smile made him want to puke. But why should he get bugged over Garmonsway and over Chambers and his little piece of ass? Didn't he *know* the white world was shitty? Hadn't Chambers in the hospital admitted as much, saying that maybe civilization had just about had it? He resented Chambers, but not because Chambers had something of value he wanted. He resented Chambers because it turned out that Chambers didn't have it. He wondered if Camus had thought of that kind of bitterness. That a person could be bitter and mean as hell because there wasn't anybody above him he wanted equality with.

Fred pattered into the bathroom for some aspirin, and knocked the soap dish to the floor reaching into the medicine cabinet.

"Hey, man, is that you?" Tommy called sleepily; he had the room next to the bathroom.

"Yeah, man, it's me," said Fred Henry. "You think it's the police?"

"Well, I was just wondering," Tommy said.

Before Tommy and Oz had agreed to join him in the SDS thing against the Chase man, the three of them had had a long argument about whether they should get themselves involved personally in something about South Africa. Joe Collier had said to the League, Stay out of this one; but Fred had told Tommy and Oz they had to fight for blacks everywhere, and if you didn't support the blacks in South Africa while the whites did, why then what sort of black brother were you? It surprised him now that he had been so vehement and emotional. Maybe it had just been habit. Maybe he wanted to get back at Joe Collier for taking over the League and being so cool and reasonable and trying to tell all the rest of them what they should do. He'd lost track of his own motives somewhere, that personal ideology that had made him so fucking proud.

Tommy and Oz had agreed to join him but said it was the blacks that everybody would be out to get and not SDS, and so they'd better be prepared for a little manly self-defense. They were already behind the times at 401½ Maple Street, they said. What they meant was that they'd join him, but to do so they wanted to have a little gun in the apartment. Tommy had found one somewhere. "Try it on for size," he said, putting it in Fred's hand. Fred had never held a real gun before, but he had been willing to go along with it. He'd aimed it at the overhead bulb with one eye shut. It wasn't much after all to hold an unloaded pistol, though to see him so stiff and out of character had given Tom and Oz hysterics. But the funny thing about it was that afterward he had felt suspicious and hostile toward them both. He had wondered if they had thought that to get a gun in his hand was the first step toward getting him to choose. He had wondered if it was a kind of symbol which, once he accepted it, meant that he was supposed to shoot any goddamn person who stood in the way. He had wondered, to tell the truth, if maybe Joe Collier hadn't put them up to it, and if maybe Joe's reluctance to get the League behind Garmonsway's plan hadn't been part of a ruse to get him to agree to the gun in order for him to get at least Tommy and Oz in on it.

It was crazy of him to be suspicious of Tom and Oz who after all had joined him even though he hadn't joined them in the League demonstration that got them into trouble, going off instead to tell Dean Chambers in the hospital about his discovery about some characters in stories. It was just as crazy to be suspicious of them as it was to think Joe Collier thought him important enough to pull such an elaborate ruse on. And weren't Tommy and Oz the closest friends he had? Still, the gun was hidden in the hall hot-air register, and it really got him uptight to think about it as some kind of bond.

But the gun had tricked him back to the dream. What he had been dreaming was this: he had been arguing with his father about the League or something, and his father had said to him, "You can't trust a nigger." That was what his father had said, in the dream. It was what his father always thought but never would say outside one of Fred's dreams. It was precisely what you'd expect from a man who insisted on being called President Henry and who lived in a big brick house and who was so desirous of placating the whites that he put down, just as if he were a sheriff, any attempt on the part of his students to demonstrate or become political. As soon as his father had said those words, Fred knew that somebody was listening, a sort of presence was behind his back, and so he turned around, and there stood Joe Collier frowning like God. Fred knew what he had to do, that pistol being in his hand. He fired twice, to prove by the second shot it wasn't any accident. The bullets exploded inside his father, flesh and blood and bone flying everywhere. A leg twitched on the floor as if it had been torn from a grasshopper. But the most terrible thing about the dream was his knowledge that in doing that to his father he had proved beyond doubt the truth of what his father had said. This is what he'd known, waking; but it was as if he'd always known it.

Mitya Karamazov had said, "I've had a good dream, gentlemen." Fred had not killed his father any more than Mitya had killed his, in fact Fred's father wasn't even dead, which ought to have been cause for rejoicing. Still Fred couldn't have one of those transcendent, glowing dreams that Russian novels were so full of. Fred's dream hadn't come out of one of his mother's books. Fred's dream made the air heavy, like a little house that enclosed him wherever he moved. He was sweating under his armpits, nigger sweat.

After taking the aspirin he had gone back to his room, but all of a sudden he found himself seated on the floor in the kitchen. He had taken the telephone from the table and held it cradled in his knees. He had this terrible urge to call home. He thought his father probably knew all about his dream, for Fred instinctively believed that other people must know what went on in his mind when his thoughts made him especially guilty. It would make him feel better to talk with his father. If it didn't make him feel worse. He dialed the number. The telephone rang and rang.

But of course it was his mother who answered. He had known it would be his mother. Late telephone calls scared his father, and he always pretended to sleep very soundly when the telephone rang after midnight.

"Hello," his mother said.

At first he didn't say anything. He was just breathing softly into the mouthpiece, so pleased to hear her voice his goddamn eyes were wet. Breathing into the mouthpiece was what maybe niggers like Sam Duncan did late at night when they wanted to scare whites, but Fred didn't want to frighten his own mother. That wasn't why he had called her. He wondered if she could hear the hum of the refrigerator, which was a better sound.

"Fred?" she asked uncertainly. "Fred?"

"Hello, mother," he said.

"What's the matter, Fred?"

"Nothing."

"Have you been hurt? What's *happened?*"

He could tell she was almost in a panic. She worried about

him being at Brangwen and in the League. She always worried. "Nothing's happened," he said.

There was a silence. Then his mother said, "But it's almost *four*, Fred."

"I'm sorry. I didn't know." There was silence again. "I couldn't get to sleep," he said.

"You drinking too much coffee again?"

"I guess so," he said.

"Well, you'd better go back to Sanka or Postum."

"Yeah," he said.

"Put in lots of warm milk."

"Sure."

And then he asked her—because he had to say something—if she was teaching this term any really *relevant* books. Which was an odd thing to ask, at four o'clock in the morning. His voice almost trembled, asking such an odd question. But she was glad to talk with him about anything if he was so lonely up there in the North as he sounded. If he couldn't sleep. He knew she would be like that. All the books she taught were relevant, she said. Right now, she said, she was teaching *A Passage to India*, and as he knew that was a relevant book. He didn't tell her that to a black committed to liberation that book wouldn't mean a thing. Probably Joe Collier hadn't even heard of it. He just asked if she thought the relationship between the white hero and the Moslem wasn't in some way demeaning to the non-white. The white after all was brighter and more practical and took upon himself the task of extricating the Moslem from the mess he was in. She said the book was really about the strangeness of being alive when you had lost the sense of God beside you. Without God the loneliness of man was unbearable, she said. Outside the window it was still dark. He could see the street light behind some bare branches. He said it was a long time since he'd read the book, but he didn't think the writer was trying to convince people to get the faith. It surprised him that he could be so peaceful, arguing with his mother about E. M. Forster of King's College, Cambridge. She said there was in that book and every book she admired a unifying vision, that men were seen as brothers even when they were lost and most hostile to each other, and if he didn't want to think of that as religious she wasn't going to argue about words. Her voice was thin and metallic, coming all that distance in a wire. It was what he had been waiting for her to say, but he replied, Did she know another writer she admired, Mrs. Gaskell, was a racist? She said if he went on like that she would have to hang up. But she could tell he was just trying to prick her on, that he wasn't angry or militant or anything. He liked to hear her defend those old-fashioned books. They were little bubbles floating up there beyond his reach. They were fantasies. Even the anguish they recorded was part of the fantasy. They were the dreams white people used to tell one another to prove their virtue. Listening to his mother talk of books made him think of the acres of grass on that Southern campus. He could smell the grass after a summer cutting, just as he had smelled it as a child playing alone under the great oak; and he could hear the evening sound of the locusts in the branches above him, just as they had sounded before his mother had called him in at dusk. Listening to his mother reminded him of clean starched sheets, and of nursery tales before the light went out. He managed to keep her talking a good long while.

Saturday, February 8

All day Chambers shuttled back and forth (driving the car himself, which put him outside the law) between suddenly called meetings of Community Action Now, which in these past few months he had been shamefully neglecting, and of the university administrative staff.

At the first CAN meeting—to which he had been summoned from bed by a seven A.M. phone call—a kind of paranoia on the part of some of the members of the large executive board made decision making difficult. The CAN offices, donated rent-free by the city because they were in a building to be demolished for a parking lot, had been occupied Friday night, it was reported, by the Philippa police. That is to say, the police had found the door unlocked (the CAN volunteers being sometimes careless), but instead of reporting the fact to the chairman by telephone from police headquarters as they had done on previous occasions, had entered the suite of offices, turning on all the lights and poking into closets. They had been discovered there at midnight by one of the board members. The secretary, Joanna Margrave, who was the wife of the general manager of the typewriter factory, was certain the minutes and copies of correspondence to state officials about violations of the state antisegregation housing law by local realtors (the mayor and some of the councilmen were in real estate) had been rifled, and it was possible even that some documents were missing; at least the drawers of her desk were all half open.

It was odd that the executive board, made up of dedicated graduate students in sociology, a dean of students, liberal wives of local businessmen and even two members of the clergy, would suddenly feel that their pursuit of decency and fair treatment for minority groups and others on welfare might make them, in the eyes of the law, subversive and underground; Chambers, though he realized that the growing tension in the city would have affected the police as much as the CAN staff, was himself angry that the police might have been ransacking the offices.

What the meeting was about was not the police behavior so much as it was the formulation of a campaign to raise bail and legal fees for Sam Duncan once again. Chambers was in agreement that the boy should be gotten out of town, though he felt that if Duncan was as disturbed as he seemed to be, that if he was inclined toward violence, it would be better to have him under someone's care. One of the clergymen said that was what mothers were for. Chambers wasn't certain about that, in Duncan's case.

At the meeting with President Doran, the vice-presidents, the proctor, and the two campus patrolmen who had apprehended Sam Duncan, the decision was made to equip the campus patrol immediately with Mace. Both Chambers and Doran had read articles in *The Nation* and elsewhere of the severe and possibly permanent effects Mace could have on eyes and skin, but the proctor and the police said it would be better to use it than to be forced to rely on their revolvers. With Mace they could have captured all three blacks. As it was they were under orders to use their revolvers only in self-defense. But Duncan had been armed. What if he had fired at them? Wouldn't they have been forced to return the fire? And even if, say, they had shot only at the legs of the blacks, wouldn't the very fact that the blacks had been shot lead to racial disorders? The two men who had eluded them were beyond doubt also armed. For that matter, Satur-

. . . *VIOLATIONS MAR VIETNAM TRUCE* . . .

day's *Daily Express* had reported a run on weapons of all kinds at the local sporting goods store. The proctor said he had investigated a charge that one of the fraternities had an arsenal in the basement; he hadn't found an arsenal, but he had found a great many rifles. The fraternity president had told him that the brothers liked to hunt squirrels and rabbits and deer in season, but had agreed with the proctor that the guns ought to be kept under lock for the present. Had the two blacks who had escaped been students or not? The patrolmen couldn't be sure, both of them thought they had recognized one of the faces, but Officer Johnson thought it had been the face of a student while Officer Schorer believed it to be a young man from town who had recently been fired from the typewriter plant. The talk went on aimlessly, dealing with Grant Powell's special issue of the *Weekly Advertiser* and of other indications of a backlash in the community.

What frightened the town was that a *citizen* had been threatened, Patrolman Schorer said. What people in town thought of was that the kind of physical harm which had earlier come to a student might now be expected to happen to any of them. President Doran said if the conditions in the following week increased in volatility, he would call a special convocation of the faculty and students, primarily in an attempt to subdue the fears of both blacks and whites. He paused to put a stick of gum in his mouth. He said the mayor had told him the sheriffs of the neighboring counties were on emergency call, and that he had begged the mayor to keep calm. At a loss to know what else to say, Doran was about to dismiss the meeting when the legal counsel made two suggestions: (1) the president should issue an order forbidding guns on campus and calling for reason to prevail; and (2) he should immediately announce that Sam Duncan, who might possibly be released on bail again, would be banned from the campus until his case was resolved. Both suggestions were passed without a dissenting vote, and the meeting was adjourned.

But at the second meeting of CAN, the executive board—to

whom Chambers, knowing that within an hour or so it would be public knowledge, had mentioned the decision to ban Duncan from the campus—felt that such a decision was, in effect, to prejudge Duncan and to make more difficult a fair trial for him. Furthermore, the board had heard that morning from an unspecified League member that the whole affair was a frame-up by the campus patrol acting in collusion with the city police. The vice-chairman of CAN, a graduate student in sociology, said that the system of law enforcement and justice in America historically discriminated against the blacks, and that if Chambers would only remember correctly, this fact was at the heart of the problem that had unsettled the campus all year and had directly led to the present crisis. Chambers, however, supported the decision to ban a student who might be deranged and who had been caught in two attempted thefts. The vice-chairman said that to penalize the student was to employ double jeopardy and was in such direct violation of the Code that Professor Freedman would be incensed. Chambers said he had talked to the campus patrolmen and had felt them to be as honest and truthful as the vice-chairman of CAN, and besides, they had seen what the vice-chairman could only conjecture about. They had caught Sam Duncan with a gun at the temple of a man, and Sam Duncan, whatever the social factors responsible for his behavior, ought at least to be guarded against as a possible threat to other people both white and black. To hold up the owner of a liquor store was hardly an act calculated to advance the black cause either in the town or the university. But his words were mere words, nothing more, to a group that already at least half-believed that police suppression was directed at them as well as at all blacks.

Chambers left the CAN meeting before it was over, feeling frustrated and hostile, thinking himself victimized in his own right. Public events were beyond his or anybody's rational control. But his anger was in some ways a relief: It kept him from thinking about private matters which—if he only had known what to do—he still might conceivably have resolved.

QUEEN ELIZABETH URGES RACIAL TOLERANCE

Sunday, February 9

Morning

After breakfast, George Chambers walked the half mile down to Hayden Wilcox's house. Mrs. Wilcox said that Hayden was out to the barns. Chambers found Hayden and his young hired helper Jonathan in the cow barn, where they were trying to adjust the automatic manure cleaner. Chambers took a wrench and tried to loosen one of the bolts, but the acid in the sodden manure had frozen it tight. Though he was wearing a good pair of flannel pants, he helped Hayden and Jonathan clean out the barn floor by the old method. They used the hydraulic loader on the Farmall wherever they could, dumping the steaming loads of dung into the waiting manure spreader and then carrying it out to the snow-covered fields. Chambers told Hayden the Ag School said it was bad practice to use cow manure on pasture lands. Hayden said he didn't care, he'd always done it that way, and it worked. In the corners of the barn, they had to dig away the manure with pitchforks. The manure cleaner had been broken for two weeks, Hayden said. It was the third time it had broken down in two years, and he still owed eight hundred dollars on it. Before he left, Chambers helped Hayden get one of the big doors back on its trolley rail. They talked of this and that while they worked.

. . . *ARAB TERRORISTS ATTACK ISRAELI*

About half an hour after Chambers had gone, Hayden, who was leaning against the tractor tire and cleaning the manure from his boot heel with a piece of shingle that had come off the roof, said to Jonathan, "Why do you suppose he came over like that?"

Jonathan said, "I dunno."

Night

The trace of snow in the air looked like dust in the headlights of the infrequent cars that because of the patches of ice near the orchard and barn came down the road very slowly. Stella, as always, had prepared a light Sunday evening supper; George and Mark, as always, had cleared the table and put the soiled dishes into the dishwasher. An elderly model, it clunked and buzzed: a homely sound but, like the flushing of the upstairs toilet, so familiar as to be unheard, though it would be distracting when the machine shut itself off. Occasionally the water pump deep in the well clicked on, sending a tremor through pipes fastened to joists in the basement; or the furnace ignited, or the motor which pumped the hot water through the radiators began to hum. The house was warm, particularly in the living room: Mark had cut down a dead apple tree in the morning, and now two large apple logs were burning. Mark sometimes tried to make a political or social metaphor out of the fact that you couldn't have a fire with one log, no matter how much kindling you used: it took at least two to radiate the heat back and forth or maybe to allow a draft between them. The fire was a good one, but nobody was in the living room to watch it.

George Chambers sat before his typewriter in his study. Mark sat before his typewriter in his bedroom, with the door closed. As for Stella, she was in the bedroom she shared with George, packing her suitcase and the bag which she used to transport her art supplies. Occasionally she left the room to wander through the house looking for something. Her bedroom slippers, for example, were under the living room couch; and in the hall closet she found, on a shelf littered with slippery piles of color slides and photographs, an almost forgotten set of new brushes. It seemed to Stella, looking at the mess, that somebody at some time should have at least tried to put the photographs into an album or something, somebody should have written on each of the slides a brief description of what it was and then got them into some kind of geographical or chronological order and back into their little yellow boxes; but of course George, though he had time—at least tonight he did—for something like that, wasn't about to do it. It seemed significant to Stella that on this night as she was packing her clothes and equipment for her morning flight with Cecil and Doris and Marjorie, that on this particular night George wasn't at least putting the photographs into an album or something.

Of course Chambers, who always preferred the camera of his own memory to any mechanical object, never took the family pictures (Mark and Mary always had) and hadn't the slightest idea of what was in Stella's mind. He had even forgotten where the photographs and slides had been put. Chambers' mind was on the letter in his typewriter:

R.D. 1
Philippa, N.Y.
Feb. 9, 1969

MR. FRANK TARBELL
Porter County Health Dept.
Porter County Hospital
Philippa, N.Y.

DEAR MR. TARBELL:

I have talked with you, and have written you in the past, about the conditions of the dump on the Fitzwater Road. I write again, to make a strong protest and also to ask for information on what has developed in the planning for county-wide dumps in Porter County. I was told a couple of years ago by our town supervisor that the problems raised by the nonconforming Fitzwater Rd. dump operation would be resolved by county action in the near future; and you may remember telling me last year of your hopes for conforming dump operations throughout the county. Some months ago, the Philippa *Daily Express* carried a news article about a proposed new dump for the eastern portion of the county; but I've read nothing about any proposals for the western portion where I live.

Meanwhile, the operations of the Fitzwater Rd. dump continue in their customary unsanitary, filthy, unsightly, and illegal manner. I read a news item a few months ago of the appointment of a township official who would prosecute individuals from outside the township who continued to use the dump; that official may have been drawing his pay, but to the best of my knowledge has done nothing to deter nonresidents from using the dump. I understand that both the townships of Forsythe and Baxter in the next county are attempting to make their dumps conform to the state legislation, which means that residents of those townships (and of the village of Waterburg, in our own county) often find it more convenient to use the Fitzwater Rd. dump: it's always open, nobody regulates its use, and there's always room for one last load of garbage or even somebody's rusted-out Rambler. There are not even signs indicating that fires are prohibited; the stench is often formidable. I believe that fires are set even by the officials of our own township, as part of their hopelessly inadequate attempts to clean it up; at any rate, the fires smoke most noxiously on the days the dump debris is pushed back. And so the rats multiply, and the stench continues; and the little stream that wanders through my woods foams whenever the rains make it run.

It seems to me that my patience and understanding of the problems have brought me nowhere, and that very probably my only recourse will be legal action against the township and possibly the county. Before I take such a step, would you tell me what your department is planning to do about what is clearly an aesthetic disgrace as well as a menace to the health of my family and the neighborhood?

Chambers wondered if the letter was firm enough. He decided that it was, signed his name, and—to make certain the Health

IN SEVERE FUEL SHORTAGE . . . JUSTICE

Department knew he meant business—added at the bottom: "Copy to Attorney J. P. Bolgano."

Meanwhile, Mark was finishing his letter, which ran as follows:

R.D. 1
Philippa, N.Y.
Feb. 9, 1969

Mr. Grant Powell
Editor and Publisher
The Philippa Weekly Advertiser
Philippa, N.Y.

Dear Sir:

About a year ago my sister Mary Chambers, becoming increasingly concerned by a high school curriculum that studiously avoided any concern with the major problems of our day, organized a group of students to work to bring these problems to the attention of students, faculty, and townspeople. Neither my sister Mary nor the students who have continued to support the activities of Information Please are Communists or members of SDS. They don't want violence, in fact they wish to understand and then help to resolve the problems in the United States which are responsible for that violence both at home and abroad.

When Information Please was formed, the idea was that it might be the nucleus not only for a change in a high school curriculum that is basically reactionary and outdated, but for a continuing public forum in which all the people of our community could discuss their opinions and exchange their experiences. If we hear only "radical" priests, boys from South Africa opposed to apartheid, and boys from the United States who have destroyed their draft cards, the reason is that representatives from the Draft Board, the VFW, the American Legion, and the Taxpayer's League have refused our invitations to participate in panel discussions. The hostility of these groups to any kind of community forum has been intensified by the untruths, innuendos, and warnings of reprisal in your newspaper. I would like to ask you this:

DEPARTMENT DEFENDS CONVICTION OF SPOCK

Do you think the *Weekly Advertiser* is really contributing to the community understanding so necessary for the preservation of a democratic system? Or is it possible that you might be appealing to bigotry and fear which can destroy all of us?

I am thinking less of your attack on Information Please and other groups in your issue of January 17 than I am of the appalling response in your so-called special issue Saturday (yesterday) to the arrest of a young black who has been accused of trying to hold up a white businessman by the campus gate. To hold him responsible (again by innuendo) for an earlier act of violence and to say that but for the intervention of the campus police the businessman "might have been killed," and to find in the attempted hold-up the "elements of a conspiracy to bring terror to a whole community and to bring that community to its knees so that a minority can do what it likes, gain what it wishes, with impunity" is to inflame racial fears. You complain that before the Black Students League came to Brangwen there were no racial problems in Philippa, which shows a lack of knowledge of the city you brag you were born in. You say that this young black should not have been released from jail while he was awaiting trial for an earlier alleged theft, and you now are so "outraged" by attempts on the part of CAN and others to raise bail for him that you are contributing to an atmosphere of fear and anger in the city that makes it mandatory for his own safety to get him out on bail and away from Philippa. You are contributing to an atmosphere of fear and anger in the city that could lead to greater bloodshed and "disfigurement" than you perhaps can possibly imagine.

I am not asking you to publish this letter. It is so long that to publish it you would have to cancel one of your ads and meet the loss by taking away Elsie's coffee break. Even if you agreed to publish it, your next issue (unless you have another "special issue," which I hope not) might be too late. I think there will be a real confrontation. The hysteria you've helped to create, the response to a young black whose guilt has yet to be proved, the fear and anger which must exist within every black student on the Brangwen campus, and—not the least—the putting of maybe a hundred sheriffs and deputies on a stand-by basis, almost make it inevitable. I'm writing this letter to let you know that if there is such a confrontation, Information Please will be there. We still value

. . . ASTRONAUTS RETURN SAFELY FROM MOON

human life and stand as always for peace. We too are on a stand-by basis. Given a confrontation, we will place ourselves between opposing groups whether the locale is the courthouse lawn, the city hall, the jail, or on the Brangwen campus; and we will be joined by any other young people in the community, black and white, who care enough for human life to stand with us.

So, if anybody gets hurt, it is likely to be one of the young citizens of the town who like most of the soldiers in Vietnam aren't old enough yet to vote. Please be advised that if bloodshed occurs, you must bear a strong responsibility for it.

Yours truly,
MARK CHAMBERS

What did Mark hope to gain from such a letter? Not even he knew. He didn't expect Powell to make a public recantation. Nor did he expect Powell to make any effort to alleviate the tensions, any more than his father expected the Health Commissioner this time to do anything more than he had done in the past about the conditions at the Fitzwater Road dump. Both letters were written with emotional conviction. If Chambers' letter dealt with a matter of less pressing importance, if in writing it he had certain selfish motives (the preservation of a bucolic view from his front porch, the elimination of occasional offensive odors), it did not mean that he was unconcerned at the moment of writing it with other issues. The fact was that Chambers thought of the dump much as John Jarndyce thought of the East Wind, whenever anything in his private relations or in the social and political world became particularly oppressive or seemed beyond his personal control. If on this night he had thought so bitterly of the dump as an infringement of his rights (or at least his rightful pleasures) as a country gentleman, the reason was that nothing seemed to belong to him anymore and nothing seemed pleasurable.

And if his fairly harmless letter to the Health Commissioner contained within it a sense, while not of paranoia, at least of persecution, so did the letter that his son Mark had just completed in the privacy of his bedroom; and for that matter Stella's behavior on this night before she flew to Nebraska with Maynard and the other artists contained some of the same quality.

At the supper table, Chambers had related the substance of his meetings with Doran and with CAN; Mark, whose relationship with his father had been strained in recent weeks, became emotionally disturbed. He didn't see how his father, after saying what he had, could ask for more oil for his tossed salad. The imminence of violence which, since it hadn't yet arrived, ought still to be averted, made him talk in a way which even he recognized as unlike himself and not always consistent. But he couldn't constrain himself. And he believed every word he said. He attacked the criminality of the American intrusion into Vietnam, he felt that all capitalistic societies were destined to destroy themselves because they could not and would not check the mindless self-interest they so vigorously fostered; he wasn't going to college no matter if his father was going to be the vice-president of one and he certainly wasn't going to Vietnam.

In the same breath that he called for peace among men, for understanding, he said a political revolution was necessary, and that it would have to be violent because of the insatiable greed not only of those in power but of the working class which when it had been poor had been a symbol of so much hope. He gulped down his food without knowing he was eating. He accused his father of sharing in the universal selfishness; he hit out in all directions. His father tried to speak, but Mark wouldn't listen; his mother, who wasn't eating, for once said nothing at all. But Mark carried out the dishes to the kitchen without breaking anything.

Then he went upstairs to the extension phone to call the other members of Information Please to convince them of the urgent necessity of his proposal for them to stand between the opposing forces if the trouble started. He was certain it would start. In fact, he almost welcomed it; he welcomed the thought that he might be killed trying to save other people from themselves. He didn't understand himself at all, and went to his room to write a letter to a man he hated with all his soul, thinking that Grant Powell symbolized all that was rotten and ignorant in the United States. Given his feelings, his letter was a miracle of soundness and restraint.

To what extent had the New Year's Eve party at Cecil Maynard's house, and its aftermath both in Harrison's office and Chambers' farmhouse, influenced Mark and Stella and Chambers on this particular night? It would be impossible to say, since statistical studies on the relationship of private affairs to public issues is vague and hopelessly unreliable; besides, there is an echo effect or a kind of resonance, by which family noises bounce off the world tumult to return reinforced to the family. The process goes on and on. One cannot push back through all that chaotic noise to get to the initial sound. Who knew what it was? Perhaps it began before the birth of any member of any given family. Perhaps the religious explanation of what happened in Eden is as good as any; at any rate it can be a useful symbol. Certainly George Chambers would have preferred an answer that put the blame long before his personal appearance on Earth. As he was beginning to see it, the problem was not with individual men but with the species. Manqué idealists make superior misanthropes.

All Mark knew was that something fishy was going on at home, because even though his parents tried not to show it and were considerate of each other, both his father and mother were apparently isolated from each other's thoughts. He could tell it in their very attempts to be thoughtful and kind to each other. He could tell this much, that it had something to do with Phyllis Christy, whom he had never liked and who now acted as if she owned his father. Well, suppose his father and Mrs. Christy had some kind of affair going. Suppose they had gone to bed together. A boy like Mark, born into the modern world, could accept that. His own generation wasn't so goddamned hung up

SOVIET DELEGATION ARRIVES IN PRAGUE . . .

on sex and the possessive relationships it had once engendered. For example, on New Year's Eve, when he had gone to Mike Martin's house to plan for Information Please in the coming year, he found that Mike's parents were away and that Mike had invited two of the Information Please girls, Stephanie Garmonsway and Maryjane Court. What had he done after they had excitedly talked politics and had a midnight snack of sliced Bermuda onions and peanut butter sandwiches and had toasted Information Please in the New Year with a bottle of Gold Seal champagne? He'd gone to bed with Stephanie Garmonsway, that's what. And it hadn't been for the first time. You could say it was the first time and a half. Had it hurt him or Stephanie or changed their old casual relationship with each other? No. It had made them both briefly feel good, and it was good to think that each had made the other feel that way. His father had told him that when he was a boy he had gone to camp with other Hi-Y leaders and had heard a lecture by a missionary in Africa who had told all the Hi-Y leaders that they ought to save their lips for the woman they planned to marry. Which was crap. His father had said as much. Mark knew his father loved his mother. Since this was what counted, why didn't his father say so and not let something that might have happened between him and Mrs. Christy louse up the whole family? To be truthful, Mark had to admit he was both proud and uncertain about what had happened between him and Stephanie, and if his father would only be open then maybe the whole family could be frank. That something was hidden was what got Mark upset and made his parents strange to each other and got Mark hostile not only toward them but himself.

Stella's response was complicated by the particular nature of her own involvement. Not only had she helped to throw George and Phyllis together beyond their professional contact in the office (she hadn't needed to be so jealous about husbanding her entire afternoon hours for painting, but had thought that since she was interrupting her mornings for George and other matters

CHINA SETS OFF 3-MEGATON THERMONUCLEAR

she really ought to have the afternoons without running after him and then looking around town for Mark), she really *had* deserted George on New Year's Eve. It was all that old business about her painting getting in the way of her family. She also could accept the likelihood that George and Phyllis had slept together that night, though she hated the radiant look of possessiveness on Phyllis' face every time she turned to George. Stella also knew that Phyllis thought her a self-centered and hopelessly inadequate wife for somebody like George. Well, Stella loved her husband; and even though she liked to think of herself as impractical, as somebody about to engage in some wild or shocking scheme, it had helped her to think of George as always tamping down garbage can lids and things like that.

Only once, and that early in their married life, had she been unfaithful to George. There had been a resident artist, a well-known, you could almost say famous, older man now either dead or forgotten, on campus for a year who had flattered her by taking an extreme liking both to her work and her personality. She loved George, though sometimes that goodness or nobility Phyllis worshipped in him *did* get Stella down. Even though at the same time she counted on it. It really couldn't damage their family if George would say something to clear up the tension and uncertainty. If the thing with Phyllis had been more or less a mistake, if it wasn't really important to George, he could say so. She might even tell him about the famous artist years before. As it was, she was holding back about the innocence of her night with Harrison because, if George really had become so infatuated with Phyllis and her thin waist and all that plastic she wore, so infatuated that he wasn't going to give her up, if he was going to ruin his family for *that*, why then the worst things he could imagine about her night with Harrison gave her, at least, the semblance of dignity, of not having been thrown over despite herself and crying into her watercolors and oils.

But she couldn't paint without the knowledge of George's loving her. Her thoughts about Phyllis and George were absolutely wild and vindictive. She would make a mess of those

Nebraska walls. She and George had been married twenty-four years. She couldn't *think* about George and Phyllis.

As for Chambers, the epitaph he once had imagined for his grave about his love for his wife and children and his affection for school buses and snowplows, was still essentially correct. In fact, on this night as he stared at the letter to the Health Commissioner on his desk, he heard the scrape of the plow pushing back the heaps of snow farther into the ditches, something the highway department did whenever a new squall was expected; liking that sense of administrative foresight and the protection being provided by people he didn't even know to keep the lanes of communication open (disaster could happen even on country roads, invalids could have new strokes, new heart attacks), he smiled and remembered the whole epitaph as he had formed it that sunny morning in the fall, only minutes before his own accident.

He had never hidden anything from Stella and wasn't going to hide this business about Phyllis, he would tell her about it after it got itself resolved. But there were problems, and he really had to face them. When people at parties talk idly about people going to bed with each other, they ignore the actual physical events which take place, and those physical events, to say the least, are of some consequence. Chambers' memory of what had happened was not much different from Phyllis', only in his mind it was he who was the more aggressive. It was a different kind of love play and love making than he had experienced with his wife, at least in recent years, and he wasn't going to forget it for a good long time, any more than was Phyllis. And when people talk idly at parties about people going to bed with each other, what the people who are doing the talking don't care to consider is that the physical intimacy of the people in bed can lead to further difficulties.

For example, if the woman happens to be somewhat fearful under a brave front, if she happens to long for permanence and really adores the man—that is to say, if she is not so stable as you

PLANES AT BEIRUT . . . ENVIRONMENTAL

would hope her to be—and if furthermore she is utterly convinced that the man's wife is selfish and indifferent to her husband's career: What does it do to that woman when the man says he's sorry, but it was just a momentary thing and that he does in fact love his wife? What does it do to that woman? Chambers became very agitated, thinking of people at parties. He didn't like parties and wasn't going to any more of them.

What he had to do, of course, was wait until tomorrow for Stella to go off to Nebraska. There would then be many opportunities for Phyllis and him to go to bed together again, particularly since he didn't have a driver's license, but he would make excuses for not doing so. She would begin to see the truth of the matter, but it would come so slowly it wouldn't hurt her. Chambers didn't want to destroy anybody. Could Phyllis really be badly hurt, emotionally destroyed, by his rebuff? He realized there was a certain pleasure to be had in thinking that it was a possibility. But if Stella could be swept off her feet by anybody who praised her paintings, he could be expected at least to have an extreme kindliness for one who not only had shown appreciation of his masculinity but who respected him in every other way.

He disliked himself for having thoughts like that. He wouldn't wait to settle things with Phyllis; he would clear up the situation the first chance he got.

What then happened was this: Mark, having finished his letter and reread it countless times, opened his door to go to the bathroom. Hearing him from her bedroom, Stella left her clothes half-packed and went to the door to smile tentatively at him. There had been such tension and queerness in the family that he had to stop, brush his hand through his hair, and smile back. Downstairs in his study, Chambers heard Mark's door open and his footsteps as well as Stella's; he put down his letter and went to the hallway below, looking up. Mark decided not to go to the bathroom but to come downstairs. Stella followed him. All three went into the living room, where the logs still burned in the

EXPERTS SAY TECHNOLOGICAL ADVANCES

hearth. In the kitchen, the dishwasher had already shut off with a hiss and a thud. They stood standing like guests at some party. Stella, who had seen Mary's guitar in the closet with the slides and photographs and her set of brushes, began talking of Mary, who had apparently been in Taormina, Sicily, for quite some time.

"She must like it there," Mark said.

Stella said, "She must be having a good time. She and her friend Sylvia must be good for each other."

"Yes," Chambers said.

Mark asked if his parents remembered the time on their trip to Yellowstone National Park that they had been unable to find the campground in South Dakota or someplace. It had gotten dark and then it had begun to thunder and rain. There had been lightning all over the place. They had got lost and it seemed best just to drive all night. He guessed Mary must have started high school that fall; he remembered being still in junior high. What he remembered, he said, about that trip was Mary playing the guitar while the rest of them made outrageous variations on an old joke about some Americans in a Moscow hotel who, having been told to be careful about bugging devices, had looked everywhere in their room and had finally discovered two wires under the carpet. They cut them and went to sleep and were asked in the morning by the manager if they slept well. They said yes, they had slept soundly; and the manager said they were lucky not to have been awakened by the crash of the large chandelier which during the night had fallen to the floor in the dining room directly below them. Chambers and Stella and Mark recounted the hopelessly bad variations of that joke they had told that night while Mary was playing the guitar and they had been lost and driving aimlessly through the rain in the car they had owned then; and they began to laugh as convulsively as they had on the night when they had thought their stories original and hilarious.

This was possibly the moment for Chambers to speak to Stella and possibly even to Mark, but so strange did New Year's Eve

THREATEN MAN'S EXISTENCE . . . SOLDIERS

appear to him as he remembered the guitar playing and the younger voices of his children, and as he remembered the smiling face of his wife faintly illuminated by the dashboard light of that old Ford they had all been so fond of, that to speak of it would be as if he were making up some new story, something that had never happened.

If Chambers had really wished to say something at that moment, it was unfortunate that he hadn't, for he was never to have another opportunity like it. There were of course so many crucial events already forming on the campus and in the town that a personal confession—as also an angry letter to the Health Commissioner because one's air and view were becoming polluted, or one to a newspaper editor who wouldn't and couldn't do anything about what it contained and which at least in the ending held the smell of martyrdom—would have been at such a point an act of indulgence, anyway.

Monday, February 10

8:30 A.M.

Though the day was cloudless for a change, it had snowed during the night and before the plane of the feeder airline could land at the Porter County Airport, the asphalt runway had to be cleared. Doris Banks and Marjorie Feidelman were in excellent spirits while the group waited in the small terminal. Cecil Maynard drank cup after cup of black coffee from the vending machine, meanwhile complaining of its quality. He told gruesome stories of what had happened in the past to people who had put their lives into the hands of this particular airline, bought four quarters' worth of insurance for himself from another vending machine, and asked Stella Chambers if he didn't really look quite elegant. He was wearing a new topcoat that fit his waist snugly and then flared out, the sort of coat, Maynard said, that a Victorian gentleman with a sense of French *joie de vivre* might have worn. Stella stood halfway between Doris and Marjorie, who were sitting on a ripped plastic couch, and her husband and Phyllis Christy, who were standing near the Hertz sign. Phyllis of course was at the airport because she had to drive George, though George *had*, Stella thought, driven by himself over the weekend and might have violated the law again this morning. But at least George was *there*; Marjorie's husband

CRASH ON ICY EXPRESSWAY . . . JEWISH

hadn't even come. Stella was so unexpectedly lonely, just before the departure, that she thought she might cry, and she thought George looked uncomfortable and sad. If he would say something, if he showed his need of her, she wouldn't go. But when the airplane finally was announced Stella felt relieved, smiled at Phyllis, and kissed George on the mouth. Maynard kissed Phyllis. Chambers stood by the gate, waving at what he took to be Stella waving back from one of the little oval windows; and he stayed there, though Phyllis went back inside the terminal, while the snow blown by the propeller blast stung his face and sent his hair flying back. He stood there until the plane left the field, banked sharply above Philippa, and became a gleam of light heading west. It was, perhaps, part of his strategy to prove something to Phyllis. Then he combed his hair and returned to the terminal.

9:00 A.M.

The student newspaper, the Brangwen *Daily Sentinel*, was delivered, late as usual, to the cafeterias at the Student Union and elsewhere on campus. It contained letters from two faculty members—Morris Freedman and Philip Durant—announcing their resignations. Both letters blamed the administration for making Brangwen an impossible center for objective research and academic study. Both spoke of a reckless politicization of the campus, augmented and even encouraged by a presidential disregard of clear principles. Morris Freedman said in his letter that he had accepted a post that had long been offered him by Yale and that if at last he was accepting it with reluctance, at least he was glad to be going to an institution which steadfastly supported scholarly work and where professors were free of intimidation because of sound and principled leadership. He regretted the inevitable decline of Brangwen as a respected leader in the academic world. Philip Durant's letter was much briefer. He was an older man, only a few years from retirement, and apparently had no other institution to talk about. Since Durant had been chairman of the Committee on Student Affairs

LEADER WARNS OF ANTI-SEMITIC STRATEGY

and Freedman its most influential member supporting the Code and judicial integrity, the implication of the resignations was that both men now believed it impossible to rescue the judicial system. What the letters implied, according to the front page editorial (which, hastily written, had accounted for the delay in publication that morning) was that the case of the three black students, which had caused such a row all year, was going to be pushed under the carpet by an intimidated administration.

10:30 A.M.

Three workmen from the Brangwen Buildings and Grounds department clipped away the branches of some evergreen bushes in the circle of the chapel road, revealing a small concrete base that had been put there some time in the past. With a star bit and heavy hammers, they made bolt holes in the concrete for some kind of iron supports. Occasionally they stopped work to slap their gloved hands against their legs. Though the day was windless, it was cold; work of the sort they were engaged in was usually done in the fall or spring. They could understand the installation of floodlights on the buildings of the quadrangle, but they couldn't understand at all the reason for doing what they were now doing.

2:00 P.M.

Sixty-five members of the Black Students League, accompanied by a white clergyman and the white vice-chairman of Community Action Now as well as several barking campus dogs, marched down the hill to the courthouse, which was connected by an underground corridor to the Porter County Jail where they believed Sam Duncan to be imprisoned. They had in their possession more than enough money for what a report in the Philippa *Daily Express* had declared to be necessary for his bail. An unusually large number of policemen, augmented by the sheriff's staff, were in the building as well as on the sidewalks outside. There was a small crowd of citizens across the street from the courthouse who jeered at the marchers. Joe Collier, the clergyman, and the CAN vice-chairman were secluded for half an hour with a judge, the sheriff, and other officials; they returned angrily to their group to report that they had been told the account in the *Daily Express* had been erroneous, that not only had bail been denied Sam Duncan but that he had been transferred to another jail outside the county where, according to the sheriff, "he was safer." They had been refused knowledge of the location of the new jail. Standing on the courthouse steps, the CAN official, self-consciously addressing not the crowd but a television camera that said NBC on it, declared that such a blatant disregard of judicial rights could not be tolerated. The clergyman, also speaking to the camera, said with less anger that what should be done was to get in immediate contact with the Civil Liberties Union. Joe Collier, speaking to the crowd, said the League would know what to do. The members of Information Please didn't hear of the affair until high school was out. By the time they arrived at the courthouse, everybody had left but the NBC crew, who were too busy lugging off their equipment to pay them any attention even though Mark Chambers tried to tell them what his group represented.

11:45 P.M.

While members of the Black Students League were still meeting in emergency session in an auditorium of one of the humanities buildings from which all whites, including members of SDS had been denied access, some unknown person or persons placed a burning cross on the lawn in front of the black girls' cooperative housing unit and fled. Upon hearing of the incident, the Porter County sheriff consulted the Philippa mayor and then phoned the executive head of the group of sheriffs from all the counties of the area that had banded together for mutual support to say that while a crisis was still not expected it was nevertheless necessary to remain at the ready.

All that night special details of the campus patrol and the local police patrolled the streets of the campus and the little city. The façades of the buildings on the quadrangle, illuminated all that night, looked from the business section of Philippa like the walls of a gigantic floodlit castle above the Rhine; the residents who saw it said the electricity must be expensive, but wasn't it beautiful? Above the illuminated buildings the stars were bright and large in the winter cold; and every hour the bells in the university clock tower told the time. The bright dial on the clock was something like a moon floating over a city that could have been any city sleeping beneath surrounding hills.

Tuesday, February 11

If he'd been in his right mind, he would have known they had no reason to trust in him. He felt truthfully he was a cipher. "Tell me, God, what's your justification of yourself?" "You are, my son." Old Zero himself, the justification of the universe. Then that long line of inane faces mirroring each other throughout infinity: God in the barbershop. God died in every one of his aliases, even as shadow or vague oversoul, the instant that man, for the best of reasons, ceased believing in himself. It had happened long before he had come along, so why worry? All he had wanted to do was to get away from those thin fingers pressed so tightly around his wrist that the knuckles were white. And of course to protect his son. All the thousands of faces might have been students or faculty or police, but they were the same face. The same face had stood in the bushes and by the door as they removed the chain. The same face was everywhere within. This face, black or white, was identical with his own and was no more nor less than the face of the disembodied gods without their eerie shine, which is why an old dream had come back. What he'd managed to achieve was a complete fusion of man and universe; but to tell the truth he couldn't care less. He could say fuck it all with any and all of the faces. He was more aware of objects than anything else. Guns belonged to many of the

MINISKIRTS . . . RUSSIA OPENS TIDAL POWER

faces, outside and in. His eyes saw the bolts of the rifles, the
triggers of the pistols, the links in the chain drawn tight through
the brass handle of the twin doors. It was a rusty chain, somebody's chain from a snow tire. They had really made a mess of
the little lobby by the door, he couldn't tell how far into the
building the wreckage had gone. "No," the face above the necklace of white tusks said. "We have this little transistor here—" it
was a white plastic Sony, on the broken glass of the receptionist's
desk—"and what we're waiting for, man, is for your great white
leader to announce over that little box to the waiting world his
acceptance of every one of our terms. Then he withdraws his
fucking army, and we leave in peace. In peace, man, when
there's not a whitey in sight." Beyond the face saying those
words was a face on the wall just like it, a poster that might
have been ripped from the bulletin board in his office. DOES HE
SCARE YOU? the poster said. It showed a wide-eyed black boy
carrying a torch. Somebody had used a spray can to write BLACK
POWER = FIRE POWER below the face of the boy. It seemed to
him odd and anachronistic, embittered writing from some sad
world he was already gone from. It would be nice, wouldn't it?
if he could see his own lack of fear as bravery. File drawers
were scattered by the elevator door. The door was open: the
papers must have been emptied into the shaft. A red and orange
gasoline container, the five-gallon kind with a flexible spout,
stood by the elevator door. "You tell them if they come shooting," the face said, and a long arm pointed toward the shaft.
"You tell them some of them die with us, then there'll be this
great big funeral pyre—"

"Somebody beat you to it," he said, being escorted to the door
while the chain rattled. He had seen the smoke before they did.

"Is that Tindall?" a voice asked sharply. And another: "Our
girls all out? Jesus Christ, the cowardly—"

He was pushed violently into the sun. The face was out of
the bushes again. He looked at it carefully, shading his eyes, because it didn't belong here. It didn't belong with him. It belonged either in the building or in the crowd. "Fred," he said.

STATION . . . PRIEST LEADS ANTI-INTEGRATION

Fred had a pistol in his hand. "They'll kill you if they see you with that," he said reproachfully. "What good are guns? You want to kill me, maybe?" He thought maybe that was what Fred had in mind, though Fred held the gun limply, down by his leg. Out there, in the sunlight, he saw the faces in the rear beginning to push forward. "Give me that gun, Fred," he said. "It won't do any good." As he was reaching for it, he saw that somebody back there in the crowd—a sheriff or deputy, somebody standing behind Mark—was aiming a rifle and he thought Mark would get killed. It was Mark who was on his mind, not Fred; but what he did was shield Fred with his body, that old instinctive response of a father. And when he looked out at the crowd of faces the funny thing was that all he could see were cows and old Hayden Wilcox, that shapeless hat on his head, leading the one in front, Ariadne or Andromeda; the unexpected presence of Hayden, smelling of manure, too tired from his labors to do anything but shuffle along, so pleased Chambers that he raised his hand in welcome, smiling.

THE PHILIPPA DAILY EXPRESS

DEAN DEAD, 2 HIT, IN BRANGWEN RIOT

BLACKS DRIVEN FROM AD BUILDING, GIRLS' CO-OP GUTTED BY FIRE, UNIVERSITY PRESIDENT RESIGNS

For several chaotic hours today Philippa and Brangwen University held the attention of the entire na- pied the Brangwen Administration tion as armed black militants occu- Building, a high administrative offi- cer was struck fatally by a bullet, two others were wounded including a student at Philippa High School, and a fire raged out of control at Tindall Hall, a black girls' housing co-operative.

In the aftermath of the morning's events, University President John Doran announced his resignation.

Dead was George Clayborne Chambers, 45, Dean of Students and appointee to the post of Vice- president for Student Affairs.

Chambers was killed at approxi- mately 11:45 A.M. by a bullet fired from an as yet identified force as from an as yet unidentified source as he emerged from the Adminis- tration Building after an apparently unsuccessful plea to the embattled black group to leave the building.

Injured were Thomas Potter, 19,

a black student from Montgomery, Ala., and Maryjane Court, 16, a junior at Philippa High School and daughter of Mr. and Mrs. Henry Court of 238 High St., Lakeview Heights. Both Potter, wounded in the shoulder, and the Court girl, struck in the thigh by a bullet that apparently ricocheted from the building, were reported in satisfactory condition at Porter County Hospital.

Another minor casualty was a bystander, Thomas Hobson, 32, an iron worker employed by the Hartsdale Construction Co., contractor for the new sociology building on campus. Hobson was struck by a rock thrown by an unidentified participant in a cordon line of Brangwen S.D.S. members and high school students standing 200 feet in front of the entrance to the Administration Building in an effort to prevent a force of 150 sheriffs and deputy sheriffs from storming the building.

MORE TO KUM

While the blacks were occupying the Administration Building despite repeated orders from University Proctor William Warren to leave, the fire swept through Tindall Hall, deserted apparently because of the Ad Building seizure. Shortly before Dean Chambers left the Administration Building flames and smoke could be seen rising above the elms on the western edge of the campus, and reports that the black girls' cooperative was burning circulated in the massive crowd of students being held in check behind the troop of sheriffs by the Philippa police. Fire Chief Max Turner called the fire "of suspicious origin."

How the shooting started—who fired the first and fatal shot—remains at presstime an unsolved mystery. Chambers was on the steps talking to an unidentified black when he was killed.

The watching crowd, which included newspaper and magazine reporters and cameramen from a major television network, heard a crack but were not aware a gun had been fired until Chambers slumped to the sidewalk.

"He's been hit!" somebody cried. One of the first to reach him was his son, Mark, 17,
see photo
a senior at Philippa High and a leader of the organization "Information Please" which, with the Brangwen S.D.S. chapter, had organized the protective cordon. Young Chambers was treated for shock at the University clinic.

The fatal shooting came after the force of county sheriffs and their deputies, eagerly awaiting the result of Chambers' conference with the Negroes, saw him leave the building alone and half their number began to advance upon the student cordon, wearing gas masks and preparing to disperse them with tear gas. Behind them, the other half had their guns trained toward the Administration Building as a protective cover for the advancing force.

Initially it was believed that the black on the steps, who was said to be armed, had shot Chambers but students in the crowd insisted that the shot had come from the contingent of sheriffs.

After Chambers fell, several other shots rang out. The building itself was apparently taken from the rear by the Brangwen Campus Pa-

SCIENTISTS PROTEST POPE'S BAN ON BIRTH

trol who forced open a little-used entry to a basement storage room and were able with Mace and tear gas to subdue the blacks without further injuries.

Joseph Quincy Collier, 20, New York City, leader of the Black Students League, surrendered himself into the custody of the Philippa police. Several other blacks have been held for questioning.

Immediately following the dispersal of the crowd by tear gas, President John Doran issued an order of a two-week suspension of classes and other activities and announced at a quickly-scheduled press conference his retirement from the Brangwen presidency.

President Doran, looking pale and fatigued, accused nervous deputy sheriffs of "probably" firing the first shot, but said that nobody should be blamed until a full inquiry was made. He said blacks and sheriffs alike had blatantly disregarded his prohibition of firearms on the Brangwen campus. He declared that his decision to resign had come in advance of today's disorders and had been made for the sake of restoring order to this racially toubled campus. "There has been too much hostility, too much suspicion on all sides of the fence," he said. "What is needed at this point is an entire new team."

He declared tomorrow—though the campus will be deserted except for a remaining contingent of the force of county sheriffs and local police, necessary maintenance workers, etc.—to be a day or mourning for Dean Chambers, whose loss he clared "will be felt for years at Brangwen."

(continued, page 7)

In addition to the main story and photographs, three other items related to the campus disturbance appeared on the front page of the Philippa *Daily Express:*

TODAY'S EVENTS: A CHRONOLOGY

7:00 A.M. Early secretaries stopped by Ad Building custodians outside building and are shown chain and locked door and placard on glass: STAY OUT. WE ARE ARMED FOR OUR OWN PROTECTION. BLACK STUDENTS LEAGUE.

7:30 A.M. President Doran phoned by Joe Collier and given following demands:

1. Full University legal aid for Sam Duncan. University to bring its full influence to bring release of Duncan and to pay his bail and to withdraw its suspension of him awaiting proof of alleged offenses.

2. University to find and punish individuals responsible for cross-burning incident at Tindall Hall.

3. University to provide armed black guards at Tindall Hall until further notice and to provide such guards to such black students who need them.

4. Immediate implementation of Black Studies Program.

5. Withdrawal of charges, with accompanying apology, to

three blacks accused in fall political demonstration.

6. Amnesty to blacks in Ad Building.

7:45 President Doran meets with high administrative officials. No decision at this time.

8:15 Vanguard of sheriffs arrive.

9:15 Philippa High "Information Please" members arrive, begin cordon.

9:30 "Information Please" joined by SDS after blacks in building deny SDS request to join blacks in take-over.

10:15 Rest of sheriff force arrives.

10:17 Proctor and Police Chief order student crowd, including cordon, to disperse. Cordon remains, but briefly most in crowd go to gym to hear various proposals

from David Garmonsway, faculty adviser of SDS. ("I just wanted to calm them down": Garmonsway).

10:45 Crowd returns to taunt police and sheriffs. Hobson hit with rock.

11:15 Dean Chambers enters building.

11:40 First signs of fire at Tindall Hall.

11:45 Dean Chambers killed, Maryjane Court and Thomas Potter wounded.

11:50 Blacks, surprised by Campus Patrol, surrender even before sheriff force breaks through main entrance.

12:15 President suspends classes, resigns.

12:30 Campus center deserted.

GEORGE CLAYBORNE CHAMBERS, 1924–1969

Who was George Chambers?

Born in Chittenango Falls, N. Y., the son of a garage mechanic, he rose to become at the time of his death Vice-President-Elect of Student Affairs at Brangwen University. A hero of World War II, he served with an artillery battalion that saw action in France, Germany, and Belgium, where he was wounded during the Battle of the Bulge. He came out of the war with a Purple Heart and five battle stars. He was the father of two children —Mark, 17, a senior at Philippa High School and Mary, 19, a freshman at a college in Massachusetts—and the husband of the well-known local artist Stella Chambers.

Dean Chambers, his associates say, was, while kindly to his ac-

quaintances and always loyal in friendship, pretty much of a "loner." A man whose social life centered around his family, he never joined the veterans' organizations or the Lions or Kiwanis. His secretary, Mrs. Phyllis Christy, referred to him shortly after his death as "one of the most Christ-like men I've ever known," and yet he had no church affiliation in Philippa. His only civic affiliation was with Community Action Now, a Philippa social action group, and at the time of his death was a member of that group's executive committee.

George Chambers was a man on the verge, it is said by those closest to him, of great work in university administration or possibly in the federal government. After nineteen years of devoted labor to Brangwen undergraduates, he was to be rewarded by a Vice-Presidency in the fall, a post traditionally used as a stepping stone to even higher positions. But that son of an obscure garage mechanic in an upstate hamlet chose to gamble his life and career for the sake of others.

The assistant dean of students, Terence O'Brien, says that George Chambers went into the Administration Building entirely as the result of a personal decision. He told O'Brien and Mrs. Christy moments before he walked through the crowd of thousands to the door that he was going to tell the blacks that most but not all of their demands were justifiable, and that he would take it upon himself to see that the justifiable ones were met by the University. What he had to offer in security was the reputation for personal integrity gained by nearly twenty years of service to Brangwen. He was going to put his own future in the balance, O'Brien said. He would promise the blacks he would renounce not only his deanship but his forthcoming Vice-Presidency if the Administration and Faculty did not back him up. "I'll live out the rest of my life as a farm laborer," George Chambers said. Recalling these words, O'Brien told this reporter: "He didn't seem to care for his own future at all. Phyllis [Mrs. Christy] and I begged him not to go in, but he did. He thought circumstances had led the blacks into a position that possibly even frightened them and that they needed somebody to help them out before somebody got hurt."

He was at least partially right. The blacks may have rejected his offer, but as the photographs of them leaving the building show they (like many whites) were under tension and fear. The "somebody" hurt was Chambers himself. His life, Mrs. Christy said, had always been devoted to mankind, and the notion of mankind for him transcended distinctions of race and nation. His dream of peace and of a world as beautiful as it was tranquil made of this man a sometimes controversial figure. He wrote many letters to the *Express* about local and national issues. His hope for the county was a county-wide sanitary landfill operation, one that would do away with litter and smoke pollution from our inadequate and non-conforming town dump operations. He supported those University students who turned in their draft cards. In a letter to the local draft board, reprinted in the *Express* for Oct. 17, 1967, he wrote, in sympathy with their action of the previous day, "I too am appalled by a military commitment in Vietnam that can be defended neither on expedient nor ethical grounds. It is testimony only to man's inadequacy as a political animal that we continue warfare in Vietnam at such a cost in men and resources for all sides involved. Compared with what the future will bring us if we can't manage our human destiny, the war in Vietnam is trivial. As humans, we all have much graver conflicts to resolve: a worldwide population increase that almost surely will alter (and in not many decades) the political structures under which all men live; major problems in racial relationships; social and economic problems in our country and throughout the world; urban problems; and problems dealing with such a fundamental matter as the meaning of human existence." Only a week before his death he was enthusiastically outlining a housing insurance plan that might help stem the hostility to integration in white neighborhoods.

It was then typical of this gentle but controversial figure that he would be the one to enter the Administration Building at a moment when tension was at its height and violence was a cat about to pounce. One of his own children, mirroring George Chambers' own beliefs, was endangering himself by standing in the cordon line. By going in, the father was no doubt protecting the high school children who were standing there, as well as reaffirming the beliefs he shared with them.

It is a tragedy that this man, lying in the shocking waste of his own blood, died before his own son could reach him and that, as his grief-stricken secretary pointed out, at the time of his death his daughter was in Europe while his wife was away on a professional visit to the Midwest with other local artists. In death as in life George Chambers the humanitarian was a "loner"; but the greatest irony of all, as Mrs. Christy has said, would be if the brutal death of this man should heighten rather than lessen those conflicts among men which throughout his life he had fought so valiantly to overcome.

—SUSAN LAMBERT,
Woman's Page Editor

SOME OTHER HIGHLIGHTS OF THE MORNING

BY DICK SUSSMAN, CITY EDITOR
(BRANGWEN, '56)

The poet W. H. Auden once described a painting by a Dutch master in which the great Icarus is a small figure falling into the sea. Of greater emphasis in the painting is a man being tortured in the foreground, a horse "scratching its innocent behind" on a tree, a farmer plowing, and, farther away, a ship sailing on "because it had someplace to go."

An alumnus of Brangwen, returning on assignment up the Hill to my Alma Mater on this tragic morning that brought death to a dean who more than a decade ago got me out of a score of scrapes, I thought about that poem ("About suffering they were never wrong, the old masters") after the death and the orders for dispersal. Many people were crying, but their tears as yet were not those of grief, but from the canisters carried by the sheriff and the campus patrol. An undergraduate was wandering through the departing crowd calling, "Here Snoopy, here Snoopy," and chasing after any dogs he saw in the distance. No doubt the violence he had just witnessed had made him afraid his dog had been hurt. "Here Snoopy, here Snoopy" lingered in my mind as somehow a significant part of what took place today.

TIBETANS ATTACK CHINESE EMBASSY IN NEW

Behind the chapel, on this frosty but sunny morning, three workmen were in the process of erecting on a concrete slab a Totem pole. Why, on this day, would they be doing that? I asked them. But they didn't know; they were obeying orders from up on high. They worked away, so intent on their task they were seemingly oblivious to what had just happened less than a quarter of a mile from their site.

By the campus gate, a young black student was struggling with campus police. "For Christ's sake, hold him!" they were crying; it took five of them to restrain him. I recognized him as a student who had been behaving strangely earlier in the morning. He had been standing, all by himself, sometimes in the bushes and sometimes on the steps of the Administration Building. He had not joined the other blacks inside; it had seemed to me as if he wanted to go in, but had been denied entrance because he was late. Or perhaps he had been uncertain all along. At any rate, he had been standing there between the blacks and the student cordon as if he were a cordon unto himself. Dean Chambers said a few words to him upon leaving the building: I remember thinking, be-fore the fateful shot rang out, that an action like that was what I would expect from a man who treated students with unfailing kindness and sympathy. It is even possible—though who can tell when even a watching reporter can't be certain?—that Chambers may have shielded that black boy at the last instant.

And here this black boy was, struggling now with the campus patrol. In his jacket pocket they found a cheap pistol. "It wasn't *him*, it's still loaded," one of the patrolmen said. The boy kept struggling and babbling to himself as they held him. "What's he saying?" I asked one of the cops, new since my time on the Hill. "Some damned foolishness, he's out of his head," I was told. "It's some damned thing about his Uncle Toby."

A boy calling, "Here Snoopy, here Snoopy," three workmen putting up a Totem pole beneath a sun indifferent to everything it was shining on, a black boy who'd had a nervous breakdown still calling for his Uncle Toby as the county ambulance took him away . . .

"About suffering they were never wrong, the old masters . . ."

Oh, you were so right, Mr. Auden.

Wednesday, February 12

The ferry having swallowed her train, Mary Chambers had left her seat to roam about the boat. It was a cloudy day. The mountains beyond Messina were dark beneath the heavy clouds, though a ray of sunlight swept across the town lighting roof tiles and church towers like a searchlight. It was too gusty on deck; Mary had retired to a lounge that reminded her of the main lobby of a large hotel. There were upholstered couches, tables and chairs and desks, and a bar where one could order food and beverages. Neither hungry nor thirsty, she sat at a desk by a window overlooking a slowly receding harbor and thought she ought probably to be writing her parents, to tell them she had left both Sicily and Sylvia.

She had in fact left Sylvia in Taormina on Sunday morning. Sylvia on Sunday could think of nothing but *calcio*, which showed how Italianized Sylvia had become: but then Gian was a local hero in the sport. Taormina might very well be an internationally famous resort with luxury hotels (though Gian's hotel, perched high on a rock in Castel Mola, high above Taormina proper, was not one of those) looking down upon a beautiful harbor and over toward the snow-capped vastness of Mount Etna; but after a month even what Mary liked best—the faint flares from the volcanic peak at night and the horseshoe of lights around the harbor—became something one had seen enough of. She had sat in the Greek theater (Greek in name: remodeled almost wholly by the Romans) looking past the columns to Etna when she had not been reading in the sun; she had wandered through the streets and enjoyed the view from the Public Gardens. She'd talked to shopkeepers, trying to work up courage to use the Italian she had learned in the little Hugo book but finding them responding always in English, even before she had finished her own brief sentence; and she had talked to other tourists, both Italian and American.

Mary's parting from Sylvia had been, if overdue, amiable. Mary had no money of her own and felt no remorse at accepting four hundred dollars in traveler's checks from Sylvia: Sylvia, really, was glad enough to be rid of her, Sylvia's Triumph, after all, only holding two people. It seemed as if Sylvia would remain in her panoramic habitat indefinitely, a beguiled guest in the drafty hotel where Gian worked as clerk, porter, and occasional chef. She would stay in the hotel until she tired of her *va bene* kick, her euphoric acceptance of the warm and impulsive Italian spirit. She had already helped out in the kitchen with Gian and two boys, friends of his, and had surprised some American guests with her idiomatic use of their language. In the evenings Gian and his friends talked and played cards in the lobby, and Sylvia made a foursome; she liked all three boys so much that Gian was jealous and sometimes cut the games short.

What Mary had done immediately upon leaving Sylvia was to go by train and bus to Piazza Armerina, just beyond the lake which had marked the terminus of her trip that day with Sylvia. The point was that she and Sylvia *had* been on their way to see the mosaics, the beautiful colored pictures in the tiled floor of what had once been a lavish Roman villa near Piazza Armerina; and even though Lago di Pergusa had ended Sylvia's curiosity in mosaics and other tourist attractions, Mary was stubborn enough to see the thing through. She saw the mosaics, approved of them, and then of course had to decide what to do next.

Rome, from her brief contact with it, was too much: the congestion in the streets, particularly the cars packed tight in all directions around the awful Victor Emmanuel monument, was pure idiocy. When the millennium came, the cars would have to go. And she hadn't cared for St. Peter's, being easily appalled by the baroque. But mainly there was too much to see in Rome; she only had four hundred dollars (not quite that anymore), so she decided to return to Florence. She had already spent more than a week there and had a good idea of what she would still like to see. And on some little street off the Duomo or someplace she had stumbled into a sculpture exhibit in a tiny gallery. In fact, she had met the artist, a young man half Italian and half Peruvian who spoke English poorly but with an Oxford accent. He'd told her the stuff on exhibit was mostly rot, ceramics and clay generally not being his true medium, but that he had been talked into the show by a friend who had just opened the gallery. If she would return in a few weeks, she could see something she might really like. He'd found an old timber with just the right knots and he was making a statue which he thought characterized some kind of duality (pagan and Christian? flesh and spirit? He hadn't been too clear) which he just might be able to bring together in one art object, though the struggle would show: in fact the struggle was the whole thing, what he was after. So in a way method or style became synonymous with meaning, which meant sculpture could be something like music. She had liked the way his eyes brightened when he talked, the almost self-parodying or at least ironic expansiveness of his gestures; and so what she thought she would do when she got to the station in Rome was to get on the next train for Florence. If she could find the gallery again, they would tell her there how to find him. At least it gave her something to think about and kept her from feeling too lonesome. A tourist needs to see people as well as things.

She ought to write her parents, but what ought she to say to them? It was easier to write when you had some awful pain inside you that you just had to get out. What she had learned from this trip to Europe was this: Americans, including herself,

TAX   CHIEF   INDICTED   ON   TAX   CHARGE . . .

worked harder than anybody to prove their innate goodness. They had this dreadful itch for purity, and when things began to go wrong they took it out either by going righteous (whether reactionaries or revolutionaries) or (like Sylvia) forgetting the whole game. And perhaps Sylvia's course was the less sinful, in some metaphysical sense. At least it was less dangerous.

Mary was still young and doubtless was wildly simplifying things, but in her opinion the righteousness that Americans were prone to was the consequence of historical accident and geography. It wasn't long ago that all Americans were thinking that modern man had reached his zenith in them. Always the American had been Renaissance man with his individualism, his interest in things of this world, carried further than anybody else had ever carried them. This sense of innate superiority affected even those who now angrily denied that the nation had ever had it. What they didn't know or didn't care to think about, not even those who hated America, was how much their Renaissance origin had had disastrous consequences from the first moments of its grand flourishings in Italy. The birth of capitalism and free enterprise, of credit and banking (of that economic system the radicals despised but which all Americans felt entirely theirs) was accompanied by greed, depravity, wars between states and between factions of the same state, the most blatant social injustices against the already weak and the already deprived, a cruelty beyond the scope of lower animals. Modern diplomacy (which was another word for the strategies and often the lies of self-interest) was born at the same time. Technology and population growth had made doubtful the survival of whatever had been born in Italy, both what was fine and what was abominable. At the end of a historical epoch, all the old sores of its birth were returning, intensified. Americans, who didn't see the connection between the early sores and the new ones, who thought of themselves as a splendid blossom fertilized by their own initiative in the purity of a natural world (didn't even those who now despised America feel at least the heritage of this provincial sense of goodness?) were appalled.

HUNT VICTIMS IN RIO LANDSLIDE ON SLUM

Americans were righteous. Whatever it did for the backbone, righteousness was an unpleasant virtue, born of ignorance and dedicated to the preservation of that ignorance. Righteousness was really bitterness, for it separated man from man and was envious of a dream that had never been. When a whole people who are inclined toward righteousness get the feeling that something has gone wrong, they splinter into a whole series of righteous groups, each feeling that it alone possesses this righteousness.

Such a generalization appealed to Mary, for at least it said the same thing about all groups and brought them under the same heading, the Birchers as well as the so-called Silent Majority as well as those who saw themselves as radicals. It applied for that matter to blacks as well as whites. The black problem was something that the whites had kept hidden under the clean and sacred carpet too long, and it hurt their trust in their goodness to have it brought out. Yet somewhere she had read a poem of Leroi Jones in which he in one breath cried out against all the materialistic shit of white America and in the next told the blacks to go out and take all the television sets they could get their hands on. That poem was one of three things: it was a put-on for the whites (it *had* outraged a judge), it was an attack on his own race, or it was about as righteous and as materialistic-American as one could get. From her point of view, the more the blacks demanded complete separation from a decadent white America, the more they favored some sense of kinship with a lost Africa, the more American (both in dreams and righteousness) they were getting. And if her native land blew itself and the rest of the world up, or if its white majority turned it into a repressive state, it would be as a consequence of that same righteousness, that striving become more desperate and terrible in the knowledge that it really no longer applied.

On the steps of the Greek theater in Taormina Mary had met a vigorous, slender, and barely wrinkled countess from Siena who had taught French and Italian at Wellesley during and after the Second War. The countess told her that the lovely

. . . ENGLISH NOVELIST E. M. FORSTER, 90,

landscape of Tuscany, which Mary had been praising as a kind of Eden, was at that moment undergoing radical change. The cypresses were doomed, like the American elms, to a hopeless blight. The olive trees could no longer be used in cultivation with grapevines because labor had become both scarce and expensive; the new method was to put the rows of vines at a greater distance and without the trees so that large tractors could get between the rows. In the future a Tuscan hill in winter would be a treeless military cemetery, composed only of concrete poles in a geometric pattern. The wealth of the old families, the countess said, was all in the land, but those families even with the new farming methods and even with state subsidies could not long maintain their estates; meanwhile the *nouveau riche* in their city apartments or suburban villas bought three cars, pretended to all the virtues of the dying class, and behaved with ostentatious rudeness if not outright hostility to those below them while cheating the government out of the taxes they should rightfully pay.

"In America there exists a more authentic sense of democracy," the countess said. "I may have laughed at it when I lived there—I may have put on superior airs, for which God forgive me—but you still have something precious in the United States, some *belief* in equality, that we don't have in Italy. No, we're too selfish, the old and new alike. As for me, I'm a Socialist."

Mary, who understood the habit of attacking everything when one was uncertain and upset (why mention the cypresses, which might or might not be doomed, when one is really criticizing something else?) thought the countess' generalizations probably a half-truth as doubtless her own (being as yet too facile for her own comfort) were. She thought the countess must not have been in the United States for a pretty long time. And yet that ideal of equality—everybody equal within some shared sense of community—lingered. She was full of it herself, wasn't she? But the odd thing was that she had thought she'd seen it realized, here in Italy, at least on one occasion.

Months ago, soon after they'd gotten down into Italy, Sylvia

NAMED BY QUEEN TO ORDER OF MERIT . . .

had been driving the Triumph over some hilly back roads some-where; they had been enjoying the sun and the views. But soon, as they neared a town, they got entangled in a traffic jam. Cars were parked on both sides of the road, sometimes not even on the shoulder so that in some places there was room for only one lane of traffic. The Italians (were their driving habits indicative of the selfishness the countess had been talking about?) wouldn't back up in either direction, so the situation got almost immediately hopeless. They blew their horns, which was typical, but apparently were resigned to such noise and chaos. What they finally did was to decide to resolve the dilemma later. They simply abandoned their cars and, laughing, trailed each other up the hill and into the town, where some sort of festival was taking place. The stands in the calcio stadium were full, boys dressed up in doublets and other costumes paraded about look-ing proud, a band was playing (not too well), and some horse-men were having a race. It was true enough that elderly distin-guished citizens—no doubt barons and other remnants of the countess' aristocracy—had special seats in front of everybody else, but the point was that the whole town, *everybody,* young and old, peasants and merchants, was there. Tickets were being sold at an admission gate, but there was also a hole in the fence which not only Mary and Sylvia but nearly everybody else seemed to be using, while the policeman stationed nearby re-mained studiously indifferent.

An old truck with extension ladders that were manually cranked stood near that hole in the fence, so Mary and Sylvia had a good view of it when it became the center of attention. A rope was attached from the last rung to something made of paper that was folded into a large wooden crate. As the ladders were laboriously raised, the object in the box unfolded. At first it looked like a gigantic Japanese fish-kite. But tubular ovals of plastic were inserted in the end nearest the ground, two men carried some kind of burner under the folds and miraculously the paper didn't ignite. Instead, the object began to swell. Sylvia thought it was a replica of an Apollo rocket, the Italians everywhere displaying extreme interest in the moon explorations; but it continued to swell until it became a balloon with a diameter of fifteen feet or so. Paper ribbons dangled from it; the name of the town—Mary could see only a few of the letters—was painted on the circumference. The burner was then attached to some kind of metal contrivance. The perspiring men who had been within scuttled out, all other activity within the stadium ceased, the men holding tightly to the plastic rim gave two trial heaves, and then—as the band began to play again and the crowd cheered—the hot-air balloon shot upward. It rose and it rose, that festooned balloon, carried up into the sunlight (for the town itself was already in shadow) while the people of the town whose name it bore watched in fascination; and then the festivities in the stadium were over. Why had Mary been so moved? The innocence, the Oz-like quality? Well, yes: and the sense that for all these people that balloon in some way represented *them*, the old barons as well as the peasants. She had been more moved certainly than by any televised Apollo launchings from Cape Kennedy. *They* had fascinated her, but *this* actually made her cry, which had embarrassed Sylvia.

She had recounted this experience to the countess, who replied, "But you have the same thing at your county fairs."

"Well, maybe we *once* did, but before my time—"

"Oh, you Americans, with your innocent dreams . . . Anyway, that balloon was the expression of a little town's pride, and who knows where it may have drifted? Perhaps into the path of a commercial airliner. Do we ever think of each other, we Italians?" But the countess smiled and put her hand on Mary's arm. She had been touched herself.

The ferry was already approaching the mainland. It was wrong of her not to let George and Stella know of her whereabouts. Desperately she fished in her pocketbook for a postcard or something and came up instead with a piece of cardboard cover from a little box of Dog Brand Mosquito Killer, made in Japan, words in English, and bought in a Syracuse supermercato (she'd gone in for oranges, toothpaste, and cheese) because

ATTACK . . . PENN CENTRAL BUYS NEW HAVEN

its phrases pleased her. What the piece of cardboard said was:

"DOG" BRAND MOSQUITO DESTROYERS

Besides bloodsucking, Mosquito is a carrier of diseases such as
MALARIA,
YELLOW FEVER,
FILARIA (Elephantiasis)
ENCEPHALITIS (Sleeping Sickness)

Also, mosquito's biting causes severe itching, swelling, restlessness, loss of sleeping and sometimes pustule formation. So, Mosquito is your enemy; a menace to you and your children. KILL HIM (Mosquito) AS SOON AS HE ENTERS YOUR HOME, OR DRIVE AWAY WITH OUR "DOG" BRAND MOSQUITO DESTROYERS.

In the margin she wrote, "Something to cheer you up as it did me. On way North, alone and glad. Will write details from Florence. Contact me there at American Express. Love, Mary," and putting the cardboard in a soiled envelope, addressed it rapidly to her parents, plastered the envelope with all the stamps she could find, and dropped it into the postal box in the lounge as she ran back toward the train.

She had her train trip to Florence all planned out, because that kind of thing still gave her some kind of security. She was, she supposed, too methodical, but if she didn't do things in proper order her thoughts became much too confused and random. So from the Italian mainland halfway to Rome she thought of the feasible activities she might undertake, at least the reforms she would work for after her return home. At roughly the halfway point she tried to use her meager Italian in conversation with an elderly lady carrying a straw basket, who simply stared at her in astonishment and said not a word.

By the time she reached Rome it was, of course, early in the morning. She had a snack at a buffet and caught the train for Florence with minutes to spare. She had thought that from Rome to Arezzo, say, she would try to plan out her personal economic problems. She needed some new clothes, and the shoes of the girl across from her caught her eyes; she liked the gold on the heels. Would she need to write home for some more money? There were special charter flights from Germany in mid-June, only sixty-five dollars a person, that cheap because the charter flights had to go back to pick up more American kids coming to Europe for the summer and sixty-five dollars was better than an empty seat. Would her money last that long? Maybe in Florence she could get a job.

She had thought that by Arezzo, daylight would come, so that she could see the Tuscan landscape before—if the countess *had* been correct—it got ruined. But it was still black outside, the train was an express. That miscalculation in her plans disturbed her; for a moment she got upset and even angry, at herself and everybody. So she looked at the gold-heeled shoes again, thought that yes, indeed, she would buy a pair in Florence whatever the cost, thought about the statue and the young artist she really didn't know at all, and finally fell asleep.

The train curled through sinuous valleys and vanished into tunnels. Above it the stars shone, those of our galaxy, and those in the hazy whirl of Andromeda; and beyond them were other galaxies unseen by the naked eye; and far beyond them, so far beyond sight they could be picked up only by radio telescope, were the quasars. At the very edge of reality you might say. Sending out messages both incomprehensible and terrifying at least for a mankind who had made its own little globe so hostile and often so meaningless. Mary, a girl not quite five feet four inches high, slept in her terrible ignorance, her terrifying innocence: dreaming perhaps of the millennium, perhaps of more immediate social reform, perhaps of her father's face or the face of a young man whose features she could only remember as pleasant as he had talked about what he planned to do, dreaming perhaps of nothing more than the message on a box of Dog Brand Mosquito Killer, a hot-air balloon, or a new pair of shoes. But looking at her smiling face as she dreamed, you could believe she was capable of meeting whatever was to come.

SIDES IN PARIS KEEP IN CONTACT . . . TURMOIL

GROWS IN UNIVERSITIES HERE AND ABROAD...

PARIS PEACE TALKS RESUME . . .